Second CHANCES

Second CHANCES

BARBARA VALANIS

Copyright © 2019 Barbara Geesey Valanis.

All rights reserved. No part of this book may be used or reproduced by any means, graphic, electronic, or mechanical, including photocopying, recording, taping or by any information storage retrieval system without the written permission of the author except in the case of brief quotations embodied in critical articles and reviews.

Archway Publishing books may be ordered through booksellers or by contacting:

Archway Publishing
1663 Liberty Drive
Bloomington, IN 47403
www.archwaypublishing.com
1 (888) 242-5904

Because of the dynamic nature of the Internet, any web addresses or links contained in this book may have changed since publication and may no longer be valid. The views expressed in this work are solely those of the author and do not necessarily reflect the views of the publisher, and the publisher hereby disclaims any responsibility for them.

Any people depicted in stock imagery provided by Getty Images are models, and such images are being used for illustrative purposes only. Certain stock imagery © Getty Images.

ISBN: 978-1-4808-7589-0 (sc)
ISBN: 978-1-4808-7588-3 (e)

Library of Congress Control Number: 2019902994

Print information available on the last page.

Archway Publishing rev. date: 3/27/2019

*To my beloved husband of forty years,
Kirk Valanis, whose constant support and
encouragement enabled me to achieve
my creative potential. Without him, this
book would never have been completed.*

ACKNOWLEDGMENTS

I would like to thank my friends, Sherrill Storhaug and Betty Fullard-Leo, who shared their thoughts and feelings during the first years after the death of their husbands, inspiring me to write this book. They may recognize something of their newly widowed selves in the thoughts and feelings of my two widowed protagonists.

Thanks to my husband, Kirk, who read multiple versions of some sections, patiently giving me feedback on grammar and the actions of my characters, suggesting plot ideas on how to move forward when my inspiration failed, and giving me a gentle push when I felt like giving up.

I would also like to thank my family and friends who gave of their time to read an earlier version of this book and provide feedback, which led to improvements in the manuscript. These include daughters Karin Fischer, Christina Weis, and Catherine Holtkamp, my sister Kathy Seraphine, my brother Bob Geesey and his wife, Wilma, and my friend Dolly Moore. Their critical comments led to revisions that improved the flow and believability of the story. Their positive reactions assured me that the story was worth seeing in print.

Chapter 1

There is only one certainty: There is very little to be certain about.

WEDNESDAY, DECEMBER 31, 8:40 P.M.

Warm air caressed Susan's face as she stepped off the Hawaiian Airlines plane into the blackness of the Hawaiian evening. The warm breeze momentarily disoriented her. It was such a contrast to the bitter cold and damp that broadsided her as she stepped out of her Seattle home that morning at six thirty, more than sixteen hours ago.

As she gingerly descended her front steps with her luggage, she had slipped on the newly formed black ice, narrowly avoiding an embarrassing fall on her butt in full sight of the airport van driver. Snow was falling heavily by the time she reached the airport. Takeoff had been a race against an imminent airport shutdown. After three deicings, the plane finally took off at 9:35 a.m., forty-five minutes late, the last flight to depart before the airport closed.

That was only the start of a harrowing day. Following breakfast service, Susan settled in with a book and read for an hour or so before she dozed off. She awoke to hear the pilot announcing that a passenger was having a seizure and the plane would take the passenger to San Francisco for treatment. Apologies for the inconvenience were accompanied by an assurance that the flight attendants would do their best to facilitate a quick offload and turnaround. Because the flight was currently approaching the halfway point over the Pacific Ocean, they would be six or seven hours late arriving in Honolulu.

The buzz of passenger chatter suddenly increased in volume. Many tried to attract the attention of the flight attendants, inquiring about arrangements at the other end. Most passengers were making connections to one of the outer islands, so they were likely to miss their connections. Worse, this was December 31, New Year's Eve! What was the likelihood of obtaining a hotel room in Honolulu without a reservation? The flight attendants assured everyone that the airline was looking into what could be done. But gloom descended.

The flight to San Francisco took nearly three hours. Another hour and fifteen minutes on the ground ensured that all the passengers missed their connecting flights. Passengers were allowed to move about the cabin while on the ground in San Francisco, but to minimize delay, they were not permitted to deplane. Despite considerable grumbling, most passengers understood and accepted the airline's decision. A few became aggressive toward the flight attendants, expressing their anger and frustration loudly enough for everyone to hear.

"A lot of good that does," said Susan's seatmate. "It's not as if the flight attendants can do anything about it. Their patience is amazing. I'd never be able to take so much verbal abuse without snapping."

Susan nodded and then asked to be let into the aisle to use the restroom. With the plane full, she felt her claustrophobia coming on. After standing briefly in the aisle and walking to the restroom, she felt a bit better. When she returned to her seat, she put on her headphones and tuned in the classical music station in an attempt to stay calm.

When her seatmate later departed for the restroom, Susan took the opportunity to call her daughter, Kristin. She had promised she would call when she got to Hawaii, but with Kristin on East Coast time, she and her family would be asleep by the time Susan got to Hawaii. There was no answer, so she left a message saying her flight had been delayed and she would call in the morning from Hawaii.

Shortly after her seatmate returned, she asked Susan, "Do you have anyone meeting you in Honolulu?"

"No, I'm going on to the Big Island. What about you?"

"I'm headed for Maui. I'm renting a condo there for a week with a friend from Phoenix. Rather than hanging around the airport to meet each other's flights, we arranged to meet at the condo. A good thing I'd say! Heaven only knows when I'll finally get to Maui. Are you visiting friends in Hawaii or vacationing?"

"Neither. My husband, Scott, and I have owned a condo in Kailua-Kona for about twelve years. Scott and I spent time there every winter before he died four years ago of a heart attack. I've been renting out the condo since his death. The suddenness of his death sent me into depression, and I've had my life on hold for several years. Now that I can finally face it, I'm going back to check on the condition of the condo and decide whether to sell it, continue renting it, or use it again for my winter vacations.

It's time to figure out what I want to do with the rest of my life. I'm hoping this time in Hawaii will help with that process."

"I'm so sorry about your husband. Losing him suddenly must have been very difficult. Hawaii is such a healing place. If there's anywhere you can think clearly about the future, I would think Hawaii is the place. But give it some time. Life has a way of telling us what we are meant to do."

"Wise words. It sounds as if they came from personal experience."

"They do. But I won't go into all of that."

Just then, the pilot asked passengers to take their seats as they were cleared to taxi for takeoff. The plane departed at 4:40 p.m. San Francisco time, 2:40 Hawaii time. After takeoff, the captain announced that in San Francisco, Hawaiian Airlines had managed to procure meal packs in lieu of a scheduled snack. These would be served on reaching cruising altitude, followed by dinner service about two hours before arrival in Honolulu. A light meal instead of snacks for this outbound trip boosted passenger morale. After eating, most passengers settled down to watch the movie or take a nap.

About two hours later, the captain announced that they should arrive in Honolulu at 7:25 p.m. Because all scheduled flights to the outer islands would have already departed, the airline had arranged to run special flights to each of the outer islands for passengers of their flight. Now, miracle of miracles, she was in Kona. It was 8:40 p.m. local time.

It had been nearly five years since Susan had come to the island with her late husband. She felt as if it had been yesterday. Some of their happiest times were spent in Hawaii. After they retired, they spent as many as five months every winter at their condo. Even while still working, they managed several weeks.

The island represented more than a physical escape for them. It was a mental oasis. In recent years, Susan and Scott often felt alienated from the world, as if they didn't belong. Several disturbing trends contributed to this, including individuals becoming tied to their electronic devices, job losses resulting from advances in technology, and restrictions on personal liberties that followed 9/11. Compounding the problem were a failing educational system and television programming that featured reality shows, inane comedies, violent adventure shows, and obsession with the activities of the rich as well as sports and entertainment personalities. The result was a citizenry less engaged and less involved in the community. The human warmth and caring they experienced in their social interactions when younger were now missing from their daily lives. Both political and personal interactions with their friends were often confrontational; it was difficult to find common ground.

In Hawaii, however, they managed to find peace. By not taking a daily newspaper and avoiding television and internet news sources, they cut themselves off from that alien world. Here, there were no cameras on every street corner or the telephone ringing several times every hour as politicians or solicitors called for money, votes, or charitable contributions. People were relaxed, kind, and thoughtful. Truly a paradise!

And now she was back. Only this time she was alone. Susan was suddenly assailed by the nagging doubts that had delayed her decision to return. Could she enjoy being here by herself? Would the memories of the happy times with Scott be comforting or reopen the wounds so recently healed? Could she reestablish relationships with her former friends and their spouses, or would she merely be a third wheel? Could she develop new friendships to enrich her time here? What did the future hold?

Susan pushed away her concerns. She needed to focus on the present.

Susan had no difficulty remembering the way to the baggage claim. The short walk through the open-air terminal was filled with the fragrance of Palani blossoms on the evening breeze. Tired as she was, she felt a thrill at the remembered fragrances, warmth, and familiar surroundings.

Passengers from the flight to Kona clustered around the baggage claim, eagerly awaiting their luggage. It had been a nearly full flight, so it was difficult for Susan to get close to the revolving baggage dispenser. Fifteen minutes passed with no luggage to be seen. Then a voice blared from the overhead speaker, announcing that not everyone's luggage had made the special flight. Those whose luggage did not arrive would need to return tomorrow morning to pick up their bags. A crescendo of grumbling arose from the crowd.

Susan leaned against a nearby wall. She was so tired ... and hungry! Normally she had plenty of energy to deal with her daily activities, although she did tire more easily than she used to. Still, for sixty-seven years of age, she thought she was doing okay.

Just as her spirits and energy began to drop further, the luggage belt began to rotate. She edged closer, trying to see if any of her bags made it. Five minutes later, she spotted one of her two cases.

"Would you please grab that blue case for me?" she asked the man in front of her.

"Sure, lady," he said, reaching for her bag. "Looks like you lucked out."

"At least I'll have something clean to wear tomorrow, even if my other bag doesn't arrive. Oh, wait. There it is! Thank heaven!"

The man grabbed the matching bag off the carousel and handed it to her.

"Thanks so much," said Susan with a warm smile. "I hope yours will also arrive."

"From your lips to God's ear! Have a good stay."

"You also," replied Susan as she waved goodbye. "Aloha."

Susan wheeled her bags to the curb, too tired to rent a car tonight. She wasn't even sure that the car rental was open this late. Ten minutes later, she finally obtained a cab, settled tiredly into the seat, and gave the address of her condo. The cabby was talkative, commenting on the lateness of the hour and how unusual it was for a flight to arrive so late. He obviously wanted to chat, but Susan was just too exhausted.

She briefly explained about the return to San Francisco and then quietly watched the passing scenery, trying to orient herself to the vaguely familiar shapes in the darkness. Although Susan did not respond to his questions or comment on his commentary, the driver talked all the way to the Keauhou district, just south of Kailua-Kona, where her condo was located.

Susan paid the fare and then wheeled her luggage to the door of her ground-floor unit. She took a deep breath, remembering the time she and Scott arrived without having arranged for a pre-cleaning, even though it had been nine months since their last visit. They had anticipated some dust, but when they had opened the door and turned on the light, she had nearly screamed! The white tile of the condo unit had been sprinkled with dead black bugs! Ants, cockroaches, millipedes, and more had to be vacuumed up before they could do anything else that evening. She had learned a lesson that night about just how many bugs there are in Hawaii, particularly in a ground-floor unit. Dealing with a few of them on a daily basis hadn't seemed like a big deal, but unattended, it led to quite an accumulation over nearly a year.

Susan forced the memory away. This time she had scheduled a cleaning for the day before her arrival. She certainly couldn't deal with anything like that tonight! After fumbling for the lock in the semi-darkness, she fit the key in the lock, opened the door, and flipped on the light switch before stepping in. After a quick glance, she saw that everything looked clean. The glass tops of the dining room table and the coffee table in the living room were sparkling, even in the dimness of the single light in the entry. Here at last!

Susan quickly surveyed the rest of the unit. Clean towels and soap had been supplied in the bathrooms; the bed had been made up with clean linens. How she longed to climb in between the smooth sheets and take a long nap! That would have to wait. There was no food in the place. She was originally to have arrived in Kona by 1:30 p.m., so she had anticipated plenty of time to rent a car, drop her luggage, and then do some quick shopping at the nearby Keauhou shopping center. Instead it was 9:15 p.m., and she had no car. She had been too tired to think ahead. She should have asked the driver of her cab from the airport to wait for her. Thank heaven for cell phones! She found a telephone directory and then called for a cab to take her to the shopping center located about a mile up the road.

While waiting for the cab, Susan quickly unpacked those clothing that had been packed on hangars and splashed some cold water on her face, hoping to feel more alert. Hearing the taxi pull in front of the unit, she grabbed her purse and went outside.

"Take me to the Royal Thai restaurant," Susan instructed the driver.

He groaned when he heard where she wanted to go. Short trips were not particularly lucrative. But when he heard that she wanted him to wait for her while she picked up some takeout and then bring her back again, he was more accepting, especially after she assured him that a good tip would reward his efforts.

Lights were still on in the Royal Thai Café, but as she entered the restaurant, she realized there were no customers. The staff were busily cleaning tables and sweeping the floor. Anxiously she explained her predicament and asked if there were anything they could make her for takeout. One of the waiters consulted with the cook and said they could do a veggie stir fry with chicken or shrimp and some rice. At this point, grateful for anything, she ordered the stir fry with shrimp, the rice, and a large container of Thai iced tea and a Tsing Tao beer.

The order was ready in about ten minutes. After profusely thanking the waiter for his kindness in providing a meal when they were officially closed, she took her bags of food and drink and returned to the cab. Briefly she considered asking the cabbie to take her to KTA, the grocery store at the other end of the shopping center to pick up some coffee, bread, orange juice, and jam, but decided otherwise. She was exhausted! She would deal with stocking food in the morning after a decent night's sleep.

"Take me back to the condo where you picked me up," she instructed the driver.

Five minutes later, the cab pulled up in front of her condo. She paid the driver, entered her unit, and immediately grabbed a glass for the beer, a plate, and a fork. She sat down at the dining table to eat. The food was as good as she remembered, but she was too tired to appreciate it.

She drank the beer but placed the iced tea into the refrigerator for the morning. It would give her something wet and refreshing while she organized her thoughts before tackling her day. In no more than fifteen minutes, she had finished her dinner, rinsed her dishes, and put them into the dishwasher. She took a warm shower to relax, brushed her teeth, and crawled into bed. She was instantly asleep.

Chapter 2

It's time to look at life through the windshield, not the rearview mirror.

THURSDAY, JANUARY 1

Susan awoke to sun streaming around the edges of the bedroom's blinds. She rolled over and reached for her watch. Blearily, she glanced at it and read six fifteen.

Too early to get up! she thought. A moment later she registered that she was in Hawaii, not Seattle. That meant it was 8:15 Seattle time, later than she had slept in years.

Thinking about the things she had to do today motivated her to get up and take a quick shower. The warm water relieved the mild muscle pain and severe stiffness in her joints that increasingly plagued her mornings as she aged.

Her doctor had offered no sympathy. "It comes with age," he insisted.

"I'm only fifty-five!" she had retorted angrily at the time.

Now she was sixty-seven, stiffer and sorer. Hot showers, activity, and Tylenol were her best friends in the morning.

Susan debated whether to wear her beige linen slacks or a pair of pale green capris. Although the morning was still cool, she opted for the capris. That way she wouldn't be too hot once the temperatures started to rise. A sleeveless cream-colored silk blouse and her favorite sandals completed her outfit.

Glancing at her image in the mirror, Susan saw a slim, well-toned figure and thought, *I don't look bad for sixty-seven years of age.* She had tried to look after herself these past two years, once she began to recover from losing Scott.

After dressing, Susan rummaged in a kitchen drawer for a writing pad and pen. Then she opened the sliding rattan curtains to allow the bright sunlight into the main living areas. She took a moment to look around. Despite being gone for five years, it felt familiar, like home. But as she considered it critically, she realized that it seemed dingy. She and Scott always kept everything in tip-top condition.

The previous evening, tired and in the dim artificial light, she hadn't noticed the wear and tear that were so obvious in the daylight. The blinds appeared discolored and worn, as did the wall paint, upholstery, and the carpet, which was endowed with several obvious stains. The sofa seat sagged, and the cane on the barstools and living room chairs was faded in spots. The room was on the verge of looking shabby!

Walking into the kitchen, Susan noticed that the wallpaper behind the stove bore streaks, as if someone had tried to use bleach to clean off grease. Even the floor tile looked dingy in the bright daylight, mostly because the formerly white grout was now grey against the still-white tiles.

Susan wandered into the two bathrooms, observing that

the glass shower doors were streaked with soap scum or hard water marks. There was a rusty-brown stain on the floor and the side of the tub in the master bath. One drawer was lopsided in the vanity in the guest bath. The bedroom's wallpaper, blinds, and paint also had seen better days. In fairness, it had been five years since she and Scott had been here, and she was aware that renters could be hard on a place. Still, she felt disappointed.

The condo had always provided a sense of comfort because of its tidiness and coziness. But face it, she had come here now because she needed to inspect the unit and decide whether to keep it or sell it. Either way, she would need to do some repairs, cleaning, and redecorating. She wasn't sure that she would get much pleasure in spending time here alone. Memories of the times spent with Scott, still fresh, were painful in view of his death since there would be no more such happy times. Nonetheless, she had learned that life does go on and one must engage with the world to have a life. Without engagement, one merely exists in a colorless day-to-day existence punctuated with pain, despair, and loneliness. She had spent two years wondering in that void before she felt able to begin rebuilding her life.

Susan slid open the doors to the lanai, stepped out, and took a deep breath. Suddenly her mood changed. She felt as if she were in heaven! The air was light, and a gentle, fragrant breeze wafted around her, the scents a gift from all the flowers growing on the grounds of the complex and the adjoining golf course. In front of her lanai was a ten-foot-deep area of grass. Beyond the grass, where the hill began to drop away to the golf course, were six purple bougainvillea trimmed into the shape of bushes. Within fifty feet of where she stood were Palani trees, Christmas-berry trees, banyans, torch ginger, bird of paradise, and crotons. A row of coconut palms marched along the edge of the cart path that bordered the tee-off area on the golf course directly in front of her. Giant monkey pod trees were scattered about the course behind a hedge of opakapaka and a row of red-flowering oleander trimmed to the shape of a hedge. The sea glistened in the distance.

Susan grabbed her Thai iced tea from the refrigerator, picked up her writing pad and pen, and walked to one of the comfortable, snuggly, although now faded and dingy, chairs on the lanai. She sipped her tea, drinking in the views and all the glorious colors of Hawaii. The sounds of the mynah birds, francolins, and a myriad of other local bird species filled her ears.

Memories flooded back of the mornings she and Scott had sat here sipping orange juice, soaking up the peace following their daily early morning walks. She smiled as an Eastern cardinal flew by in a flash of red, thinking of the days when the neighbor above them used to throw bird seed over her balcony railing, subsequently attracting small flocks of birds that settled to feed on the grass alongside Susan and Scott's lanai. There had been saffron finches, red house wrens, Java sparrows, zebra doves, mynah birds, the small red-headed Hawaiian cardinals, and many others. Their feeding had been noisy but orderly. Amazingly the birds didn't fight over the food. It was a case of live and let live, with each bird concentrating on its own needs.

Years later, when the condo board had outlawed spreading seed to feed the birds because the practice was attracting rats, individual birds would drop by the lanai to beg for handouts while she and Scott had breakfast at the lanai table. Their favorites were the small red-headed cardinals. With their red head, white ring around their neck, black back, and gray chest, they looked like they were wearing a tuxedo. She had once managed to train one of them to eat small bits of bread or Cheerios out of her hand.

The bittersweet memories brought a tear to her eye. She almost indulged in a good cry, but it had been several years since she had last allowed herself that indulgence. She didn't want to go back to those days.

Susan suddenly recalled the conflicting advice she had received from her friends. Her single and divorced friends had encouraged her to reenter the dating scene after the first year following Scott's death. In contrast, her few widowed friends urged her to take her time. They talked about how they didn't think they would ever want to date again and certainly not to remarry, preferring to live with their memories of the happy years with their spouses. They also enjoyed the freedom that came with not having someone to look after.

Like them, Susan wasn't looking for another man, although there was a substantial degree of social isolation that came with being widowed. During the initial period of bereavement, Susan had cut herself off from everyone, often spending most of the day in bed. When she finally reemerged, her married friends would invite her to socialize when they had a single man at their dinner table and needed another woman to even things out. They also they tried some matchmaking, dismissing Susan's disinterest as false.

Susan pushed aside those recollections. Returning to the pressing tasks looming in the present, she soon began a list of what she would need to do today. First was to get some breakfast. Then she would take a cab to the airport to rent a car. Next was shopping for groceries. She began making her shopping list. When she had listed everything she could think of, she finished her tea, took one last look at the view, closed and locked the lanai door, and collected her purse. It was 8:00 a.m.

Wondering whether she would encounter anyone she knew, she strolled up the driveway that threaded through the complex to the main road, admiring the tropical foliage and noting changes in the landscaping since her last visit. Her destination was the Kona Country Club, about a quarter of a mile north on Alii Drive. She planned to have breakfast at the golf club restaurant, the Vista, which overlooked the course and had panoramic views of it and of the sea. This was where she and Scott had always breakfasted on their first morning on the island. The breakfasts there had been delicious and huge! She was extremely hungry, so she had no doubt that she would finish the entire serving this morning, no matter how large.

The stroll in the cool morning air was pleasant, and she felt invigorated by the time she arrived at the restaurant, noting that the restaurant had changed its name.

"Aloha and Happy New Year!" greeted the hostess as Susan approached. "It's a perfect morning for enjoying breakfast and the view! Would you like that empty table in the front by the window? You'll get a little breeze and a splendid view."

"Yes, I'd like that. Thank you."

"Have you eaten here before?"

"Often in the past when my husband and I spent time on the island. However, it's been many years. This is my first time back in Kona since he passed away four years ago."

"I'm sorry about your loss," commiserated the hostess. "I hope you will still enjoy being here. We've changed owners since the golf course remodel, but I think the food is still as good, probably because we retained our chef!" Handing Susan a menu, the hostess pointed to an easel holding a blackboard that stood near the entrance to the restaurant. "The daily specials are posted over there on the blackboard. They will be delicious, but so will anything from the menu."

Susan took the proffered menu. "If the food is as good as it used to be, I'm sure I will enjoy it."

Susan perused the board and then the menu. *Something substantial seems in order*, she thought. She remembered the scrumptious French toast, thick but light, and enormous fluffy pancakes with sausage links, large juicy slabs of ham, or rashers of bacon. This morning, she decided something with more protein and less sugar and calories would give her energy for the day ahead, as well as be kinder to her figure.

"I'll have the eggs benedict topped with salmon, a scoop of rice, a tropical fruit salad, large glass of fresh orange juice, and coffee," she instructed the waitress.

That should hold me for a while, she thought as she looked around the restaurant. Several tables were occupied by men in sporty attire, presumably early golf foursomes. Another table was occupied by a half-dozen women, probably locals getting together while their men were golfing, assumed Susan.

Soon the waitress was pouring a steaming cup of fresh Kona coffee. The aroma stimulated Susan's already healthy appetite. Susan sipped her coffee and concentrated on the view. She spotted a mother whale with a calf playing in the distant waters. She and Scott had always enjoyed watching them. A catamaran, the *Fair Wind*, drifted into sight as it made its way to the dock by the Keauhou Sailing Club. Another half hour, Susan knew, it would be loading passengers for a trip to Kealakekua Bay for sightseeing and snorkeling. Susan also spotted a half-dozen small objects moving slowly across the bay. She knew from the past that these were outrigger canoes from the canoe club located just behind the bay, probably returning from their early morning outings.

She found herself pushing back memories. Obviously coming to terms with the past in the present was not going to be easy. Perhaps, once she had more time to indulge in memories, she would begin to find them comforting.

The waitress arrived at the table with her juice and fruit salad. "It will be only a few more minutes until your breakfast is ready. Did you see the whales? We've seen a lot this year. It was quite a relief. The past two years, counts were lower than usual. Officials were concerned that something was happening to kill them off. The increase in the numbers we are seeing is reassuring. Lack of whales had become a problem for the whale sightseeing boats. Tourists don't like it when they pay to go on a whale cruise and don't see whales. The only saving grace was that spinner dolphins were plentiful."

"I did see the whales, a mother and calf. They were doing a lot of splashing around out there! They seemed to be having a great time. I wish that I could join them!"

As the waitress headed back to the kitchen, Susan began on her fruit salad. The tropical fruit mix of mango, papaya, orange, pineapple, and banana was truly Hawaiian. Since the fruit was locally grown, it was fresh and delectable. Susan savored the flavors, subtly enhanced with a touch of lime juice. Delicious!

It seemed only moments before her main dish arrived, containing far more than she would normally eat at home. If she were to make a habit of eating so much, she'd need to think about larger clothing in almost no time! Still, after yesterday's experience, she intended to relax and enjoy her breakfast.

Twenty minutes later, her plate totally empty, Susan leaned back in the comfortable chair, took a deep breath, and relaxed as she sipped a fresh cup of coffee brought by the helpful waitress. Another fifteen minutes of pampering, and she would be off. When she reluctantly finished her coffee, she asked the waitress for the check and to please call for a taxi. She had just finished paying when the cab arrived.

Susan climbed into her taxi and directed the driver to take her to Avis Car Rental at the airport.

"No luggage?" he asked in surprise.

Susan explained how she had arrived late the night before and needed to return to the airport to rent a car for the duration of her visit.

"Since I had cancelled my original reservation when our flight was diverted to San Francisco and I wasn't sure when I'd be able to pick up a car, I didn't make new reservations. I certainly hope that I'll be able to get a car! I didn't think about the fact that it is high season in Hawaii!"

Why hadn't she thought about that? Clearly it was because she had been exhausted last night. She would have serious problems if she couldn't get a car. Perhaps she should have called this morning first thing! Now it was too late. She'd just have to hope for the best.

"Would you like me to wait while you see if you can get a car?" asked the driver.

"No thank you," said Susan as she paid him. "If I can't get a car at Avis, I'll walk over to one of the other companies to try. I really cannot do without a car this trip. Wish me luck!"

Susan walked up the ramp to the Avis office. Fortunately it didn't look too busy. After a brief wait in line, she was called to the desk. Susan gave her name and explained what had happened. The clerk looked at the computer and then walked to the back office to talk with someone.

When she returned, she exclaimed, "You're in luck! The agent who took your call entered a note in the computer about what had happened. He commented that this local office might be closed by the time you arrived at the airport and requested they hold a car for you until noon today. That's when the first flights from the mainland will start to arrive. It's good you came early! We have a Honda Accord that was dropped off this morning. I know you asked for a compact, but since we don't have one, we'll give you the midsize at the same price since you'll be here for a month or more. It's been washed and is ready to go."

Susan handed the agent her credit card.

"The car is in stall twenty-one C," stated the agent, handing her the contract and indicating where to sign. After Susan signed and returned the contract, the agent handed her a key, a copy of the contract, and her credit card. "Aloha and Mahalo."

"Aloha," responded Susan with a grin that signaled her relief.

Susan located space 21-C and briefly inspected the outside of the car, making note on her contract of a small scratch on the right rear door, the only sign of damage. She opened the front doors to let out the hot air before entering and then started the engine and the air-conditioning. No sooner had she gotten the mirrors adjusted when her cell phone rang. Picking it up, she saw that it was her daughter, Kristin, calling.

"Hi, sweetheart."

"Oh! Thank God you answered, Mom. I've been frantic! I got your message yesterday, but when I didn't hear from you today, I got really worried. What's going on?"

"I'm sorry I didn't call you this morning. I must admit that with everything that happened yesterday, being very hungry when I got up this morning, the emotional impact of being here without your dad, the pressing need to get back to the airport for a car, and the necessity of shopping for some food to fill my empty pantry, I completely forgot about calling! I'm sorry to have worried you."

Susan briefly described to Kristin her adventures of the previous day. "Now I'm sitting in my rental car at the Avis lot at the airport, just ready to head out to get my groceries. How late your time can I call you back to chat and fill you in with more detail?"

They agreed that Susan would call back before 9:00 p.m. EST (4:00 p.m. Hawaii time). Susan checked the time. It was now 10:00 a.m. That would just about give her time to get her groceries, have some lunch, and let the complex manager know that she was on-site before calling Kristin.

Susan was shocked at the food prices at KTA, despite awareness that food was always more expensive in Hawaii than on the mainland. Even in Seattle, food prices had been rising in recent years. Today, some items on her list cost two to three times what she would have paid back home. She could understand why prepared foods that had to be shipped would cost more, but for things such as local orange juice and locally grown fruits and vegetables, there was no good reason, except to make maximum profit by soaking the tourists.

"I wonder if the prices will drop a bit come February when there are fewer tourists here."

She remembered that there had been such a drop in the prices in the past when she and Scott had been here. The higher cost of living was one argument for selling the condo. She'd have to start a list of pros and cons.

Now that I have everything I need for the short term, I'll plan a trip to Costco to stock up on items I'll use regularly, and I'll hit the farmer's market later in the week, she thought as she loaded the car in preparation for heading home.

Chapter 3

*Believe that if you just show up and try
to do the right thing, things will improve.
Wait, watch, and work. Don't give up.*

THURSDAY AFTERNOON, JANUARY 1

Susan arrived back at the condo and prepared to unload her groceries from the trunk. As she lifted her first grocery bag, a car pulled into the space beside her car. A tall, slender, tanned man wearing cargo shorts, a skintight T-shirt, and flip-flops got out. The T-shirt emphasized his trim, muscular body.

His face, framed by wavy chestnut brown hair, broke into a wide grin. "Aloha. I've not seen you around here before. Are you here for vacation?"

"No, I'm here to check out the condition of my condo, which I've been renting. I must decide whether to fix it up to use or sell it. I'm Susan Brooks, by the way. I'm in 11B. Do you live here, or are you renting for your vacation?"

"My wife and I live in 21B, so we're just above you. We

bought about three years ago after we retired from our jobs on the mainland and have been fixing it up ever since. I'm Donald Sanborn. My wife is Deborah. She's at work now. She works part time as a realtor. But when she gets home, I'll have her stop by and say hello, if that's ok."

"I'd be pleased to meet her. It's been nearly five years since my husband and I were here, and I'm afraid I probably don't know many of the owners anymore."

"Actually there are a number of folks Deborah and I've gotten to know in this building who have been here for many years. I'll bet there are still people around that you know. It seems that folks really like this complex and tend to stay. Can I give you a hand with some of those groceries?"

Not wanting to get into an extended conversation, Susan responded, "Thank you, Don, but no. I really need some exercise after sitting all day yesterday on a plane. Carrying my few groceries will be about the only exercise I get today. Please do ask your wife to stop by to say hello when she has a chance."

Susan fished her house keys out of her purse and carried an armload of groceries to her door. Inside, she plunked the bag of groceries down on the counter, making a second and third trip to retrieve the rest.

Before putting anything away, she decided to check the condition of the cabinet interiors. Although generally clean, there was some dust inside and marks showing where cans had previously sat. Susan decided to scrub out all the cabinets before doing anything else. When she had finished, she washed out the interior of the refrigerator as well. Finally she decided where she wanted to keep the various items and loaded them into the appropriate places.

By the time she had finished, she was tired and hungry.

Susan glanced at her watch. It was 1:00 p.m. She made a ham sandwich, grabbed a bottle of iced tea and a napkin, and headed for the lanai. After lowering the sunscreen, she settled in at the small table and watched the golfers tee off while she ate. She did a mental review of who had been living in each of the twelve units of her building when she was last here. She knew that Rose, who had lived in the unit that the Sanborns had purchased, died about a year after Susan and Scott had returned home to Seattle that last spring. Jeannine, in the far first-floor unit had sold her unit just before Scott and Susan left so she could move nearer her seriously ill son in Oahu. Above Jeanine, Charles and Nancy Ames had also sold that spring because they bought a house on the island.

Four of the twelve units in the building had been primarily vacation rentals; their owners used their units for only a week or two yearly. That meant that the longtimers Don had referred to could be any of the four remaining units. Jack and Elizabeth Lutz had lived in the unit to her immediate left. The unit to her right had been Lynette and Buster Rustin. Above them were Holger and Suzanne Schmidt, and the top of that stack had been Gloria and Clive Pressler. Several of those couples might still be here. All four had been friends with Susan and Scott. The couples often got together for a game of cards or happy hour or to go out to a show or musical performance. It would be nice to see them. But there was still the recurring issue of memories that would reemphasize Scott's absence and what, for Susan, was the bigger concern of being a third wheel.

Susan had forgotten to bring the manager's telephone number, so after putting away her lunch dishes, she strolled up the hill to the manager's unit. Jeff, the manager, was not in, but his wife, Michelle, was. Susan greeted Michelle, who seemed not to recognize her, so Susan explained who she was. Michelle expressed embarrassment at not remembering her. Susan assured her that five years and loss of thirty pounds had probably made major changes in her appearance.

She asked Michelle to let Jeff know that she would be using her unit for the next month, possibly longer. She had Michelle write down Jeff's telephone number and requested a reserved parking spot for the duration of her stay. During the winter season when vacation renters were around, parking in front of her unit could be an iffy proposition. Often several couples jointly rented a unit and each couple rented their own car, leading to a lack of convenient parking spaces. A reserved space was essential.

Returning to her unit, Susan poured some tonic and orange juice into a large glass. It was definitely getting hot. She set the glass on the coffee table, turned on the ceiling fan, and then settled into the living room sofa to benefit from the moving air. She dialed Kristin's number.

"Hi, Mom! Thanks for calling back. I'm dying to hear the whole story of your trip yesterday and how you found things there at the condo."

Susan recounted the story of her long trip in vivid detail, knowing that Kristin liked to feel part of what was going on in her life. Then she described the sorry state of the condo and the amount of work that might be needed.

"Any idea yet whether you want to keep it or sell it?"

"It's much too early to make a decision. Either way, I need to do repairs and quite a bit of cosmetic work on the place. While the work is being done, I will have time to come to terms with my feelings and to consider the pros and cons of both options. I also need to talk with your brother. Brendon is fond of Hawaii and loves spending time here. That must factor into any decision.

"I would, however, like to decide before I purchase new carpets and furniture. I'll buy a better quality of product if I am going to spend time here than if I plan to sell. Buyers probably want to put their own stamp on the place. In its present condition, the condo is too dreary to stay very long, so it's a bit of a dilemma. While I'm pondering my decision, I'll concentrate on getting the place cleaned and repaired. After that, I'll still need to repaint the interior and either remove and replace the wallpaper or paint those walls too. Looks like I'll be busy for a while.

"Another issue for me is how many of the folks I used to hang out with are still here and how they react to me as a single. I'm really not up for starting new relationships from scratch. If I am able to resume some comfortable friendships, then I might consider spending a few months here each year."

"How are you handling being there without Dad?"

"I've had a few emotional moments, a few tears. The memories are bittersweet. It hurts sometimes, but I'm doing better than I had feared. The feelings don't devastate me like they did the first year or two after Dad died. Remembering our happy times helps. Just the fact that I was able to do this trip is a sign of the progress I've made."

"That's great, Mom! I was worried that going back might make you backslide emotionally, just as you were starting to pick up your life again. What would you think about me flying over there in a few weeks when you're closer to a decision? I haven't seen you since you were here at Thanksgiving, and I'd love to get away from this miserable Southeastern winter weather. I'd love to visit Hawaii again. Besides, we always have a good time shopping for home furnishings, so I could help you with that or with some painting or wallpapering. I might be able to swing a week, including travel time. Jim can look after the boys. This is a quiet time of year with their sports activities. It's mostly the homework issues he'll have to deal with, and they are getting better about doing it on their own as they get older. I think they are proud of their good grades, so they are motivated to keep working."

"Oh, sweetheart! That would be fabulous! It's been so long since we had some girl time, and I know how much you love this place. Your wishes must also be considered in my decision about keeping it or selling it. How about the last week in January? By then, I should have been able to complete some of the messier spruce-up work."

"I'll check airline schedules and fares and get back to you. It would be fabulous if this works out! I'll talk to Jim about it now, before Alex and Jack get back from their basketball game. I drove them and their friend Adam to the game, so Gwen will bring them back when she picks up her son. Take care, Mom. I love you."

As Susan was carrying her glass to the sink, she heard a knock on the door. It was Jeff, the complex manager.

"Welcome back, Susan! Michelle told me you had stopped by. She was so embarrassed not to have recognized you! You do look different. Fabulous actually! How are you doing?"

"I'm doing ok. Thanks for asking. It looks like I've got my work cut out for me, fixing up this condo."

"Yes, I'm afraid your tenants weren't always as tidy as you and Scott. In fact, your most recent renters didn't seem to clean very often. He was a carpenter. Neighbors seemed to think that he was doing some of the early stages of his cabinetry work here in the unit. They often heard sawing and subsequently saw him carrying partially built furniture out to his truck and bags of junk to the dumpster. The unit was often a mess when I let in the exterminator. They were both smokers as well. Some of your neighbors were quite unhappy about that. Many folks in Building One complained frequently to me about their loud and raucous arguments late at night. I was glad when they left early, apparently something about her mother having had a severe stroke and them having to move back to look after her."

"Maybe you should have told me or my rental agent about the problems. I could have talked to them or arranged to terminate the lease early. I will need to speak to the agent about renting to smokers, if I decide to rent again. I had specifically requested nonsmokers since I'm allergic to cigarette smoke. That must, in fact, be why I've been having some sinus problems and a sore throat since arriving!"

"Well, Susan, it's nice to have you back. By the way, I put a reserved sign on the parking space in front of your unit. Call if you need anything else."

"Thanks so much, Jeff. That should do it for now." Susan closed the front door, making a mental note to call her management company the next day. Feeling that she had done enough for one day, she returned to the sofa with her book.

About an hour later, she heard a knock on the door. Pattering to the door in her bare feet, Susan opened the door to find a slender blond woman in a cool peach-colored pantsuit standing outside.

"Hi, I'm Deborah Sanborn from upstairs. Don told me to stop by and introduce myself. You must be Susan. Am I interrupting anything?"

"Yes, I'm Susan. You are not interrupting anything

important. I was just catching up on some long-delayed reading. Would you like to come in for a minute?"

"Thanks. I'll only stay briefly. Wow! Your unit is so different from any that I've seen in the complex. It seems so spacious in comparison to most. I'm a part-time real estate agent, so I guess I'm sensitive to such things. I'm trying to figure out what you've done with the original floor plan. It must have been like ours."

"Funny how everyone has that reaction to this unit! We didn't do the renovation ourselves. We bought it this way. Scott and I had looked at about thirteen other condo complexes and then several units for sale in this complex. Although we loved this complex, the first units we saw felt somewhat claustrophobic. When we saw this one, we knew it was a keeper. The lady who owned it at the time had done the renovations only about two years before, so it was in excellent condition. It was for sale furnished, so we could begin using it without needing to do anything except show up!

"The sitting area over there by the wall with the Murphy bed unit was originally the second bedroom. A partial wall with an arched opening facing us and one running perpendicular to the kitchen, with a door to the hallway were removed, doubling the size of the living room. Like in your unit, a wall with a pass-through to the kitchen originally started about three feet back from where the present counter now ends. Getting rid of that and extending the counter makes the kitchen seem so much larger.

"The kitchen, living room, and dining room are all now open to the wall of windows that runs the length of the living room with views of the golf course and ocean. The remodel also gave space for the additional built-in cabinets that serve both the dining room and the kitchen, providing invaluable extra storage space and the work area with the barstools. We didn't really need a second bedroom since we didn't expect many visitors. The Murphy bed worked fine when one of our kids came to visit. They didn't seem to mind the lack of privacy."

"Yes," said Deborah, looking thoughtful. "I can now envision what was done. Would you mind if we steal some ideas? We still have a lot of remodeling to do."

"Yes, I can imagine. That unit must have been in quite a state. Rose was a dear, but she hadn't spent any money on upkeep in years, and it was already in need of attention the first time we saw it nineteen years ago. I expect it must have been pretty dirty too. As she aged, Rose couldn't do much cleaning, and those three cats of hers shed everywhere. Feel free to borrow ideas."

"My real estate sixth sense told me that our unit was a steal, despite the problems," said Deborah. "Not many people would have wanted to take on such a big remodel, so we got it at a rock-bottom price. Don was eager to show what he could do."

"Don did mention that you are working as a real estate agent. Were you a real estate agent on the mainland?"

"Yes, but full time. When we came here, Don was happy puttering around, doing most of the work needed to fix up the unit himself. He had been a contractor back home, so he was knowledgeable about what to do. He found doing this work in retirement was enjoyable, with no stressful deadlines, and it gave him something useful to do with his time. I, on the other hand, found that I was going stir-crazy with all the dust and noise in the unit. I enjoyed working with him in planning the renovations, but since I'm not very handy, I was mostly in his way when he was working. We decided it would make sense for me to work part time to cover some of the expenses of renovation while he did the labor. Life here turned out to be more expensive than we had anticipated."

"I can understand that. I nearly had apoplexy when I saw the prices at KTA today! When Scott and I were last here, we found things a bit pricey, but nothing like this!"

"Is your husband here with you now? I'm sure Don would love to meet him."

"I'm afraid not. He died four years ago, and this is the first time I've had the courage to come back since then."

"I'm so sorry. I didn't know," said Deborah, flushing with embarrassment.

"Of course you didn't! I'm doing much better now, which is why I dared to do this trip. I hope we'll have a chance to visit and get to know each other one day soon when you're not working."

"A group of us ladies get together at the pool on Wednesday mornings from ten to noon for what we call a stitch and bitch. It's a great time to meet whoever is around—both renters and owners—and to do some needlework while chatting. Please join us."

"I'd love to. That might be a good way for me to reengage here. Is the yarn shop still in the old industrial area near Costco? I need to get some yarn and instructions since I haven't done needlework for years and years."

"It's still there. The new owner is extremely helpful. Hope to see you Wednesday. It was really nice to meet you."

As Deborah left, Susan reflected that the poolside knitting group might indeed be a good way to find out about who was still around and how she might fit in. She was hungry again, so she microwaved a frozen entrée for dinner. Then she made a to-do list for the next day, before heading to bed.

Chapter 4

*If you want to get somewhere,
start with the first step.*

FRIDAY, JANUARY 2

The next morning, Susan was awakened by the eerie and raucous chorus of the myna birds clustered in the nearby banyan tree and the squeal of the golf course gate as the groundskeeper opened it for the work crew to mow the golf course. She remembered how Scott had occasionally gone down after the golf course closed for the day and oiled the gate. He'd gotten really annoyed at being awakened at 6:00 a.m. every morning. A poor sleeper, he usually slept best in the early morning hours, preferring to sleep in until at least 8:00. Susan, in contrast, liked to rise early to enjoy the morning quiet and cool air. Perhaps later she would oil the gate anyway so others could sleep.

By 7:30 a.m., Susan was taking her morning walk. She followed a route she and Scott had taken most mornings when they were in Hawaii, south on Alii Drive and then down the hill to a dirt road that led to the ocean at Land's End, the site of an ancient Hawaiian battle. Queen Ka'ahumanu had pressured her son, Kamehameha II, to end the *kapu* system (religious laws banning specific practices) that had been in effect during the reign of his father, Kamehameha I.

When he decided to end *kapu*, his cousin Kekuaokalani, a major religious leader who opposed ending *kapu*, led an army against him in 1820. Rock terraces cut into the side of the mountain were graves of soldiers killed in the battle. Wild goats now roamed the area. Just beyond the battle site by the ocean, lava rock formations from prior volcanic eruptions are pounded by ocean waves, producing spectacular sprays that rise thirty or more feet above the rocks.

From the condo it was about a half-mile walk to Land's End. Once at the shoreline, Susan continued another eighth of a mile along a barely-there dirt trail that threaded north through the lava rubble, approximately parallel to the ocean behind the lava pinnacles. This brought her to an area containing tide pools, salt pots, and other interesting oceanside sights. Usually she and Scott had explored the natural tide pools, climbing over huge lava boulders or piles of large, rounded rocks that had been tossed onto piles by angry seas. The area was strewn with broken bits of coral, shells, small lava rocks, gravel, and occasional small patches of sand. Tide pools, ranging in size from barely larger than a puddle to deep pools forty feet long by twenty feet wide, contained small specimens of several varieties of fish, tube worms, anemones, sea plants, corals, and nervous crabs that hid under rocks when they sensed motion. Each tide pool was different. On no two days was the life in any single one quite the same.

Often after exploring the tide pools, they would seat themselves on relatively flat rocks situated in the shade under trees that grew in the narrow, wooded area behind the lava piles. There they could watch the sea and listen to the sounds of waves crashing onto the shore and wild parrots squawking in the woods. They especially liked an area where the lava boulders had formed a sort of mini-canyon that opened to the sea.

When the waves came crashing in, water rushed into the canyon, filling the canyon with water that overflowed with a huge gush and then cascaded over the surrounding rocks in rivulets and rushed toward the shore. As the ocean receded and the level of the water in the canyon dropped, water from above would cascade down the inner sides of the canyon, creating the effect of waterfalls. It was spectacular!

Sometimes Susan and Scott spotted brightly colored fish swimming near the shore or spinner dolphins and whales frolicking further out in the bay. Occasionally several redheaded cardinals would come and bathe in one of the shallow pools. There was no sandy beach. The only sand here was where it collected in depressions among the lava.

Susan had followed their usual routine this morning, talking to Scott in her head as she recalled the magic of their many visits there. She noticed changes since their last visit. Piles of rocks had shifted their position; grass and an occasional shrub or small tree had invaded the shoreline. More sand had accumulated in hollows, prompting visions of sandy beaches millennia from now. Despite being alone, she felt peaceful there, one with nature. As always, she was reluctant to leave for the return climb up the hill to the condo. She promised herself she would come back one day in the cool of the evening with a sketch pad and some watercolors.

Upon returning to the condo, Susan showered and dressed. Then she had a leisurely breakfast on the lanai before returning to the bedroom to get her purse. She planned to do a Costco run and then stop at the yarn shop. Hopefully the worst of the early-morning commuter traffic was past and she could do her errands before the tourists began to clog Route 11, the Queen Ka'ahumanu Highway, known as the Queen's Highway.

She opened the bedroom venetian blind and then the window to let in cool morning air to freshen the condo. She would leave it open until she returned from her errands. As she headed for the closet between the bedroom and master bath to get her purse, she thought, *Funny, that stretch of carpet between the bedroom and the bath looks cleaner than the rest. I'd have expected it to be dirtier since it gets more traffic. I hadn't noticed it before. The bright light coming in from the window must have brought it to my attention. I wonder if a recent tenant used that scrap of carpet we left in the overhead storage area over the computer closet to replace the original carpet.*

Out of curiosity, Susan retrieved the stepstool from the laundry closet and climbed up to check the storage cabinet. Sure enough, the carpet was gone. *I guess I should be glad they cared enough to replace it if it got grubby,* she thought. *It really does emphasize how dirty the rest of the carpet has become.*

She replaced the stepstool, grabbed her purse, and headed out to do her errands. Her first stop was at the yarn store. The helpful proprietor found Susan a simple pattern for knitting a scarf and a book that clearly reviewed basic stitches. Susan selected some variegated peach yarn that she thought would appeal to her daughter, deciding that the scarf would be for Kristin. Fortunately she also remembered that she would need knitting needles. After chatting briefly with the proprietor, she carried her purchases to the car and headed up the road to Costco.

Costco was busy, as usual, and finding a place to park was a challenge. It took some time for Susan to reorient herself to the layout of the store, but soon her shopping cart was loaded with paper products, frozen dinners, and cereal. She passed over the packages of fresh produce, meats, fish, and other goodies because she could not possibly use the amount of food in a package.

After checking out at Costco, she decided to stop at Marina Seafood, the fish store at the Honokohau Harbor. She was craving fresh fish. There she selected a succulent piece of ahi tuna for dinner. This would be a rare treat. The fish sold at the store was fresh off a fishing boat, so it should be delectable.

It was rare that Susan cooked these days. Even before Scott's sudden death, she had become a reluctant cook. After cooking three meals a day for almost fifty years, she felt burnt out. When she used that as an excuse with Scott one day when she simply couldn't get inspired about what to make for dinner, he insisted, "It's your attitude that is the problem. Once you look at the creative side of cooking, your inspiration will return. I think it is fun to cook. In fact, one of these days I'll cook us a meal."

"The sooner the better as far as I'm concerned. You can even take over the meal planning and cooking on a regular basis," she encouraged.

Of course it hadn't happened. She cooked most days, although they ate out occasionally when she was really tired. But on these occasions, Scott had often complained that the quality of meals at the restaurants was going downhill. Susan had to agree. Even fresh produce seemed less tasty in recent years as genetic engineering bred for qualities that reduced bruising during shipping, losing flavor in the process.

Now that Scott was gone, things had changed. Initially, devastated by his loss, food had no interest. Her children and friends had constantly pressed food on her, later encouraging her to eat regularly to maintain her health. She had had no interest or appetite. Eventually she resumed eating, more because she felt she ought to than because she found it enjoyable. She relied almost entirely on frozen meals for dinner and a piece of fruit, a salad, or a sandwich for lunch. Breakfast was the one meal she was inclined to cook these days. She loved omelets, particularly Greek omelets with tomato and feta cheese or mushroom and spinach omelets with grated parmesan cheese and tarragon. As a bonus, the protein gave her a boost of energy to start her day and the cheese some essential calcium.

Tonight, however, would be an exception to her routine. Grilled fish with a salad and French fries sounded heavenly! She stopped at McDonald's on the way home to pick up some fries she could reheat to eat with her dinner.

As she unloaded her purchases, she saw Deborah heading out to the pool.

Deborah waved. "Don't forget the stitch and bitch on Wednesday at ten."

"I'll be there. In fact, I went to the yarn store today and bought my supplies. Have a good swim."

Later that evening, feeling satiated after her hearty and delicious meal, Susan turned on the television for the first time since her arrival. Her eyes were too tired for reading. Watching television seemed sufficiently undemanding to help her relax before bedtime. She came across a report on the day's events at the Annual Champion's Tour event held at the Hualalai Resort's Golf Course.

I haven't been to a golf tournament in years, she thought. *Let's see, tomorrow is Saturday. That means I can't reach anyone to come give estimates for work on the condo, so maybe I'll attend the tournament in the morning. That will give me something interesting to do and offer a break from errands and planning work on the condo. On my way back, I can stop at the farmer's market for some fresh strawberry papayas, apple bananas, and an orchid to cheer up this place. Then on Sunday, I can run to a hardware store for supplies and do some minor fix-ups myself. Monday, I'll start getting estimates on the bigger jobs and begin to get workmen scheduled to get this place in order.*

An hour later, bored by the programs on television, Susan called it a day and headed to bed.

Chapter 5

In the book of life, the longest chapter is on accidental occurrences.

SATURDAY, JANUARY 3

On Saturday morning, Susan decided to pass on her early morning walk. She'd probably get more than enough exercise walking at the golf tournament. Dressed in her most comfortable Earth sandals, khaki-colored capris, and a cream-colored tank top, she headed out. She carried a light cardigan. Eighty-five degrees could feel chilly in the ocean breeze. She wore a big hat to keep the sun off her face, even though she had slathered on sunscreen.

Arriving at Hualalai, she paid the parking attendant and then located one of the last parking spaces still available. Clearly interest in the tournament had grown since she last attended. She was directed to follow the signs to a big white tent where she bought a ticket for entry and was fitted with the tournament wristband. She stopped at the refreshment tent, purchased a bottle of water, and then headed out to find a shady, elevated spot where she could sit on the grass and still see what was going on. She joined a group sitting in the shade near the green of the second fairway. From that vantage point, she couldn't see the golfers teeing off but could watch them in the distance hitting their second shot. Since the hole was toward the back of the green, she could also see them putting.

After about an hour, Susan realized that the approaching players were Phil Michelson and Jim Furack. Since she enjoyed watching those players and was getting stiff from sitting, she decided to follow as they progressed around the golf course. That way she would get some exercise while enjoying the play. She could also enjoy the views afforded by this spectacular golf course where fairways and greens were often viewed against the mountain or the sea. Deep-black lava rock formations contrasted so beautifully with the white sand of the traps and the green of the grass. These sights pleased her artist's eye.

As the players were moving on to the tenth fairway, Susan was momentarily distracted by several squawking seagulls, just as she turned to move on with the crowd. Her foot hit an unnoticed depression in the ground, and she stumbled and then fell down a small rise. She landed hard on her back with one leg twisted under her. *I'm still as clumsy as ever*, she thought. *I must be a charming sight!*

As she started to recover her breath, she registered the pain in her ankle. She lay there for a minute, waiting for the pain to subside. When she wiggled her ankle, she was relieved to find that she could move it.

One of the volunteers came over to her. "Are you all right, miss?" he asked as he helped her to her feet.

"I think I twisted my ankle a bit, but it seems like I can walk on it," she replied, gingerly putting some weight on it.

"Are you sure?"

"Just give me a few minutes to stand and assess it. Then I can let you know."

She put some more weight on her ankle. The pain didn't seem too bad, so she reassured the volunteer that she could manage and began to walk slowly toward the refreshment area. There she hoped to find a chair where she could sit to rest her ankle while she had a bite to eat. It had been several hours since breakfast. By the time she got there, grimacing with every step, the place was busy with long lines for food. She saw no empty chairs anywhere. Susan painfully limped across the cart path to a shady spot near some houses. Her ankle was starting to swell now, and she needed to get her weight off it.

She sat on the grass under a tree and gasped in dismay at the rapidly swelling and discolored ankle. With some difficulty she removed her sandal. It had felt tight, and she realized that her entire foot was now swollen, as was her lower leg halfway to the knee. The intensifying pain soon brought tears to her eyes.

"Are you all right, miss?" Susan looked up and through the mist of her tears saw a six-foot, slender, fit, and very handsome white-haired man approaching her. "I saw you limping and thought I'd see if I can be of any assistance."

"I think I've sprained my ankle pretty badly. Some ice might help."

"I don't think we'll be able to get any from the refreshment area as jammed as it is. And you should probably elevate that foot for a while. My name is Walter Conway. I live in that house just over there. If you will give me a minute, I can bring my golf cart over and transport you to my house, where I can give you an ice pack and an aspirin, and you can elevate the leg until the worst of the swelling subsides."

"That's awfully kind of you, Mr. Conway. I agree that I need to do something to limit the swelling. Until that's done, I doubt I'll be going anywhere. I accept your very kind offer. My name is Susan Brooks."

Ten minutes later, Walter helped Susan hop from the golf cart to a comfortable wicker chair next to a matching glass-topped table on the lanai of his home. The lanai overlooked the ocean, and Susan caught a glimpse of waves crashing, even as she heard the roar of the ocean. Walter moved an ottoman close to her chair and helped her to position her leg comfortably on the pillow of the ottoman. A moment later he returned with two ice packs. One ice pack was wrapped in a soft towel. This he placed under her ankle. The other, he laid over the top.

"How about some iced tea and an aspirin while we wait for the swelling to subside?" he suggested.

"That does sound good. I can't thank you enough for coming to my assistance."

"No thanks needed. My mother always taught me that a gentleman should rescue a lady in distress, and I rather like the role of Sir Galahad."

"It's nice to know there are still some of them around ... gentlemen, I mean," Susan commented.

"Well, I do think that what our generation considered to be gentlemanly behavior is rare these days. The younger generations don't seem to value social niceties. A shame. I think manners and social conventions somehow made the world feel safer, certainly more predictable. One knew what to expect and how to behave, and one was more able to interpret the behavior of others. Now it's often a case of anything goes, and I often feel offended by things that were not intended to be offensive."

He headed back into the house, sliding open the doors that separated the two spaces. A few minutes later he returned with two tall glasses of iced tea and some cheese and crackers on a plate.

"I thought it might be a good idea to get a bit of food into your stomach before taking an aspirin. I'll be right back with the aspirin and hopefully an Ace bandage. My wife usually kept several in stock because she was susceptible to sprained ankles. I just need to find them."

Susan looked around her as she sipped her tea and nibbled on a cracker topped with cheese. The spacious lanai overlooked a narrow fairway with the ocean beyond, just like at her condo, except that here the ocean was much closer. Although the house was set between two other houses, it had a sense of privacy, due both to the positioning of the houses and to the mature trees, shrubs, and beds of flowering plants that surrounded it.

In addition to the table and four chairs where she was sitting, the spacious lanai had a cane bar with three cane stools, a large gas grill, and two chaise lounges. The lanai opened into the living area of the house, separated by the glass door panels that Walter had slid to the far ends of the opening, where they stacked one in front of the other. With the doors completely open, the house and lanai seemed to be one large space.

Walter returned, carrying a bottle of aspirin, an Ace bandage, and a pair of crutches, which he propped against the bar.

"It looks like you have your own health clinic here," Susan observed. "I'm so fortunate you came along when you did."

"We aim to please," said Walter with a chuckle. "Have you eaten anything?" Seeing Susan nod affirmatively, he handed her the bottle of aspirin. "Here, try two aspirin to start with. If that doesn't seem to be helping, we can try some Tylenol."

Susan obediently took the aspirin. "The ankle does feel somewhat better already. I think the ice is reducing the swelling."

"Well, just take it easy for a bit," he said, taking a seat at the table and picking up his glass. "So, Susan, I assume you were attending the golf tournament. Did you come by yourself?"

"Yes, I drove over this morning around ten. I had just been thinking about whether to call it a day or to pick up some refreshments when I fell and sprained my ankle. Now the decision has been made for me. As soon as I can walk on it, I'll get out of your hair and head home."

"Perhaps you should first see a doctor and have it looked at. Suppose you broke something. Do you live on the island, or are you here on vacation?"

"Actually, neither. My husband and I have a condo down in the Keauhou area. For many years we came here every winter. We would spend seven months in Seattle and about five here on the island."

"Perhaps we should call your husband and have him come to pick you up. Driving with that ankle probably isn't a great idea."

"I'm afraid that's impossible. He died four years ago of a heart attack. I miss him terribly! I came back this winter to check on the state of our condo. It's been rented since Scott died."

"So you're a widow! I'm a widower. My wife, Marge, died three years ago. She had cancer and was in declining health for a long period of time. I was devastated when the end came! I'm only now starting to pick up my life again. For the longest time, I didn't want to eat, socialize, or even get out of bed. My kids finally convinced me that I had to get moving and do at least one thing each day that would get me out of the house, whether a game of golf, a trip to the doctor, the grocery store, or some public event. When I came across you, I was just heading out to see a bit of the golf tournament as my activity for the day."

"I can certainly relate to what you described. I was almost a total recluse for the first two years. This trip was the first time I could face coming back here. It sounds like your kids and mine think alike. I got similar advice. How many children do you have, Walter, and are they living on the island?"

"We have three, and none of them lives on the island. Two, my oldest son and a daughter, are in California, and the younger son is in Chicago. They were all really good about coming here when Marge was ill. Then they came to visit me several times during the year after she passed away, taking turns looking in on their old dad. Last year for the first time, I managed to go and see them and the grandchildren. I have four grandchildren, two boys and two girls, aged five to thirteen. What about you, Susan? Children? Grandchildren?"

"We have two children, a son in California and a daughter in North Carolina, and three grandchildren, aged two to ten, two boys and one girl. Their lives are so busy that I usually do the travelling these days, although they had to do it the first two years after Scott died. But it's uncomfortable to visit with them for too long. I feel as if they are putting their lives on hold to spend time with me. How long have you lived on the island, Walter?"

"Almost twenty years. Marge and I had a lovely life here. We both enjoyed playing golf and taking long walks on the beach. She enjoyed theater and volunteered with the Kona theater group, mostly helping with publicity. I did some volunteer work with the local Rotary Club and got involved with the local county planning group."

"It sounds like we have some things in common. Scott and I also enjoyed taking long walks on the beach and attending theater and musical performances. We were not really able to get involved much with volunteer work because of our nomadic lifestyle. We weren't in either location long enough that organizations wanted to invest time in orienting us for any long-term activities. So any volunteering had to be mostly one-shot things, for example, environmental projects like removing nonnative plants or maintaining trails. I've recently started tutoring preschool children back in Seattle through one of the programs for low-income kids that prepares them for starting school. Apparently having some school-like activities during the summer helps them to do better when they start school. It feels good to be doing something useful again. After I retired, I missed being involved in meaningful activities that let me feel like I was contributing to the community."

"What sort of work did you do, Susan?"

"I taught statistics and research methods at the university. Scott was also a professor, but in physics. We met at the University of Nebraska, where we both got our first teaching job after we finished our PhD programs. What about you? What sort of work did you do?"

"I did a variety of jobs in my life, including a short stint as a policeman in New York City. My last job was as a consultant to international companies that required computer systems to protect proprietary data. That work required that I do a great deal of traveling. When I retired, my wife wanted me to stay put so we could enjoy what was left of our lives. Hawaii was the perfect place to spend retirement. Anyway, enough about me. How is that ankle doing?"

"It feels much better." Susan removed the ice pack, and they peered at the ankle. "It looks as if the swelling has gone down considerably."

"Yes, I agree. But judging by the discoloration, I'd say you did some major damage to the tissue. It's my judgment that you ought to keep it elevated for a bit longer, maybe without the ice pack, and see how it does. I'm not sure the swelling has reduced sufficiently for you to get your shoe on. I have a suggestion. I'm hungry, and I'll bet you are too. How about I call over to the restaurant with a takeout order? Then we can have something to eat here while you keep that foot elevated. Afterwards we'll see how you're doing. What do you like to eat: seafood, steak, a sandwich, or a salad?"

"That's a very kind offer. I must admit I am a bit hungry, and cooking might be a bit of a problem at the moment. I like almost anything, so why don't you order for me since you know what is good?"

"Are you comfortable there, or would you prefer to sit in a softer, more comfortable chair?"

"A soft, comfortable chair would be most welcome. I am feeling a bit tired, but maybe that's because I'm hungry."

Walter assisted Susan to move inside to a comfortable recliner, which allowed her to elevate her foot. After making her comfortable, he refreshed her iced tea and placed it next to her before placing a takeout order.

As he prepared to leave for the restaurant, he asked, "Would you like something to read while you wait? Or a television program? Some music?"

"No, thank you. I think I'll just sit here and close my eyes while you're gone. No, on second thought, some quiet music might be relaxing."

"I hope that classical will do. That and some occasional light jazz, country music, old favorites from the forties and fifties, and, of course, Hawaiian music are about all I listen to anymore."

"Classical would be perfect! Thank you."

As Walter left, Susan settled back into the recliner with her eyes shut, drifting asleep to the sounds of a Chopin sonata.

Thirty-five minutes later, Walter gently awakened her. "Dinner is served, Sleeping Beauty. Sorry to wake you, but I thought you'd like to eat the meal while it's fresh and hot."

He helped her to the dining room table where he had set up a virtual feast that included shrimp scampi, baked ahi with mango sauce, rice, a spinach salad, and fresh bread.

"Goodness! This is amazing! It looks scrumptious! There's enough food here to feed a small army!"

"I wasn't sure what you might prefer, so I selected several dishes. If you're as hungry as I am, we'll make it disappear in no time. Their food is really good, and I tend to get carried away when I order. Besides, leftovers always come in handy! Will you have some wine with dinner?"

"Perhaps just a small amount since I'll be driving home."

"About that. I don't think it is safe for you to drive with that ankle, so I took the liberty of asking the tournament officials to arrange for you to leave your car until tomorrow. We just have to call and give them your license plate number. After we've eaten and gotten your foot iced again for a bit, we'll wrap it in the Ace bandage. Then I'll drive you home. Tomorrow, if your foot is much better, I'll pick you up and drop you at your car."

"Are you sure that isn't too much of an imposition? You've

already been so kind to a stranger. I could just take a cab home tonight and one back tomorrow to pick up my car."

"No arguments, please. It's my pleasure. It makes me feel useful, something that doesn't happen often since Marge died. Now dig in and enjoy."

An hour and a half later, after a satisfying dinner and an easy flow of conversation that included a wide variety of topics, including family, Susan's pending decision about her condo, discussion of current events, and stories of favorite travel experiences, Walter settled Susan comfortably on the sofa with a new ice pack on her ankle and then began cleaning up the dishes.

"I haven't been so pampered in years. You have spoiled me. And I haven't enjoyed an evening's conversation so much since Scott died. Perhaps one day you will let me thank you by accepting an invitation to dinner. I'm still a decent cook, although I must admit that I don't entertain much anymore."

"A homemade meal would be a treat to look forward to, not to mention your company. You are so easy to talk with. I've been so uncomfortable around women since Marge's passing. I always feel that they have an agenda, and I'm not ready for or even interested in dating. For some reason, I haven't felt at all that way with you. I feel as if I've known you for years."

"Perhaps it's because we're both feeling the same way about new relationships because of what we've been through. Neither of us is ready for a long-term commitment. We still feel too much loyalty to the past. But it's nice to be able to share those thoughts and feelings without feeling that you are boring your listener."

"I think you've hit on a major element of why I'm so comfortable with you. Anyhow, I want you to know that while I'm sorry you have experienced so much discomfort with your ankle, I view it as fortuitous for me that you happened to have your accident just before I came along and that I was able to help. I have certainly enjoyed your company. Now I expect you must be feeling a bit tired, so let's get that ankle wrapped and get the crutches adjusted. Then I'll bring the car around. Hopefully you can get to it using the crutches."

Before leaving to get the car, Walter asked Susan for the make and model of her car as well as the license number so he could call the tournament official to confirm about leaving it overnight. He also requested her address and telephone number so he could call and arrange to pick her up the next day to retrieve the car, assuming she was up to it.

When they arrived at Susan's condo, Walter insisted on accompanying her into the unit and getting her settled on the couch with a glass of orange juice, the TV remote, her book, and her cell phone on the adjacent table. He placed the crutches within easy reach.

After she thanked him for all his assistance and assured him that she could manage to get herself from the sofa to bed using the crutches, he reluctantly departed.

Chapter 6

It is one of the beautiful compensations of life that you cannot help another without helping yourself.

SUNDAY, JANUARY 4

The next morning Susan awoke later than usual. Despite taking two Tylenol before going to bed, her sleep had been restless. She sat on the edge of the bed and tentatively put her foot on the floor, gradually putting her weight on it. The pain was considerably reduced from that of the previous afternoon. She hobbled to the bathroom and sat on the edge of the tub. Then she ran some warm water into the tub while she unwrapped the bandage.

Although barely swollen, her ankle resembled a rainbow, with streaks of yellow, purple, and blue. The warm water felt good on the ankle, so Susan slipped into the tub and indulged in a long soak. By the time the phone rang, she had dressed and eaten a bowl of cereal.

"Hi, Susan. It's Walter. How is the ankle this morning?"

"Much better, thanks. I can walk on it without the crutches, but will continue to use them for a day or two if that's ok with you. The crutches will give the muscles a chance to heal before I abuse them. I do think I'm ok to drive today, however."

"I'm pleased to hear that you are on the mend. Just don't try to do too much for the next few days."

"Actually I already had planned to spend tomorrow calling workmen and scheduling them to come give estimates for the work I need done on this place. That will keep me on my butt rather than on my feet!"

Walter chuckled. "Sounds like just what the doctor ordered. I have names and telephone numbers for several guys who have done some work for us. If you like, I'll bring them along when I pick you up to take you to your car. How about I pick you up at eleven thirty and take you to brunch? After we've eaten, I'll take you back to Hualalai for your car. Please say yes."

"I'd love to have the names of some reliable workmen. Thanks. And I'd enjoy having brunch with you. But you've already done so much for me!"

"It really is my pleasure. Like I told you last night, I feel very comfortable with you. In fact, I can't believe I've known you for less than twenty-four hours! See you at eleven thirty."

Susan spent a pleasant hour and a half sitting on the lanai with her book and some tonic, occasionally reading, but more often watching the golfers tee off, watching for whales, or chuckling at the antics of the birds. It was particularly funny to see the blue-headed male rock doves strutting and bowing as they courted their females, only to be unceremoniously ignored as the females moved away and continued their search for tasty tidbits.

By 11:15, she had changed clothing and freshened up in preparation for Walter's arrival. *Strange,* she thought. *I'm not at all uncomfortable about going to lunch with him.*

Then talking to Scott, as she was prone to do these days, she said, "Scott, I hope you don't mind. This in no way reflects on my feelings for you. They haven't changed a bit. I still miss you. But it is so nice to have someone to talk with who understands what it's like to lose a loved one. I've had little of that in the past four years, and frankly that makes me feel very lonely."

A knock on the door returned Susan's thoughts to the present. She greeted Walter at the door on her crutches. "I'm glad to see that you are taking care of yourself. May I escort you to the car, my lady?" he asked, bowing low.

"Thank you, kind sir," she replied with a grin and an awkward curtsy.

"I hope you like the food at Antony's. There were other places I'd have preferred to take you, but the parking is problematic. At Antony's I can just drop you in front of the door. Their food is not bad, and it's between here and Hualalai, so it is convenient. Also because of its location, I thought there might be fewer tourists, and we might be able to get a table outside."

"That's fine. It was thoughtful of you to think about the logistics."

Brunch was lovely. They sat at an outdoor table on the patio where they could hear and watch the waves crashing on the rocks below. A green-and-white striped market umbrella provided shade. The restaurant featured seafood. Susan's ahi fish sandwich was fresh and topped by a flavorful pineapple coleslaw and accompanied by a generous salad of mixed greens, avocado, and yellow pear tomatoes, with a green goddess dressing. To drink, she had a tonic with a slice of lime.

Conversation flowed freely, and before she knew how much time had passed, it was midafternoon and time to go for her car before traffic got too heavy on the Queen's Highway. After Walter saw her safely to her car, Susan again thanked him for lunch and all his hospitality and care.

"I will be busy with getting work set up and executed at the condo these next few weeks, but by Friday of next week, the worst of that should be over. By then, I should no longer need your crutches. Why don't you plan to come for dinner around six o'clock, not this Friday, but the following one. I think the date is January 16. We can start with cocktails on the lanai, followed by our dinner. When you leave, you can take the crutches with you."

"I do hope this isn't your way of letting me know that you won't want to see me again after that?"

"Of course not! I value your friendship and am so pleased to have someone with whom I can converse so easily. You are one of the most thoughtful people I've ever met. But I really do have an extremely busy few weeks ahead of me. And after so many years of avoiding relationships, I prefer not to move too fast. Can you understand that?"

"Of course, Susan. I'll see you on Friday, January 16, at five. Get home safely. Please give me a call to let me know you got home without mishap. Here's my number. It's unlisted, so don't lose the card. And when you have identified what kind of service people you will need, give me a call, and I'll see who on my list might be of help. I'm afraid I forgot to bring the list with me." Walter kissed her cheek. Then he closed the car door and walked back to his car.

Susan touched her cheek where Walter had kissed her. What was that all about? She certainly had been taken by surprise. She did think that he was enjoying her company as much as she enjoyed his, but the kiss seemed inconsistent with his expressed feelings that he wasn't ready to develop an intimate or long-term relationship. Maybe it was just a nice but relatively meaningless gesture.

Susan hoped that she hadn't been too abrupt when she suggested setting the invitation to dinner for almost two weeks away, but she really did feel that she wanted to move slowly in continuing to develop a relationship with Walter—on any basis. Some breathing space would be helpful. Further, it was essential to make some progress on fixing up her condo. She found its present condition depressing and couldn't enjoy living there without sprucing it up. Besides, there was no way she could sell if in its present condition, in the event that was what she decided to do.

Kristin's anticipated visit toward the end of the month prompted Susan's plan to complete at least the dirty and disruptive work before then. The condo had only 1,050 square feet, including the lanai. Unless it were neat and tidy, it felt overcrowded and unsettling. She'd like things to be in order so Kristin could relax and get some of the rest she had indicated she craved. Also they couldn't very well go furniture shopping if the place were not in condition to have the new pieces delivered. She just had to get most of the basic cleaning and fixing completed before Kristin's arrival.

Once at home she pulled out her notepad and began a list of work to be done, separating those tasks that she could manage from those that needed professional assistance. For each of the latter chores, she added columns to list potential companies or individuals to contact for estimates, their phone numbers, a column for their estimated costs, and the date they could do the work. Then she called Walter to let him know she was safely home and again and thank him for all his kind assistance. She also gave him the types of workers she needed and obtained a list of possible individuals to contact.

"Feel free to tell them I referred you," said Walter. "Do you mind if I call to see how you're coming along later this week?"

"That would be fine. Thank you for wanting to. Talk with you soon. Good night."

Susan smiled as she hung up the telephone. It was a lovely feeling to know that someone besides her children was concerned about her welfare.

Chapter 7

*Healing has begun when the past
no longer appears perfect.*

WEDNESDAY, JANUARY 7

By three o'clock on Wednesday, January 7, Susan had managed to have a house phone installed, get an internet hookup, and obtain multiple estimates for grout and upholstery cleaning, interior painting, window cleaning, replacing the lanai door, and fixing the broken vanity drawer. Since calling for the estimates didn't require her to walk and showing the men who came to do the estimates around her small space to look at the work to be done had required only minimal walking, her ankle hadn't received much of a workout and had been healing well. Today she hadn't even used her crutches. She continued to wear the Ace bandage since she occasionally still had twinges of pain.

Now, before all the businesses closed for the day, she started calling the chosen workman, hoping to complete the scheduling today so that tomorrow she could go out to look at window blinds and carpet. Then on Friday morning, she could shop for some groceries and stop by the farmer's market for the produce and orchids she had planned to pick up last Saturday, before she sprained her ankle.

By the time she gave up phoning, she had scheduled the painting, grout, carpet, and upholstery cleaning, along with a handyman to repair the drawer and replace the lanai door. She decided to leave the window cleaning for after all the dusty work, including replacing the carpet, was completed.

Now that she had finished her day's work, she intended to reward herself with a swim. She dearly missed daily exercise. After the swim, she would treat herself to dinner at the Italian restaurant in the shopping center. That would also alleviate the problem of what to cook tonight; she was running low on groceries.

After changing into her swimsuit, Susan went hunting for the beach towels she knew had been left for the tenants as part of the apartment's inventory. They were not where she used to keep them. She rummaged through all the drawers in the bedroom, the drawers and cabinets of the Murphy bed unit, and the bathroom drawers. Not only did she not find any of her beach towels, but she realized that at least half of the bath towels seemed to be missing as well. Annoyed, she made a mental note to look for some towels next time she went out on errands. Then she grabbed a bath towel and headed for the pool.

As she unlocked the pool gate and entered the enclosure, she saw Deborah Sanford waving from across the pool deck.

"Hi, Deborah! How are you?"

"I'm doing well. Thanks, Susan. We missed you at the stitch and bitch this morning."

"Oh my! I'm afraid I completely forgot! I've been so busy

with getting estimates for the work on my unit that nothing else entered my mind. I really do want to come. I need to buy a calendar so I can post my scheduled workmen's appointments. Then I can add the Wednesday morning get-togethers on the calendar as well. I'm so tired that I can't remember if I scheduled anything for Wednesday of next week or not. If no one will be here working, I'll be there."

"I was telling the gals who were there that I had met you. Lynette, Suzanne, Elizabeth, and Gloria said they remembered you from when you and your husband were last here and are looking forward to seeing you again."

"So I've been the topic of gossip? I'm so glad they are still around. I will enjoy seeing them again."

Susan showered before gingerly entering the water—cool but not really cold. After thirty laps of the pool, she dried off, said goodbye to Deborah, and headed back to her unit. She was just dressing for dinner when her cell phone rang.

"Hi, Mom! How is it going?"

"Hey, Kristin! I'm doing well, although these last six days have been quite an adventure!" Susan brought Kristin up-to-date with her mishap with the sprained ankle, meeting Walter, and her progress with getting the unit back to some semblance of order.

"Mom, I can't believe you actually had a date. That's great news!"

"It was hardly a date, just a kind, helpful, and lonely man going out of his way trying to make my life a bit easier. I must admit, however, that it was nice to have someone fussing over me again. It has been such a long time. I've invited him over for dinner for Friday, January 16, to thank him. That way I can also return his crutches."

"Ok, so it wasn't a date. I'm glad for you nonetheless. You never know what could happen. Even if you just have a new friend, that is good for you. You need someone you can talk with who can really understand what it has been like. And you need to start having some fun!"

"I'm sorry, Kristin. I didn't mean to jump at you. Guess I'm feeling a bit guilty that I enjoyed the time with him as much as I did, like maybe it's a betrayal of your dad."

"That's ok, Mom. I understand. Anyhow, the main reason I called is to tell you that I found some reasonably priced tickets for February 6, returning home on February 13. Will that work for you?"

"That is just about perfect! By then I hope to have this place in reasonable order. I've decided to go ahead and replace the carpet with a decent medium-grade carpet. That way it can work whether I keep the place or sell it. I'll have the carpet installed before you get here, so if we find some furniture, it can be delivered."

"I'm so glad those dates work. I'll go ahead and book my tickets and will email you the flight information. Don't plan a busy schedule for us, please. Getting the boys set for school after the holiday break took some doing. These long breaks get them used to a lack of routine. After all the holiday activities, they don't want to go back to the more regimented lifestyle. This year was particularly busy since Jim's daughter Michelle and her husband came to town with their two kids. Each of Jim's relatives felt they had to hold their own party for her while she was here. It was a real social whirl, and the boys got all wound up and lost a lot of sleep. I'm exhausted, and I need some downtime."

"I understand. We'll have a quiet visit, and you can soak up some sun. Hopefully you'll join me for an occasional morning walk down to the ocean. You can just tell me if there is anything you want to do when the mood strikes. Anyhow, I'm so excited about you coming for a week. It's been such a long time since we've had the chance to just hang out. And Jim and the boys are ok with your plans?"

"The boys are fine, except that they'd like to be coming too. Jim grumbled a bit at the idea of my being away, but he'll do ok. As he gets older, he seems more and more reluctant to have me be away. But I've made it clear that occasionally I need time to spend with my family. We see his all the time since we live in the same town. And as you know, he's not a great socializer. He prefers to sit in front of the TV with the sound loud enough to be heard across the street, so it's a bit of a drag if I bring him along. Besides, someone must stay with the boys and see that their homework gets done and that they get to their sports activities. He'll survive."

"You are so good at communicating your needs and setting limits. I could never do that with your dad. We were both from the olden times when a wife's role was to look after her husband and keep him happy, subverting her own needs if that is what it took. In many ways I was fortunate. Aside from grumbling about my being tired at the end of a long workday or about my leaving him alone when I had to travel for work, your dad was generally supportive of my career, for which I was grateful. That support, however, was largely dependent on my keeping up with the expected wifely chores, especially breakfast on the table in time for us to have a leisurely breakfast before leaving for work and a proper dinner every night. When I had to travel, I made sure there were homemade, prepared meals in the fridge or freezer that he could just heat and eat. Even so, more often than not, he'd eat out. Fortunately he did mellow and loosen up as time passed. The one thing I did hold fast on was insisting on a housecleaner once per week. There was no way I could take that on while working full time."

"I know. I remember. I often wondered why you weren't more assertive. Especially when he had his jealous reactions to what seemed to me to be inconsequential events."

"That was the one thing about him I couldn't handle. I just never knew when he would misinterpret a situation and get upset, so I was often on edge worrying. He would withdraw without any obvious reason and sulk for several days before finally telling me what I had done. Meanwhile, I'd be worrying about when it would finally come out, trying to figure out what might have set him off.

"I was usually blindsided. Sometimes he misinterpreted or misheard something I or someone else had said. There was no point in trying to correct his impression. He would accept no other explanation than his own. Sometimes he insisted that someone I was talking with had touched my arm several times while we were talking. He saw it as some sexual overture rather than the innocent mannerism it probably was. He'd be angry that I hadn't rebuked the person at the time, but I was totally unaware of the contact since I was absorbed in the conversation. Many people have a habit of touching people when they are talking. But he was always sure he was right, and he fumed for days and insisted that I had no respect for his feelings. That was a frequent theme.

"As a result, I dreaded social events because they often were a trigger to set him off. At those times, I felt like he never knew or understood anything about me. He was always the only man I loved, but he sometimes behaved as if he thought I might run off and have an affair with any man in sight. Although I was always careful to be proper, he still found things to get upset about. Many were the nights that I silently cried myself to sleep. That is one thing I don't miss since he is gone. I resent it even now, although I long ago concluded that he must have felt some basic insecurity that made him feel unworthy of love. I know that he had lots of negative feelings about his mother and believed that she didn't really love him.

"His behavior did give me occasion to consider leaving him several times when I didn't think I could cope anymore. But then it would pass for a time, and all the wonderful things about him became my primary consideration. If it hadn't been for those, fortunately infrequent, episodes, I'd never have even considered the possibility of leaving him. I did love him so much. He was my best friend as well as my husband, and when he wasn't being jealous, he was such a pleasure to be with. He was so intelligent and had such interesting ideas about the world and everything in it. Still, it is nice not to have to worry about such things now every time I go out or do something with other people."

"Well, at last you've recognized something positive about being widowed!"

Susan laughed. "That and not having to cook a proper meal several times a day. Not only is it easier to control my weight, but I've really enjoyed the extra time I get from just heating up a frozen dinner rather than spending hours in the kitchen. Also I like being able to go out shopping, especially to browse in a store without worrying about how long I've been gone and what he may be thinking about where I might be, what I might be doing, or when I'm coming home. I can just wander around a store for inspiration rather than hastily grabbing something off the shelf as I dash through. I had forgotten how much fun it can be just wandering through a store and seeing what is new. I believed that I hated shopping, but it was the constant pressure to get done quickly and get home. Anyhow, enough time spent reminiscing about the past. It's been a long time since I thought about all of that.

"On another topic, I wanted to tell you that it appears that several of our old friends are still living in the complex. I plan to attend the women's weekly Wednesday morning stitchery gathering by the pool next Wednesday so I can reestablish contact with them. I'm really looking forward to it. I even bought some yarn and some knitting needles so I can fit in."

"Good for you, Mom. That's a terrific idea. Reestablishing contact may lead you toward a social life there in Hawaii. If that works out, you may decide that you want to spend winters there in future years. You know that Brendon will be happy with that decision. He's always liked spending time there. In fact, he may also want to come out for a visit this winter if you end up staying on into March." Kristin paused. "I wish I could talk longer, Mom, but Jack is calling for me. I better go see what he wants. It's getting late here, and I need to get these guys ready for bed. Talk to you soon. Love you."

"I love you too, Kristin. Hugs to the boys, and hello to Jim. I'll keep an eye out for your email. Bye."

Chapter 8

*The great comfort of friendship is
that one has to explain nothing.*

WEDNESDAY, JANUARY 14

The days passed quickly. Some days Susan was at home supervising workmen. When no work was scheduled, Susan went out to look for carpet, new blinds, and towels. In between, she perused the internet looking for suitable wallpaper to replace that in the kitchen and some grass-cloth to provide texture on the long living room/dining room wall. She found a reasonably priced carpet that she liked and was able to schedule the installation for the following week. She also bought a product for wallpaper removal and began stripping the kitchen wallpaper in her spare time, since she hadn't found anyone to do that job.

She did not, however, forget about the Wednesday morning stitchery group. She found some instructions on the internet for a simple scarf and started working a few rows on Tuesday evening to refamiliarize herself with the stitches before she embarked on the pattern she had bought at the yarn shop. She didn't want to appear completely inept! She had gathered from Deborah that many of the women were experts at needlework. But knitting wasn't why she was going. This seemed a non-threatening way to reengage with her old friends. After all, five years is a very long time!

Just as Susan was finishing off the breakfast dishes, she heard a knock on the door. Susan quickly dried her hands and headed toward the door. When she opened it, three women standing outside shrieked, "Susan!"

Susan did a double-take. She recognized Lynette, Elizabeth, and Suzanne, her old comrades. After hugs all around, Susan said, "Come in. How nice to see you again!"

"We won't come in. Thank you," said Lynette. "We just came to take you down to the pool. Deborah said you had promised to come, and we came to make sure you keep that promise. All the other gals want to meet you, and we have a lot of catching up to do."

"So I'm being shanghaied, am I? Ok, let me grab my knitting." Susan shoved her knitting supplies into a tote and dutifully followed her friends across the parking lot to the pool.

As they arrived, she noted that there were about eight women already seated around several umbrella-covered tables on the pool deck, busily chatting away as they knitted or crocheted. She vaguely recognized one or two. Sitting alone at one table was Gloria, another good friend from the past.

"Gloria has saved us a table, as we instructed," said Lynette, moving toward the empty table.

Gloria enveloped Susan in a bear hug. "Welcome back, girlfriend. It's wonderful to see you. You were missed!"

"Before you sit down, let me introduce you to everyone."

Lynette took Susan from table to table, introducing her to the other women.

"Don't worry about remembering all our names," said a woman named Mona. "We'll remind you until you've had a chance to get to know us. Welcome back. We've heard a lot about you, and we look forward to getting to know you. It appears, however, that Gloria, Lynette, Elizabeth, and Suzanne intend to monopolize you today."

Susan settled in at the table with her friends. As they knitted, they chatted comfortably about their lives during the past five years. Since the inevitable questions about her post-widowhood life were framed by concern for her welfare and how she was coping with being alone, the conversation was less stressful than Susan had feared. Further, she realized with some relief that thinking about the past few years was now more than a dull ache than an acute pain. Voicing her feelings about those years to her friends was a sort of catharsis.

Eventually the conversation turned to her future plans, especially regarding her condo.

"We really hope you will be coming back in the winter like you used to do. I'd love to do more of our antiquing trips," said Suzanne.

"And I need a companion for going to the theater," said Lynette. "Buster still has no interest in culture. His interests are pretty basic."

"Besides, if you're here, we won't have to worry about noise from your renters or their smoke drifting up onto our balcony when we're trying to have breakfast or enjoy the sunset," said Suzanne. "Your last renters were really an issue. They smoked like chimneys, and they ignored our requests to smoke inside the unit or away from the building. And their arguments! Ever since they moved in last March, we'd frequently hear them shouting at each other. Recently it had gotten worse. They seemed to be arguing about money all the time. We could only hear snatches of conversation, but it sounded like she wanted to limit his access to funds she felt were hers. We were really glad when she left to look after her grandmother and even happier when he moved them out of the unit a short time later in order to follow her to the mainland!"

"I'm so sorry you had to endure them. I had given my rental agent strict instructions not to rent to smokers because of my allergies. As for the noise, if someone had let us or the rental agent know that there was a problem, we'd have tried to terminate the lease. Anyhow, their leaving early was a good trigger for me to come back to check on things and to make some decisions. Once I get the place livable, I'll either sell it or come here in the winter like I used to."

"We, of course, hope you'll come back," said Suzanne. "Holger and I will organize a happy hour get-together for this weekend so we'll have the old gang together again. How does Sunday at five o'clock sound for all of you?"

"That would be great!" they chorused.

"No need to bring anything. We'll keep it simple. All of you think about whether you would like to go out as a group for a simple dinner afterwards—just as we used to. Give me a call after you've talked to your spouses."

"Thanks, Suzanne," said Susan as they began gathering up their belongings. "It's thoughtful of you to get us all together. I must admit that I'm a little concerned about whether it will feel awkward without Scott."

"Don't you worry about being the odd man out, Susan. The guys are eager to see you again, although they will miss Scott.

We girls will do our thing and resume some of our outings as soon as you have time. On Thursday mornings, some of us go to water aerobics down at the retirement center. Maybe once you're finished some of the repairs on your condo you will join us. There will be a hula class at the pool again starting in March. Do you remember the fun we used to have doing the hula performances when you were here?"

"I do. It was not only fun doing hula but also great exercise. I look forward to all of that, Suzanne. Thanks so much for making me feel wanted. I was worried that I would no longer fit in."

"You needn't worry. We are excited to have you back with us. See you Sunday."

Feeling a warm glow both from her reunion with her friends and the mild sunburn that resulted from sitting in the sun for two hours, Susan returned to her unit and took a quick shower. Following lunch, she reviewed her to-do list, checking off what had been accomplished. Since Walter was coming for dinner on Friday, she had scheduled the carpet/upholstery cleaner to come on Thursday at 11:00 a.m., so she would have things looking reasonably clean before his arrival. There had been no time to get the new carpet installed; it would not arrive on the island from the Oahu warehouse until next week. She began a new to-do list for the remainder of the week, moving forward those items that she hadn't completed from the previous list.

A crucial chore for today was to prepare a menu for Friday's dinner and then do her grocery shopping. She would also pick up a few pretty candles and some flowers to brighten the place. Realistically, that was probably all she could hope to accomplish. She would resist her usual tendency to try to do more than she reasonably could. Maybe she was getting wise in her later years.

Chapter 9

Remember the moments of the past, and look forward to the promise of the future, but most of all, celebrate the present, for it is precious.

FRIDAY, JANUARY 16, 5:00 P.M.

Susan took one last look around before heading off to the shower. The small table on the lanai was covered with a bright Hawaiian-print tablecloth and set with the small white plates from her dinner set and her crystal wineglasses. The ice bucket was in place by the table, and the sun screen was pulled down to keep out the hot afternoon sun. Her hors d'oeuvres were plated and refrigerated, ready to serve.

Inside, a Hawaiian table runner was laid across the center of the glass dining room table. Rattan place mats set off the two place settings of white china plates, simple stainless flatware, flowered napkins that matched the runner, and crystal wineglasses. A low bouquet of white plumeria blossoms in a green vase was surrounded by a circle of votive candles in crystal holders. A dendrobium orchid sat on the end of the kitchen counter, and a decorative candle held center stage on the coffee table. The room was tidy, and Susan thought the whole effect was somewhat festive.

The opakapaka fillet was marinated and ready to grill, along with asparagus spears and small Yukon gold potatoes. She had prepared a salad of baby field greens with dried cranberries, candied walnuts, and gorgonzola cheese as an accompaniment. For dessert, she would serve papaya halves sprinkled with lime. Just before serving, she would fill these with fresh Waimea strawberries topped with whipped cream.

Deciding that everything was in order, Susan proceeded to shower and dress. After a few last- minute touches to her hair, Susan put on her small pearl and gold knot earrings and a pearl pendant on a gold chain. She took one last look in the mirror and headed for the kitchen. She had no sooner filled the ice bucket with ice and put in the bottle of white wine she had selected to go with the hors d'oeuvres when the doorbell rang.

When Susan opened the door, Walter greeted her with a bouquet of tropical flowers. "The lady seems to have recovered from her accident," he said, smiling. "I'm so glad to see it."

"Yes, I'm so much better. The ankle still has a little purple color if you look closely, but it's functioning well. I stopped using the Ace bandage two days ago. It's so nice to see you again. Please come in. And thank you for the flowers. I do love the tropical colors!"

Walter looked around the room. "I'm not sure what you have done since I was last here, but everything looks so fresh and smart. I like the effect."

"Thank you, Walter. I've had the walls painted, grout and

carpet cleaned, and a few repair jobs done since you were last here. That achieved the freshness you detected. Also paint to replace the wallpaper I removed in the kitchen helps; that old stuff was yellowed and dog-eared. I found the ground-in dirt depressing. A few added women's touches like fresh flowers, candles, and crystal finished the improvements. I am much more comfortable living in the place now."

Susan led Walter to the lanai. "I thought we could start with some wine and cheese on the lanai while we watch the sunset. Then we could move indoors when we're ready for dinner. I'll do the fish and veggies on the grill. That way I can keep an eye on it while we talk. Please make yourself comfortable. Is white wine ok, or would you prefer a mixed drink?"

"White wine is perfect, thank you. I don't drink much alcohol other than wine these days."

"Excuse me a minute while I put your lovely flowers in water. Afterwards, I'll bring wine and the opener out. Would you open the wine while I get the hors d'oeuvres? I'll be right back."

"You have a lovely view from here," Walter observed when she returned with the wine and opener in hand. "I almost prefer it to my close-up view of the ocean. This panorama is spectacular. And I note that you can still hear the waves and see whitewater. At this distance you don't have to worry about the corrosion from the saltwater that comes with being closer to the ocean. Yes, I think this is just lovely."

"Thank you, Walter. I really do love this location. Not just being close to the ocean. More important is the privacy, which is very important to me. Because of the way the units are positioned relative to each other, I get a complete sense of privacy when sitting here on the lanai, despite being in a complex. It's almost like having a private estate."

Susan handed Walter the opener and went to collect the hors d'oeuvres. By the time she returned, he had opened and poured the wine. As Susan set the plate of hors d'oeuvres on the table, Walter handed her a glass of wine.

"To friendship," she toasted.

"To friendship!" he responded.

"You know, Walter, friendship is one thing I have really come to appreciate since Scott died. Friends can be annoying when they insist on pressing their views when you don't agree with them, like when my friends thought they knew what was best for me as a widow. However, one comes to realize that they press their point of view not just because they think what they are suggesting is best for you but, more importantly, because they care. The comfort of having someone who will be there for you when you most need companionship makes it worth biting one's tongue when they become annoying. Comfort and companionship mean more than does having your point of view understood."

"I agree completely. But I think that perhaps you were better at it than I was. There were times when I got really exasperated with some of Marge's friends who tried to get me to reengage with life before I was ready. I fear I alienated more than a few of them!"

They reminisced comfortably while they sipped their wine and enjoyed their hors d'oeuvres. Later, as the sun began to set over the sea, they waited to see whether the fabled green flash would appear as the sun dipped below the horizon. Neither of them had ever seen it and agreed that it was probably just a story spread for the tourists. Just as the sun touched the ocean, the sound of the conch came from an upper balcony to their right.

Susan chuckled. "Holger celebrates the sunset in the ancient tradition every night when he is here. It's nice that so many people try to learn about the ancient Hawaiian culture."

Moments later, just as the sun dipped below the horizon, they saw a flash of green cross the horizon where the sun had been.

"I don't believe it!" Susan exclaimed. "Neither of us ever saw that before, but now we saw it together!"

"There seems to be something magical about the two of us together. Maybe we should give some thought to the significance of that," mused Walter. Pausing for a moment to glance at her with a twinkle in his eye, he returned to Susan's previous comment. "As you were saying, the resurgence of interest in the Hawaiian culture is a good thing for the islands. There is increasing support for protecting physical remains of the old culture. Also, for highlighting the culture in educational offerings, festivals, and other events, such as the canoe races. Did you know they have constructed a facsimile of the ancient Hawaiian sailing ship, the Hokuleá? It is used to teach young Hawaiians the old ways of seamanship and navigation. Each year now, young Hawaiians are trained as they sail the ship to Tahiti and back."

"Yes, I read about that. It amazes me that they could sail such vast distances without compasses or any of the other aids used by the early European sailors. Those early Hawaiians had a lot more knowledge than most people give them credit for.

"Excuse me, please, Walter, I must get the dinner on the grill. It will get dark quickly now that the sun has set." Susan poured another glass of wine for Walter and then began grilling their dinner as the sound of music drifted on the breeze from the luau at the Sheraton hotel down the hill on Keauhou Bay.

When dinner was cooked, they moved into the dining room to enjoy the meal. After eating, Susan and Walter companionably cleared the table and rinsed the dishes before placing them in the dishwasher. They carried the remainder of their wine to the lanai. Susan put on some music, turned on the outdoor lights, and dimmed them to a soft glow. They sat in comfortable silence as they listened to the sounds of Pavarotti singing Italian folk songs. It was nearly ten before Walter regretfully took his leave.

As Susan finished cleaning up after he left, she reviewed the evening in her mind. She decided it had been a success. She felt as if she had spent the evening with a cherished friend.

Chapter 10

*Three essentials to happiness
in this life are something to do,
something to love, and something
to hope for. (Joseph Addison)*

SATURDAY, JANUARY 17

Walter poured himself a glass of red wine and sat in his favorite recliner. For a moment, he basked in a warm glow of contentment. The dinner with Susan had been everything he had hoped—relaxed, convivial, and totally comfortable, like being with an old friend. Susan reminded him of Marge in many ways. She was organized, a good cook, and a classy dresser. Her home showed excellent taste in its décor. She was intelligent and a good conversationalist who exhibited a wide range of knowledge on a variety of topics. Her discussion of issues considered all sides. While she held strong opinions on some issues, she did not appear judgmental of differing opinions. She seemed to enjoy his company and made no demands of him.

In fact, she had a way of making him feel that he was the total focus of her interest when he talked, drawing him out with questions or rephrasing his thoughts to clarify that she had understood his point.

After spending so many evenings, weekends, and even holidays alone, it was refreshing to have spent such a congenial evening. His only companions most days were a few of the guys with whom he played golf and Ralph, a crotchety bachelor friend with whom he occasionally went to dinner. He didn't particularly enjoy those evenings because Ralph was very self-centered and talked mostly about himself. On the few occasions when the conversation wandered into more general areas like current events or politics, Ralph always propounded his opinion forcefully and at length. When one's opinion differed from Ralph's, he was always too willing to tell you why you were wrong. Thinking about it now, Walter wondered why he had so often tolerated those evenings. He supposed it was because he was lonely. Since Marge's illness ended in her death, he had often felt so lonely that any human companionship was better than another evening alone.

During the first year after Marge had died, some of his golfing companion's wives had invited him to join them for dinner. After the first such occasion, they might invite him again for a dinner party as the odd man to be paired with an unaccompanied woman. But he didn't really enjoy these occasions. He often suspected that they were trying to play matchmaker. When they learned that he had little interest in continuing these relationships, they stopped inviting him.

Some single women had invited him to dinner or to go with them to a show, but he could never relax with them. Some of them were clearly on the make. They probably wanted to develop a relationship because they could see that he had money. Many wanted to be part of the island's upper-class social scene and seemed to think he could provide them with productive introductions. Few realized that he and Marge had largely avoided that scene.

Some of the women were merely lonely and wanted companionship or an escort for a community event. He had, at times, agreed to such excursions out of kindness or loneliness but found that he had but little in common with most of the women. Conversation often had been an effort. Thus, for the past few years he had contented himself with a quiet life of golfing, reading, walking, playing online chess, and reminiscing ... until now.

Susan's fortuitous entry into his life had made him look outside himself and his overwhelming sense of devastation. He felt like he wanted to rejoin life. Susan was a breath of fresh air, and he felt alive again. He had laughed more tonight than he had in the entire past year! It was wonderful.

The question now was how to pursue things from here. Susan had made clear that she was not looking for romance. He wasn't sure that he was either, although to be truthful, the thought had entered his mind tonight. Susan had looked so fresh and appealing. Following the lovely dinner at her place, they had enjoyed after-dinner drinks on the lanai. As they talked, they listened, first to the Hawaiian music drifting up the hill from the hotel on the bay and then to Pavarotti as they watched the stars twinkling in the night sky. He had experienced an almost irresistible urge to reach out and take her in his arms. He had actually wanted her, and amazingly, the thought of Marge hadn't entered his head until now.

Please understand, Marge, he thought. *No one could replace you, but I would like to enjoy life again. I believe you would approve.*

Perhaps he could still have a life. There were many places he and Marge had wanted to visit. They had been in the midst of planning a trip to Europe and one to Mexico when Marge had begun feeling ill and had been diagnosed with cancer. So they had never managed to take those trips. While his work had taken him to Europe, he had never had time to do much sightseeing, and he was usually alone.

Perhaps someday he and Susan could travel together. She had described some of the traveling she had done with Scott. Clearly she loved to travel. Her descriptions of the scenery, the people she had seen, their customs, and the food—all had been so illustrative that he could see it all as she talked. She had said she missed traveling and that one of the sorrows of the past four years was that she did not have a close friend with whom she could enjoy traveling. She had gone on one trip with her sister and longed to take a trip with her daughter, but said that until her grandchildren were out of school and in college, her daughter couldn't really spare the time.

But he was getting ahead of himself. First, he had to figure out a next step for evolving the relationship. Occasional lunches and dinners were all very well, but a broader agenda was needed. He would do some research on what cultural events might be scheduled in the next few weeks. Perhaps he could invite Susan to one of those. She had said she loved theater and concerts. He would look for something about two weeks out so it didn't appear that he was being pushy. Meanwhile, he'd send some flowers with a thank-you note for last evening. Good manners were always appropriate. Content with his decision, Walter headed for bed.

Chapter 11

*When among friends, there is no urgency
to fill each minute with constant chatter;
rather there is calm familiarity and
companionship in moments of silence.*

SUNDAY, JANUARY 18

Susan took one last look in the mirror. Satisfied with her image, she lightly sprayed her hair and then took a deep breath to calm her nerves. Funny that the prospect of meeting with her friends should give her butterflies! She supposed it was because she would be a single in a crowd of people with whom she had always been part of a couple. Well, she was as ready as she'd ever be. She picked up her purse, returned to the kitchen to collect the flowers she had bought for Suzanne, and then left the condo. A short walk across the parking lot brought her to the Schmidt's condo. She raised her hand to knock on the door.

Before she could knock, the door opened. "Welcome, Susan!"

said Suzanne. "No one else has yet arrived, so Holger and I get a chance to chat with you for a few minutes alone. Come in."

Susan handed her the flowers. "Thanks so much for organizing tonight's get-together. I appreciate your facilitating my reintegration."

As she stepped into the apartment, Holger enveloped her in a bear hug. "So wonderful to see you again! We've missed you guys. Losing Scott must have been an awful blow for you. But we're delighted that you've finally been able to return. We often talked about calling you but were afraid that you would find it difficult to talk to us, so we settled for sending flowers and a card and then later the few letters Suzanne sent. Maybe we were afraid it would be awkward for us, to be honest," admitted Holger. "Anyhow, we're delighted you're here now."

"I do understand, and I did appreciate your card and letters. Just knowing that you two were thinking of me helped me feel less alone. If we had talked during the earliest days after Scott's passing, I'd probably have been crying or complaining. I went through an extended period of wanting to avoid being around people, so I wasn't very sociable in any case. But it is wonderful to see you again and good to be back here. I've enjoyed the peace and quiet, in addition to the pleasure of seeing old friends. Chatting with Lynette, Suzanne, and Gloria earlier this week by the pool felt just like old times!"

"Speaking of peace and quiet, we're so glad your last tenants left," said Holger. "They were anything but peaceful! Has Suzanne told you anything about their fights? In the week or two before they left, it was almost every evening. Once we even called the police on them. They were keeping everyone in this end of the complex awake!"

"I do apologize. If I had known ..." Susan was interrupted by the arrival of the other couples.

Following greetings and hugs from Jack and Elizabeth, Lynette and Buster, and Gloria and Clive, Holger took drink orders. He and Jack prepared the drinks and passed them around. Then they all settled on the lanai after filling their plates with a sampling of the various appetizers that Suzanne had prepared.

"When you arrived, we were talking about the arguments that Bart and Carole used to have," explained Holger to the rest of the group.

"I'm amazed they never came to blows," said Clive. "A few nights before they departed, I remember hearing Carole scream, 'No! No!' I thought I heard some other voices and then a door slamming and a car leaving. After that it got quiet for a while. Later I heard power tools. I guess Carole went out for a while and Bart worked on some of his carpentry projects to cool his temper, although he was usually good about not using power tools after about seven. On the subsequent nights, everything stayed quiet, and there were no more arguments. Hopefully they sorted it out. Bart told me that Carole had left abruptly to go back to the mainland to look after her grandmother. She never said goodbye to anyone as far as I know. Anyway, I'm glad they left."

"That's odd about going back to look after her grandmother," commented Lynette. "I'm sure Carole's grandmother died last year and left her a small inheritance. That's what some of the arguments were about. Bart owed money on gambling debts and wanted Carole to give him money to pay off those debts."

"I heard that Bart told someone Carole had gone to help get her mother out of some trouble having to do with drugs," said Buster.

"No, that can't be true. Carole and her mother were estranged," added Lynette.

"Enough about the Selwyns, if you please," said Gloria. "We want to visit with Susan, not revisit the unpleasantness of the past."

"So, Susan," said Clive, "tell us how you're adjusting to life as a single woman and fill us in on your plans. Then before the evening is over, we'll update you on our major life events. I know that Gloria brought pictures of the new grandchildren. She was sure you'd want to see them."

"You can be sure I do," said Susan with a grin.

For the sake of the husbands who hadn't been party to the conversation at the pool, she briefly summarized highlights of the past four years, minimizing the pain of the first two and concentrating on the aspects of rebuilding her life and the decisions that lay ahead.

The rest of the evening passed in a flash. Everyone wanted to tell her their stories of travels, births, deaths, and other significant events. Conversation flowed easily among the couples. To Susan, the evening felt like she had stepped backward in time. She felt no awkwardness. By the time they returned from dinner at their favorite hangout, it was after 9:30 p.m. Promising to make plans for another get-together after Kristin's visit was over, everyone returned to their own home.

Susan was pleased that the evening had gone well. She had not felt like a third wheel. It was clear that the men missed Scott, but she had been comfortable with the group and thought that while the group would never seem the same, her female friendships would endure. All four women had individually suggested getting together with Susan for some excursion or another in the coming weeks. It was a good start. Rather like old times.

Chapter 12

Things happen to you, but also for you. It is wise to see the positive in negative events.

WEDNESDAY, JANUARY 28

It was midafternoon on a Wednesday nearly two weeks after the dinner at Susan's when Walter received a telephone call from Susan. He had been thinking of calling to invite her to accompany him to the upcoming production of *Fiddler on the Roof* at the local playhouse in Kainaliu but hadn't yet gotten around to it. He had decided to wait until any workmen who might be at her condo had finished up for the day and gone home. That would give them a chance to chat. And now here she was. She sounded upset!

"Walter, I need some advice, and I didn't know who else to call. I remember that the first time we met you mentioned that you once worked in law enforcement. As a policeman, I think you said. I'm hoping that whatever you did might be useful in dealing with an issue that has arisen here. Or maybe you know someone who could offer some advice."

"What has happened? It must be pretty awful for you to sound so upset!"

"The carpet installers are here this afternoon to install my new carpet. They removed the old carpet and then installed the new carpet in the living and dining room areas. They were ripping out the old carpet in the bedroom when they came to find me. When they removed the strip of carpet that runs down the hall from the master bedroom to the master bath, they discovered that the padding underneath has extensive rusty red-colored areas and an odd smell. One of the workmen said it was the smell of blood.

"The floor underneath the padding has those same stains, although less extensive. They wanted to know if I knew what it was. I don't. The carpet was here when we bought the place. However, shortly after I arrived in early January, I noticed that particular strip of carpet in the hall looked cleaner and less worn than the rest. A piece of the original carpet had been left in our overhead storage compartment when we bought the condo. We decided to keep it in case we ever had a stain that couldn't be removed so we could patch in a piece rather than replace the entire carpet. When I looked for it, it was gone. I assumed that someone had spilled something and had used the carpet to replace that which had been damaged rather than report the damage to the rental agent."

"Interesting. But what has you so upset?"

"One of the installers insists that it is blood. 'Lots and lots of blood!' was the way he put it. He remembers the color and odor from a prior job where he was installing new carpet in an apartment that was being rehabbed after a murder had been committed there. If it is blood, I would agree that it's a lot of blood! There is also a reddish-brown stain of about the same color in the tub of the master bath. I had previously wondered why all of my beach towels and many of my bath towels were missing, but just assumed that someone had stolen them. Now I'm wondering whether they were used to clean something and then discarded. Particularly after hearing my friends talk about heavy-duty arguments that my last tenants engaged in just before breaking the lease and moving, I'm concerned.

"As I mentioned to you on the telephone last week, it seems that Carole, the wife, just disappeared without saying goodbye to anyone. That seems odd. My friends thought the whole episode of their departure strange, especially the different stories that the husband, Bart, told about why they were leaving. Maybe I'm letting my imagination run wild. But I can't help but wonder whether this shouldn't be looked into. Do we just ignore this and put down the new carpet? If this is blood, my gut tells me that this amount of blood had to be from some major blood vessel bleeding out!"

"Susan, if Carole and Bart broke their lease quite abruptly and you heard that Carole just disappeared without saying goodbye to anyone, I think you should report this to the police. They may not take you seriously, but at least it will be on record. Keep the installers there until I arrive. Perhaps they will talk to the police for you. They'll probably be taken more seriously than you will. I'm sorry to say that some police officers still tend to treat women as hysterical twits.

"I'll head on over to take a look. I'd like to talk with the installers. Do not let them throw out that piece of padding. It might be a good idea to hang on to the replacement piece of carpet as well, if they can identify it among the pieces they have removed. Perhaps also keep a piece of the carpet from elsewhere in the bedroom. Take pictures of the pad and the area underneath.

"Ask the installers to hold off on putting in the hall carpet until I get there. Offer to pay them for any time they spend waiting after they finish installing the main section of bedroom carpet. Also have them contact their employer to let him know what's going on and assure him that they will be paid for their time. I'll leave immediately, so I should be there in thirty to forty-five minutes, depending on the traffic. If the police won't come out to have a look and interview those involved, I'll do it."

"Thanks so much, Walter. I've never encountered anything like this before. But it may be much ado about nothing. Maybe I am being a hysterical twit!"

"Sounds to me like one of your carpet installers is taking it at least as seriously as you are. I'll see you soon."

Susan hung up the phone and relayed Walter's request that they wait to install the bedroom's hall carpet until he arrived, even if they had finished with the other areas. Since she was willing to pay for their time, they were more than willing to have a paid rest and wait. The lead installer agreed to call the police for her, and one of the other men went ahead and called their employer. Susan offered the workmen drinks and began to assemble beverages for the men to sip while they waited around after installing the carpet in the bedroom.

The police declined to come. They had no reports of any crime or missing person, so they would not open an investigation. Their conclusion was that someone might have experienced a serious accident that caused the blood stains, if that were indeed what they were. There was no reason to delay laying the new carpet.

Walter arrived forty-five minutes later. He introduced himself and apologized for the delay, the usual problems with the heavy afternoon traffic on the Queen's Highway. He looked at the pictures Susan had taken, examined the carpet pad and the cement underneath, and compared the relatively clean piece of carpet that had been removed from the hallway with pieces from the rest of the unit. He talked briefly with the two installers, inquiring why they suspected the stain was from blood.

Reiterating what they had told Susan, they indicated that they had once worked on rehabbing a house where a murder had been committed. The odor and color of the stains reminded them of that experience. Walter agreed with their opinion that the stain was blood. Whether it was significant remained to be seen.

The senior installer asked Walter about his law enforcement experience. He said that he had been a detective in New York for about ten years. "Even though it was a long time ago, the instincts and the process of an investigation never leave one."

Walter told the men to go ahead and install the new pad and carpet in the bedroom hallway since the police weren't interested and Susan had already taken pictures. In any case, that particular stretch of carpet could easily be pulled up if there were reason to test the cement floor underneath. He took possession of the stained rug pad and the old hallway carpet, along with several smaller pieces from other parts of the condo, just in case. These he wrapped in plastic wrappings from the new carpet and placed them in his car trunk.

Later that evening, Susan and Walter sat talking on the

lanai. They had gone to the Italian restaurant at the shopping center for a pizza and a salad once the installers had finished and gone. The dinner had been a good distraction for Susan after the events of the day.

Walter asked Susan many questions about her recent and previous tenants. She related that she had no information about any of her renters except the last couple whose early exit from their lease had led to her trip to the island. She filled him in on what she had been hearing from her neighbors—about the arguments, including Clive's comment about hearing Carole yell "No! No!" followed by voices, a door closing, and a car leaving, followed by the sound of power tools. Carole disappeared soon after that.

She also repeated the conflicting stories told about the wife leaving to return to the mainland to care for her ill grandmother, who was already deceased, and another about leaving to get her mother (from whom she was estranged) out of legal trouble. Susan told him that the rental agent had told her that the husband, Bart, had notified the agency that he would be breaking the lease, packing up, and moving their things in order to follow her there.

Susan also reported that she had asked the rental agent whether during any of her inspection tours she had noticed the newer piece of carpet in the hallway. The agent said that she vaguely recalled thinking that the hallway carpet looked new when she inspected the condo just after the husband, Bart, had left. She was sure that she hadn't noticed any new carpet on inspections after prior tenants left.

"I might not have thought anything about their story, if it weren't for all that apparent blood, despite my friends' comments about the departure seeming odd," Susan commented to

Walter. "Both stories of why they were leaving sounded plausible to me, although it seems odd that Bart told inconsistent stories."

"Family crises often do require sudden changes in lifestyle and routine. However, I think that this merits some follow-up, just to be sure that all is as it seems," Walter said. "I suppose it could have resulted from some serious accident, for instance, if the glass mirrors on the closet doors broke and cut someone badly, but those don't look new to me. Did you leasing agent ever talk to you about the mirrors needing replacement?"

"No, I had to replace some furniture and a mattress, but never a mirror."

"Please talk with your other neighbors who knew them. See if they remember either Bart or Carole having been injured and, if so, when. Also see if you can find out where this ostensible grandmother lives or whether she really is deceased. You might also want to ask when the wife left and whether anyone has heard from her since. Perhaps she had a friend in the complex who has heard from her since her departure and knows where she is now. Ask if anyone remembers seeing carpet with red stains in the dumpster and, if so, when that was.

"Finally talk with your real estate agent. See if you can get a forwarding address for the couple and a license number for their car. That could provide a lead to help locate them if they shipped it back to the mainland. If they didn't ship or sell it, then perhaps I can find it here on the island. If something happened to Carole and Bart is still here using the car ... well, that could indicate something is truly wrong!

"Meanwhile, I'll go ahead and contact a friend who still works in law enforcement and can probably get a test done on the carpet pad to assure that it is blood. I don't know whether there is a test that could be done on the rusty-colored areas on your tub, but I'll try to find out. If it is blood on the pad, I'd like to talk to the husband. Perhaps he has a plausible story about where it came from."

"Walter, do you really think that there might have been a crime committed here? I'm not sure how I feel about living in a place where a murder might have occurred. That is what you're thinking, isn't it?"

"I'm afraid it is, Susan. I do hope that I'm wrong. While you're gathering information from your neighbors and I'm waiting for the blood test results, I'm going to try to determine whether either of these individuals had been seen in the emergency or urgent care facilities in the past year with any accidental injury that could be consistent with the blood loss that must have occurred. If they had, we can lay this whole thing to rest. If not, I'd like to pursue it further.

"In the meantime, I know it will be difficult, but please try not to let this upset you too much. I'm sure you feel as if your hard-earned serenity has been invaded. Call if you feel a need to talk, ok?"

"Thanks, Walter, I will. I'm grateful to have you to turn to. I'll try to talk with some folks in the complex tomorrow. Working on the problem will help me deal with it. Let's check in at the end of the day to see what progress we might have made. Will you call me, or shall I call you?"

"I'll give you a call tomorrow evening, Susan. Oh, by the way, I had intended to call you this evening, even before you called. *Fiddler on the Roof* is showing at the playhouse next week, and I hoped you would agree to accompany me to see the production. It's on Thursday through Sunday. Will any of those evenings work for you?"

"How very thoughtful of you, Walter. I'd enjoy doing that.

Thursday would probably be best. My daughter arrives on Friday evening for a weeklong visit."

"I didn't know that she was coming. How nice for you. Any chance that I could meet her?"

"Of course. I'm sorry if I didn't mention her visit. I've been so caught up in the condo rehabbing that I didn't realize how fast the month has gone by. I'll try to schedule a dinner one evening while she's here so you'll have an opportunity to get to know her. Probably for some time early next week, if that works for you."

"I'd like that very much. Early next week is fine. Just let me know when. Meanwhile I'll see if I can get tickets for Thursday's performance. Talk to you tomorrow evening."

Susan walked Walter to the door. As he reached for the doorknob, she said, "Walter, I could really use a hug right now. Would you mind?"

"I'd be delighted! I wanted to offer but didn't want to appear pushy." He opened his arms, and she stepped into his embrace. Walter felt her begin to relax as he wrapped his arms around her and held her close. Moments later she pulled away. Reluctantly he released her.

"Thank you, Walter. I feel better now. I was really stricken by today's events. I don't think I could have dealt with it all without your help. You are a wonderful friend! Thank you."

Chapter 13

*The main trait that makes us interesting
is the courage to be ourselves.*

LATER THAT EVENING

As he drove home, Walter reflected on the day. The investigation of the circumstances surrounding the bloody rug pad could throw him and Susan together fairly often for a while. Only last week had he been looking for a hook to see her more often. This wasn't quite what he had in mind, but he'd take what he could get. He was gratified that Susan had thought to call him and was somewhat amazed that she had remembered his comment at their first meeting about working in law enforcement. Obviously she had listened when he talked, something many women didn't do, in his experience. Marge, of course, had been an exception.

He had never elaborated on his background during prior conversations, and Susan had not pursued it. In fact, he had worked as a New York City detective for fourteen years when he was a young man just starting out after college. Subsequently he joined the FBI. Because of one particular case in which he had witnessed a crime that involved a Mafia don, he had been entered into the witness protection program. Although the don was now in prison, having been convicted of the crime as a result of Walter's testimony, he had sworn to get revenge.

Walter and his wife had been given new identities and moved to the big island to protect them. He continued to receive a retirement stipend from the FBI. It was under this assumed identity that he had done the international consulting work he told Susan about. Because of his past, he had some contacts he could draw upon to get some information about the former renters. But he would have to be careful. There was still some personal risk should his whereabouts be known by certain individuals.

Walter looked forward to meeting Susan's daughter. He wondered whether Susan had told her daughter about him and, if so, what she thought about her mother seeing him socially. Strange that at their advanced age he and Susan should have to worry about what the children might think! Well, he supposed that would all sort itself out next week. It would be informative to see Susan with her daughter; he would see another aspect of her character.

Once home, Walter called a private number that he hadn't used in years.

"Jim Breem here," said the voice on the telephone.

"Jim, it's Chuck Morris, alias Walter Conway. I'm calling to ask a favor."

"Are you in trouble, old friend? What do you need?"

"No, I'm not in trouble, and I know I shouldn't be calling unless I really need help, but my sense of justice won't let me rest, and I didn't know who else to call."

Walter filled in Jim on the day's happenings and requested

help in getting tests done on the carpet pad to determine whether it was blood they were dealing with. He also requested that Jim agree to help with tracking down the information on the previous tenants and the grandmother once Susan obtained more information to begin a search. He also asked for help in tracking down the car driven by the couple if they were able to obtain a license plate number. He provided Bart and Carole's names as a place to begin a records search.

"You really think this could be murder, don't you? I can understand why you want to follow up. You never could leave a possible crime alone, even if it meant you had to track down a victim or find a body. I'll do what I can to help. Give me your number there, and I'll check in with you tomorrow to see what information your lady friend was able to obtain. Meanwhile, clip off a piece of the rug pad and send it to me. You know where to send it. But for heaven's sake, keep a low profile. We heard recently that Morelli still has people looking for you. We've been able to keep you hidden for more than twenty years, but he hasn't given up. He believes in retribution!"

"I'll be careful. I plan to let Susan do the poking around for information, and I'll be sure to ask her to keep my involvement out of any conversations."

"You do that, friend. I'll keep an eye out for the piece of the rug pad. Meanwhile, you'll hear from me tomorrow evening or the following morning so you can update me on what your lady friend found out. Remember, I'll call you. Do not call me."

"Thanks, Jim. I appreciate it."

Yes, he would be careful. Life was looking up, and he didn't want to do anything to jeopardize his future. But on the other hand, if this were a murder, he couldn't bear to let someone get away with it unpunished. It was against all his principles.

Chapter 14

You usually learn more by letting the other person tell you what he knows than by your telling him what you know.

THURSDAY, JANUARY 29

Susan organized her day around a list of information she had promised to gather for Walter. She had already taken her morning walk and showered before breakfast. Now she was ready to begin on her list.

First, she called on Pamela, her rental agent, at her office. She told Pamela that she had come across some personal items left behind by a tenant, probably Bart and Carole Selwyn, since they had been there most recently. She asked about any contact information that the couple provided so she could locate them and find out whether the items did belong to them and, if so, return them to the couple.

Pamela perused the file and found both a license number for the car and a next of kin for Carol, the wife. The person listed was identified as her sister. She lived in Montana. Pamela was reluctant to provide Susan with the contact information. She said she needed to talk to her supervisor to obtain permission, so she walked down the hall to talk with her.

While she was in the other office talking with her boss, Susan quickly opened the file. There, in addition to a license number for the vehicle, was an account number at the Bank of Hawaii that had been listed on the credit check form submitted when the couple had first applied to rent the apartment. There were also two credit card numbers, one for Carol and the other for Bart, and information on the sister as contact person. The final piece of potentially useful information was Bart's employer on the island, the Hupuna Prince Hotel.

Susan quickly copied down the license number, the name, address, and telephone number for the sister, along with the bank account and credit card numbers. Then she closed the file just as she heard Pamela coming back down the hall.

Pamela said that the supervisor had agreed that she could give Susan only the name and telephone number of the sister. This she wrote on a piece of paper and handed it to Susan, who then asked Pamela whether anything during her dealings with the couple had seemed unusual or triggered any concerns about them.

"Why would you ask that?" asked Pamela.

Susan said she was just curious because she had heard such strange stories about the couple from others in the complex and wondered if they could be true. She briefly told Pamela about the reported arguments and inconsistent stories told by the husband.

Pamela replied that when the couple first had applied they seemed very nice. She had few dealings with them while they were renting, as they never called to complain about anything or to ask for information, and they paid their rent promptly by check each month. However, she commented that when Bart came to return the keys, he had dealt with an assistant in the office who subsequently commented to Pamela about his abrupt manner. In fact, the assistant recounted that when she politely inquired about where the Selwyns were moving to on the mainland, he had been downright rude.

Susan made a mental note of the comment about the rudeness, thanked Pamela for the information, and left. Checking Pamela off her to-do list, Susan ate a quick lunch and then changed into her swimsuit and headed for the pool. There were usually folks there in the morning, and it was a good place to strike up a casual conversation that would possibly allow her to catch some gossip about the couple.

None of the folks that Susan knew were at the pool. There was a woman who looked to be in her late forties sitting in one of the lounge chairs. She looked up as Susan entered the pool enclosure. She waved at the chair next to hers and introduced herself.

"Hi, I'm Della Jonis from unit 24D. I haven't seen you around here before. Are you renting?"

"No, I'm Susan Brooks from unit 11B. I haven't been coming to the island since my husband died, so I rented our unit. Since my tenants recently left, I decided to come and spend some time this winter."

"Oh, you're the new resident in that unit! I'd heard that someone had moved in after Bart and Carole left. I was really sorry to see them go. Carole and I were friends and used to paint together at my place once a week. I really miss her and those painting sessions."

"I'm sorry about your friend leaving. Have you been able to keep in touch?"

"No, unfortunately she left without saying anything about her plans. She didn't even let me know that she wouldn't be coming to the last Monday painting session we had arranged. Normally she would have called and, if I didn't answer, would have left a message. I called both the condo phone and her cell phone but have heard nothing back since she left. I only found out that she had gone when I ran into Bart in the parking lot packing up his things and asked about what he was doing. He seemed a bit embarrassed and said that he was supposed to give me a message from Carole to let me know that her mother had been arrested back in Montana and that she had to go back on short notice to untangle things. He said he would join her once he had put their things in storage.

"I was so stunned that I didn't think to ask how I could reach her. Later it occurred to me that what he said did not make sense. Carole had been estranged from her mother since she was a child. Her grandmother had raised her and her sister from the time Carole was six and her sister was three. Then last year her grandmother died. She willed everything she had to Carole and her sister. Besides, why would it be necessary to move out of the apartment if she had only gone back to untangle a legal problem?"

"Interesting. My rental agent said that Bart told her Carole had gone back to the mainland to look after her sick grandmother and that he would follow. That was the ostensible reason he broke the lease. I've heard the same story from several other folks."

"I think that Bart says whatever serves his purpose at the time. Carole had told me he has a serious gambling problem and that he often would lie to her about why he needed money. She said she told him that she would longer function as his banker and arranged for a trustee to handle the account containing her inheritance so he couldn't draw on it. But she said he would frequently plead for funds to pay his creditors. Apparently he feared that there would be physical reprisals if he didn't pay.

"Carole was at her wit's end. She didn't want anything to happen to Bart, but she wanted to save the funds inherited from her grandmother for their future. No matter how many times she tried to get him help for his gambling addiction, he would refuse to follow through. She recently confessed that she was considering divorce because she feared he would never change."

"It sounds as if she needed you as a friend to talk to as well as a painting partner, Della. No wonder you miss her! It does seem strange that she would leave without contacting you. Even if she had to leave on short notice, she could have called or texted you later.

"I am also an amateur painter. Back in Seattle, I often paint with a small group of widowed friends. The get-togethers act as therapy sessions, allowing us to talk out our problems, in addition to critiquing our painting efforts. I can imagine how you must miss those sessions with Carole, especially since you seem so concerned about her. In what medium do you paint?"

"I prefer watercolors but have tried oils and done a fair amount with acrylics. What about you, Susan?"

"I have done mostly watercolors, although I've tried acrylics, pastels, and silk painting. But I especially enjoy working with watercolors. They are a continuous challenge!"

"You can say that again! Maybe that's what keeps drawing us back to them. Would you like to get together to paint? We can do it at my place, if you like. My husband works during the day, so it's quiet there. Carole and I always painted at my place. If her husband were working on his cabinetry at home, it could be dusty. The dust wasn't good for the paintings."

"I'd love to get together. I could do it early next week. Then I'm out of commission for about a week because my daughter's coming to visit. I could resume after she's gone. When do you suggest we get together?"

"How about we get together Monday morning at nine thirty?"

"That sounds great! I'll see you then. Can I bring anything other than myself and my painting supplies?"

"No, that should do it. I look forward to it. Now I'd better head back before I fry to a crisp. I've already been out here for over an hour. See you Monday."

As Susan resettled into her chair, she thought about what Della had told her. She felt sure that Walter would find it of interest. She thought it was unlikely she would obtain much else useful from hanging out at the pool since she was now alone. Also her friends had told her that few residents had much to do with Carole and Bart.

After a brief period of sunning while reading a novel, she went for a short swim and then returned to her unit to write some notes about what Della had said, before she forgot the details.

While she was writing, Walter called. "How about I come over and bring us a light dinner? We can catch up on the day's events over our meal. I'll also be able to reassure myself that you are ok."

"Thanks, Walter. What a lovely idea. You are very thoughtful. I appreciate your concern for me. What time shall I expect you?"

"Does six o'clock sound good?"

"Perfect! That gives me time to finish writing my notes of what I learned today, have a short nap, and then freshen up before you arrive. See you soon."

When he arrived, Walter admired the new fresh look created in the condo by the newly installed carpet and Susan's decorative touches. He inquired as to how Susan was feeling after the ordeal of the previous day. Then he handed her a bottle of wine he was carrying in his right hand. His left arm was wrapped around a bag of groceries. These he carried over to the kitchen counter where he deposited them.

"I told you I'd bring something to eat, and here it is. I hope you like it."

"I'm sure I'll like it very much since we seem to share a common taste in food," said Susan. "But it appears that you've brought enough to feed an army rather than the light dinner you said you were bringing!"

"I'm afraid I get carried away whenever I see a deli counter. I'm sure you can use whatever we don't manage to consume tonight. Besides, I'm starving. I had a late breakfast, so I skipped lunch."

Walter and Susan were enjoying the deli selections that Walter had brought when Susan commented, "We seem to spend much of our time together eating and talking."

"Seems to me that's a big part of life. I see four essentials for a good life. First is eating to sustain the body. Then talking and sharing one's thoughts and feelings to sustain one's soul. The other two are exercises to help maintain the body and actions directed at helping others, essential to peace of mind—at least for me.

"Some might say I left out God. Now there's a can of worms!

God! A concept shared by people the world over. But God to most people means religion. Organized religion is not something shared, but something that has divided mankind throughout history. Even though most modern religions subscribe to the idea of one god and share ideas about God as Creator, as Protector, as Giver of Wisdom and Rules for Living, people view as alien anyone not of their faith. They are compelled to convert others to their way of thinking and persecute those whose religion differs from theirs."

"My! You are a philosopher, Walter. Isn't that need to persecute those with different religions related to the fact that organized religion has been used by those in power to maintain control over their adherents? Christ taught general tenets or principles of living. Organized religions, in contrast, promote layer upon layer of rules that try to regulate every aspect of people's lives. The differences in those rules obscure the commonalities of religions, leading to persecution of those whose detailed rules are different. How I wish the world could focus on commonalities rather than differences!"

"You are very perceptive, Susan, and I agree with you. However, we digress. We wanted to catch up on where we are with our investigation into the strange case of the Selwyns."

Susan and Walter exchanged updates on their information-gathering activities. Then they began a list of what to do next. Walter would follow through on the license plate information Susan had obtained in hopes of finding out in which state the car was now registered. He would also determine whether there had been recent activity on either of the credit cards. Finally he would call the hotel where Bart had worked, pretending to be a friend of Bart's who was visiting from the mainland and wanted to get in touch with him.

Susan would call Carole's sister, using the pretense of finding items left behind. She would ask the sister how she could get in touch with Carole to determine if the items were actually hers and where she would like them to be sent. Walter would have his FBI contact see if the Bank of Hawaii account had been closed and, if not, would obtain information on recent activity.

Walter was particularly interested in what Susan had learned from Della about Carole's background, the money issues in regard to Bart's gambling, and the discrepancies in Bart's various stories. They agreed that it seemed odd that Carole would leave, even on short notice, without contacting her close friend, Della, either before or after leaving. They hoped that Susan might obtain useful information from Della during their painting session the following Monday. Susan would also see what she might learn during the upcoming Wednesday knitting session at the pool. Additional women there might have known the couple.

Following their working session, Susan and Walter retired to comfortable chairs on the lanai, listening to the waves and the music from the Sheraton as Susan described her plans for her daughter's visit. At the mention of the probable furniture shopping expedition, Walter suggested several furniture stores that should definitely be on their list of businesses to visit. They reconfirmed that Susan would schedule a dinner for Walter to meet her daughter early in the week following Kristin's arrival.

Walter mentioned his concern about whether Susan had mentioned him to Kristin. He asked how Kristin might feel about her mother seeing a male friend. Susan assured him that

Kristin would be most positive since for some time she had been encouraging Susan to expand her circle of friendships.

After Walter left, Susan made her to-do list for the next day and then prepared for bed. She had already decided that because of the three-hour time difference between Hawaii and Montana she should call Carole's sister Monica first thing in the morning before her walk. She needed to catch Monica before she left for work.

Susan slept restlessly, replaying in her mind the events of the previous day. She hated to think that murder was the explanation for the apparent blood on the carpet pad. But try as she might, she was unable to envision an alternative scenario that would produce so much blood. *Maybe it wasn't blood at all*, she thought. But she was defeated in her efforts to think of another substance that might have produced the stains. And then there were Bart's inconsistent stories. Susan dozed off, trying to make sense of it all.

Chapter 15

*Any road is bound to arrive somewhere
if you follow it far enough.*

FRIDAY MORNING, JANUARY 30

Susan felt bleary-eyed the next morning when she awoke at 5:00 a.m. She took a quick, hot shower, hoping it would wake her up before she placed her call to Monica. It didn't seem to help much! After dressing hurriedly, she called the number she had obtained from Pamela.

A terse voice answered after the fifth ring. "Hello."

Susan introduced herself and identified herself as the owner of the condo Carole and Bart had been renting in Hawaii. She explained that she was trying to locate Carole to determine whether some items she had found in the back of the closet belonged to her.

"I'm glad to hear from you. I've been worried sick! Carole and I usually talk by phone at least once a week and email several times weekly. I haven't heard from her for more than a month. I've called her cell phone and left messages numerous times. I also tried calling her landline in Hawaii several times, but only got a message saying the phone has been disconnected. I didn't know the name of the agency they rented from or any of their friends there, so I've been a bit frantic! I didn't know where to start looking for her. It's not like Carole not to call. But apparently you don't know anything about her whereabouts either if you're calling me!"

"Unfortunately you're right about that. About six weeks ago, Bart told the rental agent that Carole had returned to the mainland to look after her ill grandmother and that, since it looked as if it might be a long illness, Carole would be gone for a considerable time. Therefore, he asked to break the lease so he could return to the mainland to be with Carole. You were listed as her contact person on the rental application, which is why I called you since we didn't know how to reach her."

"Now I'm really worried! Bart's story is a bunch of crap! But then, much of what he says usually is. Our grandmother died several years ago. Carole and I have only each other. And now she seems to have disappeared from the face of the earth! I'm sure something is terribly wrong. Carole had confided to me that Bart was constantly trying to get his hands on her money. We both inherited something from Grandmother. Carole arranged for hers to be put into a custodial account so Bart couldn't get his hands on it. He gambles, and their savings kept disappearing because he'd take it to pay off gambling debts. He was pressuring Carole to give him money from her inheritance, and she refused. She was actually considering a divorce. Where could she be? Maybe she's hiding from Bart. But I can't believe she wouldn't contact me! She would know I'd worry about her!"

"It sounds as if you are right to be worried. Such a sudden

change in her behavior along with the lies Bart told about her whereabouts raises several concerns. I think you should contact the police here in Kona today. Tell them your story, officially report Carole as missing, and ask for their help in trying to locate her. Hang on for a minute. I'll get you their telephone number. Because of the time difference, it's only five fifteen here. Eight local time would probably be a good time to call."

Susan also gave Monica her own number and told her that she could call any time. She assured Monica that she would ask around among the folks at the complex and call her if she obtained any information that might help locate Carole.

Susan was shaken when she hung up from her conversation with Monica. All indications now were that murder was indeed a strong possibility. She ought to call Walter, but it wasn't even six, so she decided to have breakfast first. She also wanted to revisit the report of the blood on the carpet with the local police but thought that she should wait until Monica had a chance to report Carole missing. She didn't feel much like eating but forced down some toasted bread left over from Walter's visit the previous evening and a cup of coffee. She decided to skip her morning walk and wait at the condo until she could safely call Walter without waking him.

Finally, at 7:00 a.m., Susan decided to take a chance on calling. Walter sounded sleepy when he answered. "Did I wake you?"

"No, Susan. I was awake, although I'm still in bed. I'm a slow starter in the morning."

"Would you rather I call back later?"

"No, I'm fine. What can I do for you? You sound a bit edgy!"

"I'm quite edgy. I called Carole's sister this morning. What I learned seems to confirm that something is definitely wrong." Susan recounted the conversation with Monica for Walter.

"I agree with you that this situation seems serious. At the least, we appear to have a missing person. I think you should wait until noon to call the police. That gives Monica time to report her sister missing. It might be best to go to the station in person and ask to speak with one of the detectives. Organize and then write down all the information that you have obtained so far. Make several copies to save the work of rewriting it later. You might need it for someone else. Mention your conversation with Monica this morning and the inconsistencies in what Bart has said. Ask if Monica has yet filed a report on her sister. Then tell the detective about what you found when changing the carpet and the fact that you had called at the time to see if you should file a report, but were told no. Let him know you kept the carpet pad, just in case.

"I hope they will want to do a luminol test for blood on the carpet pad. They may want to test your condo bathroom and nearby walls as well, if they take all this seriously. Give them Della's name and how to get in touch with her. You'd better not tell them that you got the car license number and the credit card information since what you did to get them is, at the least, unethical. I'll have my contact follow through on that as soon as he calls back. You might suggest the police contact your rental agent for additional information on the couple. The agency would probably have the credit check information from the rental application, which could be useful in determining their present whereabouts. The detective would have the authority to get that and other information from the agent."

"Would you come with me to the police?"

"I'd better not. We don't want to overwhelm them, especially since they showed no interest on your previous contact. In fact, I'd prefer you not mention me or my involvement, if you don't mind. The fact that I'm an ex-police officer might get their back up. These local officers often react to ex-officers as if we're trying to nose in and tell them what to do, especially if they know one was with a big-city police force like that of New York City. If it's just you, the detective may want to be helpful to a pretty lady so he can seem the hero by solving the case."

"My but you are cynical! I do, however, understand your point, Walter. I'll call you after my visit and report on what happened."

Walter breathed a sigh of relief as he hung up the telephone. Jim had told him to keep a low profile, so he had to avoid getting involved with the local police force. Thank heaven that Susan had accepted his rationale and that she wasn't a suspicious person. He couldn't tell her the truth now. If their relationship should ever evolve to consideration of marriage, he'd have to tell her since it would affect her life as well as his. However, at present, it was best to keep his secrets to himself. All it would take is an idle remark at the wrong time and he could have problems.

Given recent developments, he was going to find it difficult to sit tight and wait for Jim's call. But Jim had made it clear that he was not to call again. Since Jim hadn't called last night, he should be calling this morning. Walter was eager to update Jim on these recent events.

Since he wanted to take Jim's call at home, Walter decided to make a light breakfast of toast, jam, cheese, and tea. Over his meal, he settled in with the copy of *West Hawaii Today* that had been delivered to his door this morning. An article about the theater group in Kainaliu caught his attention and reminded him that he needed to pick up the tickets for next Thursday's performance. That way he and Susan could go for a leisurely dinner at the nearby Strawberry Patch restaurant prior to the performance instead of rushing through dinner in order to wait in the box-office will-call line at the theater. He needed to go to Captain Cook anyway this afternoon, so could pick up the tickets on the way.

Once he had finished breakfast, he called the Hapuna Prince Hotel, where Bart had worked. He asked to speak with the manager, identifying himself as Cory Sithers, an old friend of Bart's from the mainland. He explained that he was visiting Hawaii and would like to see Bart while he was here but forgot to bring his phone number and address. He did remember that Bart had told him he worked for the hotel; therefore he was calling in the hope that he could reach Bart there or get his phone number so he could call and arrange to see him. He asked the manager how he could get in touch with Bart. The manager indicated that they could not give out information on their employees but said that if Corey would care to leave his name and number, he would be happy to have Bart get in touch. Walter gave the manager the name Cory Sithers and the telephone number of an old pay-as-you-go cell phone that he maintained for the few times he made calls that he didn't want traced to him under his present name and address.

Now at least he knew that Bart was still on the island and working at the hotel. So whatever stories he had told people at the condo complex and the rental manager were not true. Why would he lie unless he was trying to cover up something? Walter was sure that Bart would not call him since he would not recognize the name. But news of the call could make him very nervous.

Walter's thoughts were interrupted by the ringing of the telephone. He grabbed the phone and glanced at the number.

"Anonymous" read the inscription on the face. *It must be Jim*, he thought, hitting the phone button.

"Hello."

"Ok, old buddy, it's Jim. Not much news to report, I'm afraid. I'm still awaiting the piece of carpet pad you sent. Hopefully it will arrive tomorrow. I ran a search on your couple and found an arrest for the husband, Bart. He has a prior for illegal gambling in Montana. But nothing else turned up. There is a truck registered in his name with the Hawaii DMV. There is no indication that he sold it. The address of record is in Kona, at a condo complex on Alii Drive."

"Sounds like the address where they were renting my friend's condo."

"Since there is no indication that he sold the truck, he may still be on the island. He could probably get away with not registering the new address until he renews the registration, even though he's supposed to report the change within thirty days."

"Actually, Jim, I'm almost positive that he's still here. While you've been getting that information, I've been eagerly waiting to tell you some interesting information that Susan and I have turned up." Walter related everything that Susan had told him that morning and the upshot of his telephone call to the hotel.

"Well, my friend, it looks as if your instincts were right again. What are you going to do next?"

"I'll wait to see what the local police do with the information. Meanwhile, here are the numbers of the two credit cards and a bank account that Susan copied from the rental file. Perhaps recent activity will give us a clue as to where they are now. We won't pass them along to the police because of how Susan obtained them. They may contact the rental agent and get this information, but if you don't mind checking the card and bank activity for me, it may put us a step ahead.

"If there is activity on Bart's card, it will reinforce our conclusion that he is on the island and could lead to a new address. No activity on Carole's card could suggest that something has happened to her. But if there is activity, the location of such activity would be important. If it's being used on the island, it could mean that Bart is using it when he needs extra credit or that Carole is in hiding for some reason."

"I agree with you, Walter, and I'm impressed with the ingenuity you and your friend have shown in your sleuthing activities. I guess you're not out of practice after all, despite being retired! I'll check back in with you tomorrow night. By then you should have heard from Susan about her visit to the police and hopefully will know what the police plan to do. Also, by then I should have information on the credit cards and hopefully the carpet pad. But we'll need to give some thought as to how we use whatever information we obtain on Bart's address. I don't want you going to his residence or to the hotel where he works. We could sit tight and see if the police look for the credit card and other information from the rental agency files and follow up on the information they obtain. If they don't, we need to find a plausible way to share the information with the police."

"Good point, Jim. I'll give that some thought until I hear from you. Thanks for your help."

"Glad to contribute to seeing that justice is done, as long as I can keep you safe. I know how important this is to you. Talk to you tomorrow."

Chapter 16

Every man feels instinctively that all the beautiful sentiments in the world weigh less than a single lovely action.

FRIDAY, FEBRUARY 2, 6:00 P.M.

Susan and Walter sat on his lanai enjoying a salad of baby greens with avocado and mango that Walter had made, along with the fish and chips that Susan had picked up from her favorite fish restaurant at the Honokohau Harbor on her way to his place. Because early evening traffic can be heavy when driving south, Susan had suggested they meet at his place to discuss the day and offered to pick up dinner on her way. Now they were sitting companionably at the same table where they had initially gotten to know each other. A bottle of pinot grigio was already about half consumed.

"It seems such a long time since that Saturday when I sprained my ankle and you rescued me," said Susan. "So much has happened in less than a month. I'm beginning to feel as if I've known you forever."

"I share those sentiments. Do you believe in fate? I never did but am beginning to now."

"Whatever it was, I'm grateful to have met you. Your friendship has enriched my life and made it easier to keep moving forward. Only I wish it weren't a potential murder that brings us together so frequently."

"That wouldn't have been my choice of a way for conducting a friendship, but I must admit that I'm enjoying the fact that it throws us together so often," Walter said, chuckling.

"What a story to share with our respective families someday when this is all over!" said Susan. "Anyhow, let me fill you in on my visit to the police station. I approached the man at the front desk and said I was here to follow up with the police on a missing person report that should have been filed that morning by Monica Jessup. I asked to speak with the detective in charge of the case. After checking his records, the desk officer said that it had not yet been assigned, but he introduced me to a Sergeant Hanaka, a pleasant young Hawaiian sergeant. The sergeant said that although he hadn't yet been formally assigned, since he had been the officer on duty when the call had come in, he was likely to be in charge of any investigation. He was interested in hearing what I might know that could be of help.

"I told him the relevant details about the Selwyns breaking the lease, Bart's story that his wife had to go back to the mainland to care for her ill grandmother, and he was going to follow her as soon as he packed up their belongings. I also told him that I had been told by Carol's friend and her sister that the grandmother had died several years ago and that Bart told a different story to a friend of Carole's who knew about the grandmother's death.

"I recounted the reports of the arguments and particularly of the night shortly before Bart left when Carole was heard shouting 'No! No!' and that Carole had not said goodbye to even her closest friends. I also told him that when a friend of mine had called the hotel where Bart had previously worked to obtain information on where Bart could be reached, he learned that Bart is still working there. Then I told him about the carpet pad episode and the attempt to report it to the Kona police. I said that in view of the other information, the stained carpet pad, for me, seems to be potentially relevant to Carole being missing.

"I was quite relieved when he agreed with me and asked if I had kept any of the carpet pad. I said a friend was keeping it for me because I had no storage space for it in the condo. I promised to deliver it to him on Monday morning. He seemed quite amused that I had been 'playing detective,' as he put it. But he did seem to take me seriously, I'm happy to say. He even congratulated me on my efforts. And he promised to keep me informed of any progress they make, although he indicated that little could probably be done until Monday, when he would visit the rental agent and see what information he could get that might be of help in tracing the couple. Per your suggestion, I specifically neglected to mention the information I had obtained when I visited my rental agent and copied information out of the file."

"I'm relieved to hear that. Besides, it will be useful for the police to visit and ask questions of the rental agent. Who knows what she might let drop that she didn't want to share with you. Unfortunately I've little to add since I last saw you. I'm hoping to hear from my contact tonight."

Just then the phone rang. "Hello, Jim. Susan and I were just sitting here discussing where we are with the investigation. Carole's sister has officially reported her to the Kona police as missing, and Susan met with the police detective on the case earlier today to fill him in on her inquiries to date. They won't be doing much until Monday. Susan will deliver the piece of the carpet Monday morning—at their request—so they can run tests on it. They also plan to question the rental agent. Apparently they were amused by the work of our amateur detective but seem to think she is on to something and have promised to keep her informed of their progress. What did you find out, Jim?"

Walter listened as Susan watched him.

"I see, no activity on her credit card or her cell phone. That seems to support what we feared—that Carole may be dead. Did you get the test results from the rug sample? So it is blood. More confirmation of what we thought."

A pause as Walter listened to Jim and then, "As we surmised, Bart indeed must still be on the island. His credit card being used here would confirm that. Yes, I agree. We will allow the police to take over from here. Of course, Susan may stumble on some more useful information during her interactions with condo residents at the complex or from Della when they do their painting session on Monday. She will share anything she discovers with the police. As you suggest, I will stay out of it. Thanks, old buddy, for your help. It is much appreciated. You'll check back with me in a week or so? Yes, I do think that might be a good idea. Thanks. Talk to you soon. Bye."

Walter hung up the telephone and turned to Susan. "Did you get the gist of that conversation? Just as we feared, there is no sign of Carole anywhere, but Bart's credit card is being used on the island, so he must still be here—consistent with what I learned from my call to the hotel. There is a new address for him in Hawi. Also the red stain on the carpet is blood, but without a sample from Carole, they can't confirm that the blood is hers. Still it reinforces the need for further investigation. You might ask Sergeant Hanaka whether testing Monica's blood could help identify whether the blood on the carpet is Carole's."

"Yes, I was able to understand what you were being told since you helped along my understanding by repeating what he said and adding the context of what he said to your restatement. I am sorry that all indications point to murder. I guess I was hoping that the evidence would indicate otherwise. However, I've begun to get over my feelings of creepiness about it when I'm in the condo, thank heavens."

"I'm sure that must be a relief. Still you're too sensible to worry about ghosts or anything like that. But I do understand what you are saying."

"Actually I do believe in ghosts. When I was about sixteen, I lived in a house that was built in 1806. One day I saw the ghost of a Civil War soldier walking down the hall. But that's another matter. In any case, I'm not afraid of them, and I've seen no indication that the condo has any supernatural visitors. It was just the horror of murder in my private space that made me uncomfortable. I do realize it wasn't my space when it happened, and I don't dwell on thinking about it. I no longer give it more than a passing thought."

"Tell me about your ghost sighting. That must have been something for a sixteen-year-old girl!"

"It was simply strange. Not actually creepy or anything the way it happened. I was home alone, sitting in the upstairs bedroom. I had been reading a book when I heard a sound that caused me to look up. My chair faced the open door to the hall, and I saw a bedraggled soldier dressed in what looked like an old, faded Union Army uniform walking unsteadily down the hall. He was very pale and looked exhausted. He passed in front of my door and then continued until he was out of sight. I didn't move for a few minutes since I was a bit stunned. When I got up to look out into the hall, there was nothing there.

"I told my mother about it when she returned home, expecting that she'd think I was imagining things and would tell me so in no uncertain terms. Instead she looked at me with a stunned expression on her face and said, 'Thank heaven you've seen him too! I've seen him several times during the years we've lived here and thought I was going mad. After all, I don't believe in ghosts. But what you describe is exactly what I saw. Given the history of this house as a station on the Underground Railroad and the fact that there were Civil War battles not too far away ... well, who knows about these things. But the fact we've both seen him suggests he may be real, perhaps a ghost of someone with a connection to this house. I've never felt anything malignant about him, never felt as if he represented a threat or wanted to harm us. But I didn't say a word to your father or anyone else because of what they might think of me. They commit people to the asylum for things like that!'

"Then she gave me a hug and asked me to keep it our secret. I never told anyone about it before now. Those were the days before it was acceptable to discuss such things. It must have been hard for Mother to keep it to herself for so long. Somehow I never gave it much thought after that. I tend to just move past experiences and forget about them unless something triggers a recall. It never felt like a very odd thing to have seen. So that's why I believe in the reality of ghosts."

"I always thought of people who believe in ghosts as hysterics," said Walter. "But you certainly don't fit that category. Maybe I need to rethink my prejudices."

"My father was like you in that regard. Quite a while after Mother died, he confessed to me that she had come back several times at night during the first few months after she died. He said he would awaken and see her in the room, usually sitting on the edge of the bed. If he reached for her, she would move away or disappear completely. He felt she wanted to reassure him that she was looking out for him. Because he didn't believe in ghosts, he was afraid he was losing his mind. So he said nothing to anyone until one day when he was visiting with his friend John, who had lost his wife the previous year. John confessed to Dad that sometimes in the first few months after she died, Shelly had visited him at night. He asked whether Dad thought that was possible. Dad was so relieved to hear that someone else had such an experience that he confessed to John that he had also had visits at night from Mother. He said they both felt better after that conversation and were able to hope for future visits rather than fear them. Unfortunately there were no more visits for either of them. Having heard of those experiences, I had hoped maybe Scott would visit me after his death. I missed him so much and would have felt consoled by his presence. But he never did."

Walter chuckled. "Well now that you've told me those stories, I must confess that Marge did visit me several times after she passed. I considered myself mentally unbalanced at the time due to my grief. Since I also didn't believe in ghosts, I decided I was just conjuring up her presence in my imagination because I missed her so much. I did find it consoling, but also feared I was imagining things, so I never told anyone. Maybe it really did happen. It was only a few times spread over several weeks. You've reassured me of my sanity!"

"Glad to have been of help! Back to the conversation about the investigation, if you don't mind," said Susan. "I wonder if we should ask Carole's sister to talk with the people at the bank that manages Carole's custodial account. Perhaps she can find out if Bart tried to access the account without success and, if so, just when that occurred. Everything we've heard suggested that he needs money for his gambling debt. I assume he can't access the account without her written permission or a death certificate and copy of her will. Since he would be unlikely to have the former and certainly can't produce either of the latter two documents if her death hasn't been reported, someone might remember the contact. Also it might be worth talking with the sister about whether Carole made a will and whether she knows its contents."

"Those are some good ideas. I suggest you contact the sister and start with the questions about the will, where Carole might have kept a copy, for example, with a lawyer, and whether she knows what is contained in the will. If a lawyer has a copy, obtain his name and office number if you can. Also see if Monica would allow you to give that information to the local police. They might be able to get a copy. Then again, they may not since there is no proof that Carole is dead. If we're really lucky, Carole gave a copy to her sister, and she'll share it with you."

"Okay, I'll call her on Monday. That will give her thoughts time to settle following her conversations with the police. Meanwhile, I need tomorrow to finish off some preparations for Kristin's arrival next Friday. I still have to strip some wallpaper. Then I must vacuum the Murphy bed unit and clean the wall behind it. The good Lord only knows when it was last used and what manner of dust, dirt, and bugs may have accumulated back there. I also need to go shopping for some clean linens for the Murphy bed, along with towels and a new bath mat for the guest bathroom. And whatever else may be on my to-do list that I can't remember just now."

"It all sounds daunting to me, a guy who has someone in every week to clean and who has seen no need to replace anything in the house. Are you sure you can handle the Murphy bed on your own? They can be quite heavy, especially those older ones. And who knows what you might find back there. Maybe something really scary!"

"It sounds to me as if you are lobbying for an invitation to come over and help. If so, feel free. But once you are there, you risk being asked to scrape wallpaper as well as help to manipulate the Murphy bed and serve as my protector from scary things!"

"How about I come over around one? That way, you can sleep in, read the paper, take your walk, or do whatever else you would find relaxing. We'll go to work when I arrive. If I can use your facilities to freshen up when we're finished working, I'll take you out for pizza at Bertolini's. Deal?"

"How can I refuse an offer like that?! You are really spoiling me. And I'm enjoying it. It's been a while since anyone has wanted to take care of me—except for you during these past few weeks! I'm grateful to you."

"No need to be. I want to spoil you a bit. Believe me, it's nice to have someone to look after besides myself for a change. I'd like it to become routine! Now it's time for you to be heading home. You were up early today and must be exhausted. I don't want you falling asleep on your drive home. Let me escort you to your car."

"Thanks for being so considerate, Walter. I am tired."

On her drive home, Susan reflected on how fortunate she was to have found a friend like Walter. He was intelligent, kind, amusing, supportive, good company. He was comfortable to be with, and while he seemed adept at finding ways to bring them together, he was not at all pushy about moving the relationship to places she wasn't ready to go. He was truly a treasure!

Chapter 17

Happiness consists more in small conveniences of pleasures that occur every day, than in great pieces of good fortune that happen but seldom. (Benjamin Franklin)

FRIDAY, FEBRUARY 6, 3:30 P.M.

Susan sat on the stone wall by the door where arriving passengers would come through on their way to the baggage claim area. Kristin's plane was due in about fifteen minutes. As she waited, Susan reviewed the events of the past week. She and Walter had finished repapering the living and dining areas on Sunday afternoon. The job certainly had gone more smoothly with two people working. The steamer that Walter brought simplified the removal of the old wallpaper enormously, saving hours of scraping!

As promised, Walter had helped her with the Murphy bed so she could prepare it for use during Kristin's visit. The bed unit had been heavier than she had remembered. It would indeed have been difficult to manage the lifting on her own. Even so, by the time they finished, she had been too tired to change her clothing and go out for pizza. Instead Walter had picked up a takeout pizza that they ate in the condo with a simple salad that he had prepared.

Monday morning's painting session with Della had been fun. It had felt great to again engage in that creative endeavor. It was also pleasant getting to know Della, who had been a magazine illustrator in the days before computers had lessened the demand for people in that profession. Subsequently, as her illustration jobs began to disappear, Della had done some editing work for the publication where she was working at the time. While it helped pay the bills, she did not particularly enjoy the work. For a hobby, she had taken a portrait-painting class and began to do portraits of her friend's children, often giving them as gifts. It turned out that she was quite proficient at catching the unique spirit of each child. Other parents who had seen these gift portraits had approached her about doing portraits of their children. Eventually she was able to support herself by taking portrait commissions.

However, despite several hours of chitchat, Susan learned very little more that was helpful regarding Carole. On the positive side, she did catch up on a lot of what had been happening in Kona during the years she was gone. Della confirmed that there had been a population explosion, despite the recession. That helped explain the increased traffic congestion. Della had pointed out that the congestion would be much worse without the recently opened middle road, which facilitated traffic flow between downtown and the upper industrial area. The new shopping plaza, Kona Commons, had improved the shopping options with the addition of a Target, Ross, Office Max, and a Petco, in addition to a variety of small boutiques and other shops.

In addition, local governmental services had been centralized at the new West Hawaii Civic Center, which also provided a venue for a weekly senior citizen painting group that Della attended. During the previous year, the artists had been allowed to hold a show featuring their work in the courtyard at the civic center. Susan had promised Della that she would try to attend some of those painting sessions after her life settled down a bit. Susan had enjoyed Della's company, so she scheduled another morning painting session at Della's condo for the week after Kristin's scheduled date of departure.

On Tuesday afternoon, Susan had called Carole's sister, Monica, to ask her to find out whether anyone had tried to access the custodial account in which Carole kept the money inherited from her grandmother. She learned that Carol did have a will. Both Monica and a local lawyer had a copy. Although Carole had been intending to update the will, she had not done so. Monica agreed to mail a copy of the will to Susan, who would pass it along to Sergeant Hanaka. She would call Susan early next week with information about whether anyone tried to access the custodial account or contact the lawyer since Carole's disappearance. She would also provide the lawyer's name and phone number.

On Thursday evening, Susan and Walter had attended the performance of *Fiddler on the Roof*, following a lovely dinner at the Strawberry Patch, a recently opened restaurant in Kainaliu. It was a great find! Not only was the food and service excellent, but the restaurant offered a takeout service. So this morning before she went to the airport, Susan had picked up some prepared meals that she could use this week while Kristin was here. Earlier in the week, she had gone to Kona Commons to shop for linens, dropped by Costco and the Kailua-Kona Village Farmer's Market for groceries and produce, cleaned the condo, and made a list of things she and Kristin could do, if Kristin wanted to do some touristy things while in Hawaii. Susan would give Kristin all her attention while she was there! Follow-up on the investigation would have to wait.

The sound of voices interrupted Susan's musings. She saw a group of passengers emerging through the gate from the arrivals area. She glanced up at the electronic arrivals board and noted that Kristin's flight had arrived. She hastily opened her purse and grabbed the plastic bag containing the lei she had bought to welcome her daughter. She withdrew it from the plastic bag, shoved the bag back inside, and then hung her purse over her shoulder.

Holding the fragrant lei, she turned to watch the emerging passengers. People streamed through the gate—mothers and fathers trailing children of all ages who were looking excitedly about them; elderly couples walking slowly, some with canes or walkers; single men in business suits; and groups of teenagers in skimpy attire, prepared for the warm tropical air. Finally she spotted Kristin just at the moment she spotted her. They ran toward each other and hugged, unwilling to let go after a long absence.

When Kristin finally released her, Susan slipped the lei over Kristin's head. "Welcome to Hawaii, my darling. I'm so pleased that you are here!"

"Oh, Mom! It's so wonderful to see you again! And so exciting to be back in Hawaii! Not to mention being where it is warm. It was in the forties this morning when I left for the airport and raining as well. This is heavenly! It must be eighty degrees here. And this lei is so fragrant. It's Palani blossoms, isn't it? It smells just like I remember the early-morning aromas of Hawaii when the cool humidity releases the fragrance of the flowers."

"Yes, darling. I remembered that was your favorite Hawaiian scent. It's funny how that heavenly scent can always evoke the feel of the islands. Did you have a good trip? Can I carry something for you?"

"The trip was long and tiring but uneventful. As usual when flying into Kona, I felt I was landing on the moon. All that bare lava everywhere! Even though I've seen it so many times before and patches of grass have begun to grow in places, the view from the air still has a sense of desolation! Would you please hold my coat for a minute, Mom? I want to go over to that bench and get my sandals out of my carry-on bag. These closed shoes are too hot for this weather."

Kristin plunked herself on the bench and rummaged in her bag. Finding her sandals, she quickly substituted them for her traveling shoes and shoved the latter into the bag. Then she removed her jacket, rolled it, and stowed it in the bag as well.

"Ok, that's more appropriate attire! Let's see if we can find the luggage."

An hour later, they were sitting on the lanai at Susan's condo, sipping mai tais. Kristin, now attired in shorts and a sleeveless shirt, sat lounging in one of the basket chairs with her feet up on the hassock.

"How wonderful it is to be sitting here looking at the sun on the ocean and the palm trees silhouetted against the sky! And to have no one saying, 'Mom will you ... ' all the time. I can't believe I have a whole week of this to look forward to!" said Kristin.

"I want you to do exactly as you please while you're here, sweetheart. The only thing on our calendar is dinner here at the condo with my friend Walter on Monday night. He is looking forward to meeting you. But otherwise don't feel obligated to do anything. I know we talked about going out to look at furniture. I can do that after you leave, if you'd rather not go running around. It is a rather exhausting activity after all."

"I look forward to meeting Walter, Mom. You haven't exactly given me much information about him, you know. All I know is that you've sounded happy these past few weeks. If he is the cause of that, I know I'll like him. As for furniture shopping, I'd be happy to spend a morning with you looking around. That would be fun for me. It's been a long time since we've done anything like that together. Maybe we could plan on doing it after I've been here a few days and have caught up on my rest. Incidentally you have the condo looking great. I was quite surprised, having heard your description of the sordid state in which you found it when you arrived. You've apparently been quite busy these past few weeks. It wouldn't surprise me if a little rest sounded good to you also."

"Early to bed, a leisurely morning while we chat, an afternoon sitting in a comfortable chair on the sand under a tree reading and watching the waves, and a late-afternoon nap followed by a quiet drink here on the lanai before a good dinner ... I think I could handle a few days of that! I have been running pretty much nonstop since I got here. I never made it to the beach even once, unless you count my morning walks down to Land's End. But I do think all the activity has been good for me, both mentally and physically."

"You do look great! Better than I've seen you look in years. There is a healthy glow about you, a spring in your step, and a sense of life that has been absent far too long. These last few weeks have been good for you."

"I feel better than I have in years. I've been so engaged with life's tasks that I haven't had time to be sad. I've even lost a few pounds and toned up some flab. Then there has been the social stimulation. Between time spent with old and new friends and Walter's companionship, I haven't felt lonely. It's been nice to spend some time with a man without having to worry about him pushing for sex. With Walter, it's just comfortable companionship, not to mention shared empathy and understanding of where I'm at psychologically in my healing from your dad's death. I'm not yet ready for anything except friendship, although I'm honest enough to recognize that I'm physically attracted to the man. He is quite handsome!"

"You are so fortunate to have found someone like that. I'd say a man willing to settle for friendship is a rare commodity these days."

"You are so right. At least I never encountered anyone like that before. I have missed a man's perspective on the world since your dad died, so Walter's presence in my life has filled that gap. He's a really nice, kind, and helpful man as well as a charming, interesting companion. I shall miss him when I return to Seattle. But perhaps he would consider coming for a visit. It would be fun to show him the city, go to a symphony concert, visit some of my favorite restaurants, or go to the Chilhuly Museum … Just listen to me! Who ever thought I'd be thinking of a future that includes another man having any role in it?"

"It's a healthy sign, Mom. Life is for the living. Although you'll always have a big empty spot in your heart that belongs to Dad, if you find meaningful companionship in your life, you need to take advantage. Constant loneliness and dwelling on the past are not living. Now you said something earlier about having picked up some food for dinner. How about I make a salad while you heat it and set the table? I'm starving!"

Chapter 18

*The person who makes an effort to
keep smiling usually winds up with
something good enough to smile about.*

MONDAY, FEBRUARY 9, 5:30 P.M.

Kristin had finished setting the table and Susan was adding lemon juice to the bowl of salad dressing she was preparing when they heard a knock on the door.

"That must be Walter, Mom! Let me get it," said Kristin as she headed toward the door. Opening the door, she was greeted by an attractive older man holding a bouquet of heliconia.

"Hello! You must be Kristin. I'm Walter. I've been looking forward to meeting you. In honor of your visit, I've brought you some tropical flowers." Walter handed her the bouquet.

"Well, thank you," said Kristin, blushing. "I've also been looking forward to meeting you. From what I've been hearing, you and my mother have been spending considerable time together. Are you sure these weren't meant for Mom?" she asked, glancing at the flowers.

"Not this time," Walter said. "I wanted to get in your good graces from the start. I've always heard that flowers predispose a woman favorably toward the man who gives them to her."

"If you've had anything to do with the smile on my mother's face, I'm already favorably disposed. I haven't seen her so relaxed and happy in several years. Please come in and make yourself comfortable. Can I get you a drink?"

"A glass of white wine would be perfect, thank you." Walter walked over and gave Susan a kiss on the cheek. "Just checking out that smile Kristin was telling me about."

"Don't take too much credit. Kristin's visit has done a lot to make me smile," joked Susan.

"I have no doubt of that. But I've seen my fair share of that smile these past few weeks. I've also seen a considerable improvement in your outlook since I met you. Whatever it's due to, I like it. Speaking of outlook, I'd say mine has also improved. We've been good for each other."

"You won't get any argument from me on that point. But enough of this mutual admiration society. Come have a seat and chat with Kristin. I'll bring out something to nibble on. Then I will finish making dinner while you two get to know each other."

The evening passed quickly. Conversation flowed freely over dinner, covering topics that ranged from stories about their respective families, favorite places to visit, changes in the genre of popular music, and the state of the world.

As they were finishing their dessert, Kristin commented to Walter, "Mom was telling me about the blood found under the condo carpet and the investigation of what happened to Carole.

It seems that murder has been assumed and that Bart Selwyn has been the primary suspect. I can't help but wonder what would be his motive. Since he apparently needed money to pay his debts, murdering Carole and hiding the corpse would make it difficult, if not impossible, to get money from her, either from a life insurance policy or her inheritance. Without a valid death certificate, he would have no access to any money."

Walter's eyes met Susan's across the table. "Your daughter has hit on an important point. We should have thought of it ourselves! Since Bart's major issue in recent months had been on getting money to pay his gambling debts and Carole was his major source of funds, her disappearance, whether through voluntarily leaving or by having been murdered, would totally frustrate fulfilling that need. I'm afraid we got carried away by our focus on his inconsistent stories and trying to confirm that there was a death."

"But if she left voluntarily, certainly she would have contacted her sister," said Susan. "They were in touch frequently, and Carole wouldn't want Monica to worry. I also think she would have contacted her friends. Della said it was so unlike Carole not to let her know she wasn't going to show up for their painting session. She certainly wouldn't leave the island without saying goodbye in person or at least sending a text or calling."

"I agree," said Walter. "Clearly we need another hypothesis. I still believe that she must be dead or she would have surfaced by now. It's been more than a month since she was last seen or heard from. Who else might have a motive to kill Carole? And why has Bart been saying she left the island? He must know something or he'd be looking into things himself instead of developing the cover story he's spreading around. His behavior under the circumstances suggests that he may be afraid of something or someone."

"Mom, have your conversations with the condo residents turned up anyone with a grudge against Carole?" asked Kristin. "Could she be afraid of something or someone and be in hiding and unable to contact anyone? Could Bart be helping her to hide?"

"I haven't heard any suggestion of a grudge against Carole," said Susan. "She wasn't a great socializer. Many of the folks I talked with said they didn't really know her well. Those who did said she was pleasant, easy to get along with, and loyal and reliable. Her closest friends saw her as a martyr to Bart's gambling habits and constant debts. As to Bart helping her to hide, that's an interesting idea. But I can't imagine a circumstance that would lead to that."

"Walter, what is the likelihood that some of Bart's creditors would threaten to hurt Carole as a way of getting him to pay up?" asked Kristin. "That would give him motivation to take her into hiding."

"I suppose things like that do happen, but in my experience, it's more likely they would threaten to harm him." said Walter. "And I can't imagine that she couldn't at least let her sister know she is ok. Perhaps it is time that your mother has another conversation with Sergeant Hanaka. Would you mind doing that, Susan?"

"I'd be happy to talk to him. I just hope he doesn't feel I'm an interfering busybody. I'm expecting to hear from Monica in the next day or so with the information about the bank, lawyer, and so forth. I can use passing that information along to the sergeant as my excuse to call him. That may offer a convenient opportunity to bring up what we've been discussing. Maybe I'll just give her a call."

"Good idea, Susan," said Walter. "It will be interesting to see how Hanaka reacts. But enough about Bart and Carole tonight. It has been a lovely evening, and I really enjoyed meeting Kristin. Let me help you clean up. Then we can relax with an after-dinner drink before I head home."

"Many hands make light work," commented Kristin as she rose from the table. "Thanks for offering to help, Walter. If you'll carry the dishes to the kitchen, I'll rinse them, and Mom can load the dishwasher. I'll pour us drinks, and the two of you can take them to the lanai while I put away the last of the leftovers and clean the counters. Then I'll join you outside and enjoy your company for a while longer. Will I see you again before I leave the island?"

"I promised your mother I wouldn't interfere with her time with you, so that's up to her. If she agrees, I'd love to take the two of you to dinner on your last evening here."

"I accept with pleasure and will convince Mom to say yes," responded Kristin, playfully glancing at her mother. "That would be a lovely way to end my visit. Mom and I will still have the following morning together before I need to head out for my afternoon flight. Now to work!" Kristin picked up several dessert plates and headed toward the kitchen.

Chapter 19

*A man should never be ashamed
to own he has been in the wrong,
which is but saying that he is wiser
today than he was yesterday.*

TUESDAY, FEBRUARY 10, 9:30 A.M.

Bart sat on the edge of the cot in his jail cell, his head resting on his hands, elbows on his knees.

"Stupid, stupid, stupid!" he berated himself. "How can I have done this to myself? Why was it so important to go to that cockfight last night? Not only did I lose more money, I had the bad luck to be there when they raided the place. Now I'm stuck here with no money for bail and no one to call for help, and I am liable to lose my job when I don't show up for work today.

Carole was right when she told me I was a loser. I should have listened to her and gone for counseling about my gambling. With her gone, I have no one. Lord how I miss her!"

Just then Bart heard someone walking down the hall outside his cell. Looking out, he saw Tony, the pal he had accompanied to the cockfight. Tony was being escorted by a police officer.

Seeing Bart peering out of his cell, Tony called out, "Hey, Bart! I just made bail, so I'm going home. Jerry said he will post bail for you later today. Shall I call the hotel and tell them you can't come in today?"

"Yes, please do, Tony. Just say I'm sick. That should save my job. Tell Jerry thanks. I owe him ... again!"

"Move along now. We haven't got all day for a social call" said the officer to Tony, giving him a slight shove.

"I'll give you a call when I get home," Bart called after his departing friend.

I wonder how long until Jerry posts my bail? thought Bart. *Getting me out of here is in his self-interest since I can't pay him what I owe unless I'm working. I was hoping to win big at the cockfight so I could pay some of my debts. I really felt lucky last night. Thought I would have a good night and make back much of which I've lost the past months. Carole always told me it didn't work that way.*

Why can't I learn from my past mistakes? Maybe this is my time to turn over a new leaf and try a new approach. If I start saving every extra penny from my job at the Hapuna Prince and pick up part-time work, perhaps I can start to dig out of this hole. Then I can think about a normal life. Some hole! Ten thousand dollars! With what I make, even if I save every penny I earn, paying my debts would take forever! I have to find a way to cut ties with Tony and Frank. They are a bad influence. But they have been my only pals recently, so it will be lonely without them. They will certainly have something to say about my cutting them out of my life. This won't be easy. If Carole were here ... No use thinking of that. I'm on my own now.

Bart looked up to see a deputy approaching his cell. Unlocking the cell door, the officer said, "There is someone to see you, Mr. Selwyn. He is waiting for you upstairs in the interview room."

"Who wants to talk to me?" asked Bart. "Is it someone about posting my bail?"

"Nope, it's Sergeant Hanaka, a detective from the Kona station. I have no idea what he wants to talk with you about. What have you been up to besides illegal cockfights?"

"Nothing that I'm aware of. Can't imagine why he should want to talk to me."

As Bart entered the room, a Hawaiian officer rose from his chair at the table. Bart heard the door close behind him. "Hello, Mr. Selwyn. I'm Sergeant Hanaka of the Kona Police Department. Please sit there opposite me. I'd like to ask you a few questions about your wife, Carole."

"My wife?" said Bart. "What can I tell you about her? She left me more than a month ago. I have heard nothing in that time."

Observing Bart closely, Sergeant Hanaka thought he detected tension, surprise, and confusion in Bart's demeanor. "Your wife's sister has reported her as missing. She says she always heard from Carole several times a week and hasn't heard a word for more than a month. So naturally she is concerned."

Bart frowned. "Missing? I thought she went back to Montana to be with her sister. At least that's where I assumed she would go when she walked out on me. I certainly haven't heard from her, although I keep hoping she will relent and give me another chance."

"Why did she leave?"

"We were arguing a lot about money. I had accumulated gambling debts, and I was under pressure from my creditors to pay up. They threatened me with bodily harm if I didn't pay soon. I was very frightened, so I asked Carole for money. She had some she had inherited from her grandmother, and she refused. She said she had already given me all she intended to give me. I said that if she loved me, she would give me the money to save my skin and, if she did, I would get counseling and try to stop gambling. I don't think she believed me. She said I had made such promises before, but as soon as I got the money, I just went back to gambling. Unfortunately she was right about that!

"Carole had been asking for years that I go for counseling about my gambling habit. I kept refusing. I was sure that I could stop if I wanted to. Gambling was something I did with friends, and I enjoyed the thrill of it. I thought that if I stopped, I might lose my friends since it was about the only activity we did together. Now it's clear to me that she was right all along. I can't seem to stop on my own. As you probably know, I'm in here because I was at the cockfight that was raided last night. With Carole gone, it's even harder to quit. I thought maybe she left to try to shock me into doing something about it and that she would be back eventually. At the very least, I thought she would get in touch to let me know where she is and what she plans to do next. I'm pretty sure she still loved me. But I've heard nothing from her."

"Well, Bart, in your favor, what you've told me about the arguments is consistent with what we've heard from residents at the condo complex where the two of you lived. However, I need to clear up some discrepancies in the stories that you told various people when you were preparing to leave the complex. None of the stories we've heard as to what happened to Carole and regarding your plans is consistent with the story you just told me.

"You apparently told some people that Carole was going back to the mainland to look after her sick grandmother. Others reported that you said her mother had been arrested and she had to go back to deal with that. Apparently you indicated to all that you stayed behind to move your possessions, close up the unit, and negotiate a release from the lease, but you planned to join her once all that was accomplished. Obviously you did not return to the mainland to meet up with her."

"You are correct that I told inconsistent stories. I was upset at her leaving and embarrassed that she would walk out on me. I wasn't thinking clearly and said whatever came to mind at the moment, hoping to avoid a lengthy discussion. I couldn't afford to keep the condo without Carole's income, so I temporarily moved in with a pal who lives in Waimea until I found my present cheap accommodations in the town of Hawi."

"Did you try to get in touch with Carole after she left?" asked Sergeant Hanaka.

"I tried calling her mobile phone numerous times over several weeks, but she never answered and never called back. I thought about calling her sister, but Monica doesn't like me, and I couldn't bear the thought of talking to her. I decided that Carole was trying to teach me a lesson and I'd just have to wait until she finally relented and got in touch. As I said, she never did. I still can't believe she would just disappear like that. Every time my phone rings, I expect it to be her. But it never is." Bart swallowed hard, fighting to hold back tears.

"We will need to confirm your story. This is a missing person's investigation after all. Who is the pal you stayed with when you left the condo complex? How do we contact him?"

"Do you really need to contact him? He isn't supposed to have anyone else living at his place and could get in trouble if his landlord finds out I had stayed there."

"Yes, we do. I will try to be discrete. If you give me his phone number, I can call rather than go there in person."

"His name is Antonio Marrato. I'll write down his phone number for you."

"Thank you for your cooperation, Bart. Give me your phone number as well. I'll get in touch if we have any further questions or information on Carole's whereabouts. If you hear from her, let me know." Sergeant Hanaka handed Bart his card. "In the meantime, don't leave the island."

"Yes, sir. I will do as you ask," said Bart.

As Sergeant Hanaka left the room, the deputy appeared at the door. "Come with me, Mr. Selwyn. Bail has been posted for you. Your friend, Antonio Marrato, is waiting for you in the reception area. You and I must stop in the front office on the way out. You have some papers to sign, and your personal items will be returned. Afterwards you are free to go. You will be notified about your court date by mail. If you don't appear, your friend who posted bail will lose his money, and you will be subject to arrest."

"Don't worry. I'll be in court when the time comes. I want no more trouble with the law," said Bart.

As Bart entered the reception area after signing the papers, Tony rose from his chair. "Hey, Tony!" exclaimed Bart. "Thanks for coming. I was worried about how I was going to get home. I had no cash left on me when the fight was raided!"

Tony frowned. "We need to talk—once we get to the car."

Nuts! thought Bart. *Hanaka must have already called him. I had no chance to warn him. My luck!*

As Bart settled into the passenger seat of the car, Tony turned to him. "What the hell were you thinking—to give my name and telephone number to that cop?"

"Simmer down, Tony. I had no choice!" Bart briefly explained what had transpired. "So as long as you confirmed that I came to stay with you for a few days after Carole left me, there can be no problem. You were just a friend helping out a friend in need. That's all I said. As long as our stories are consistent, I don't see a problem."

"The boss isn't likely to see it that way. Why the heck is that policeman asking about her anyhow? How did he find out she's missing?"

"Apparently her sister contacted the cops here since she hasn't heard from Carole for some time. They usually talked several times a week or texted or emailed frequently."

"Never thought about that, did you? There was probably no way to have done anything to head that off, at least not for the long term. You could have sent some texts initially, but the whole thing was so upsetting for all of us. Too late now. Just keep your trap shut, you hear? I'll keep quiet about the fuzz calling. No need to get the boss more upset. But you better find a way to start paying what you owe or you're in deep doo-doo!"

"Yeah! I decided while I was in there that I need to stop hanging around with you and Frank for a while. Just until I start paying off some of what I owe. I'll miss you guys. I thought I'd get a part-time job in the evenings to supplement my income. If I stay away from gambling venues, I can stay off the police radar. Further, if I stop spending on recreational activities with you guys until I've reduced what I owe, it will make it easier for me to save money to make payments. If I promise to scrimp and save most of my income so I can pay a good chunk of what I owe each week, perhaps Jerry will let me start paying on an installment plan. I figure that at least that way he gets his money. Any other way he gets just my hide. He probably figures that would send a message to others, but hopefully he'll be willing to accept money instead. With the interest rates he charges, he'll do well. I'll miss spending time with you guys, but it's not forever—just 'til I dig my way out of debt."

"I get it, but I don't like it. If you can arrange a payment schedule with the boss, you'd better stay in touch with me and Frank. If we're not going to see each other regularly, we still need to maintain contact. And keep your mouth shut! Remember, we know how to find you. Don't try to leave the island!"

"Don't worry, Tony. I have nowhere to go. It's ironic. The last thing Sergeant Hanaka said to me was the same thing: don't leave the island!"

Chapter 20

It's easy to take for granted the simple beauties that surround us. Take time today to feel the warmth of the sun on your face, to smell the flowers in your path, to watch with wonder the butterfly's dance.

WEDNESDAY, FEBRUARY 11, 9:30 A.M.

Susan sat at the dining table, preparing to call Sergeant Hanaka. She wanted to report on her conversation with Carole's sister, Monica. She had called Monica's cell phone at 7:00 a.m. Hawaii time and reached her at her workplace. Susan also wanted to raise with Sergeant Hanaka the issues discussed over dinner last night. She dialed the cell phone number he had provided and heard the sound of ringing.

After three rings, the phone was answered. "Hanaka here."

"Sergeant Hanaka, it's Susan Brooks. I'm the woman with the condo on Alii Drive who discovered blood on the carpet last week."

"I remember you. You were going to find out from the sister about a will and a bank account as I recall."

"Yes, that's why I'm calling. I spoke to Monica, the sister, this morning. She does have a copy of the will. She will send me a copy, along with information on the bank account, name of the law firm, and telephone numbers for the lawyers who were involved in establishing both. I will bring it by the station as soon as I receive it. She said it's the original will. Although Carole told Monica that she was considering divorce and was going to change the will, she never did so. Bart remains the primary heir. Also Monica says that no one has tried to withdraw money from the restricted account.

"That reminds me. Last evening, my friend Walter Conway, my daughter, and I were talking about this situation over dinner. I don't know why it didn't occur to us earlier, but we began to wonder if thinking of Bart as a suspect makes sense. After all, if Carole is dead, what does he gain? If he killed her and hid her body, there would be no death certificate and therefore no way to claim her money. If he had killed her, wouldn't he have done it in a way that looked like an accident or suicide so he could inherit?"

"You make a good point. I've been thinking along those same lines. I interviewed him yesterday afternoon. He had been arrested while attending an illegal cockfight in Waimea on Sunday night. Perhaps you saw the article in *West Hawaii Today*. Anyway he seemed sincerely fond of his wife and quite unhappy about her being gone. Either he is a good actor or a truly unhappy man. However, there are parts of his story that don't quite ring true. I'm sure there is something he's not telling me. There are several things he told me that I will be checking on.

"In the meantime, we are obtaining a blood sample from the

sister. We will have it tested and compared to the blood on the carpet. There is a good chance that the test can confirm whether the blood on the carpet was likely Carole's. These days, familial similarities in blood components can be detected to pinpoint such a likelihood with a high degree of certainty. Meanwhile, there has been nothing to indicate that Carole was treated at any medical facility for an injury that could lead to so much bleeding. This whole situation is certainly a mystery."

"It is that! I'll give you a call to arrange to pass on the will and other information from Monica as soon as I receive it. Thanks for the update on your investigation. I'll be glad when this is all resolved."

"So shall we all!" replied the sergeant.

As Susan sipped her coffee, she thought about what Sergeant Hanaka had said about his interview with Bart. Assuming that Bart was hiding something as the sergeant surmised, what could it be? If he had done nothing wrong, why would he need to hide anything? She kept coming back to the thought that someone might have kidnapped Carole to put pressure on Bart to pay his debts. But that didn't make sense. Surely his creditors must be aware that without Carole's funds, his only way of paying off his debts was through systematic savings from his earnings. Could they be holding Carole and be pressuring her to pay his debts? If Carole had been kidnapped and was being held until he paid off his debt, wouldn't Bart have avoided gambling venues in order to save enough to pay up more quickly and get Carole released? Would he have gone to the cockfight where he might lose more money?

Of course, thought Susan, *I suppose gamblers are convinced they will soon have a big win to make everything all right. I guess I just don't understand their psychology. And Walter did say that racketeers don't generally go after the family members, but try to threaten the debtor.*

Hearing footsteps in the hall, Susan turned to see Kristin emerging from the bedroom. "Good morning, sleepy head! I'm glad you were able to sleep in this morning. Did you rest well?"

"I was lulled to sleep almost instantly by the sound of the waves and slept soundly until a few minutes ago. I thought I heard the sound of voices."

"You must have heard me on the telephone. I first talked with Monica and then Sergeant Hanaka. He agrees with your thought that Bart really had no motive to kill Carole. Like you said, he would benefit only from her being alive. I'm sorry if I woke you."

"Don't be. I was ready to wake up. I feel more rested than I have in months! Your bed is so comfortable. Did you do ok on the Murphy bed, Mom?"

"I slept well, but you know that I'm an early riser. Besides I wanted to catch Monica before we got caught up in our day's activities. You will need to help me to put up the bed. I'll make breakfast for us while you shower. What would you like?"

"Toast, cheese, fresh tropical fruit, and a cup of freshly brewed Kona coffee would be heavenly. Thanks."

"I'll set us up here in the dining room. The morning sun filtering through the tropical foliage into the room is almost magical this morning."

"I'll be ready in fifteen minutes max!" said Kristin as she headed for the shower.

Susan rose to prepare breakfast. She was setting the last of the food on the table when Kristin reappeared. "You look refreshed and ready to take on the world," observed Susan as Kristin settled in at the table.

"Thanks. That's how I feel! Is the plan still to go looking at furniture this morning?"

"Yes," replied Susan. "Then when we get tired of furniture shopping, I thought we might pick up some sandwiches and go to the beach by the fishpond in the Kaloko-Honokohau Historical Park. There's a nice shaded area under the trees behind the beach where we can sit and stay cool. I'll throw a cooler with some water, my beach chairs, and towels into the car. We can take some books too. Maybe we'll see some sea turtles. They often come ashore there in the afternoons. If you think you'd like to swim, you probably should wear your swimsuit under your street clothing since there's nowhere to change."

"That would be heavenly!" said Kristin. "I haven't had any beach time this trip. Maybe I'll pick up a bit of suntan so I can look healthy when I go home. Eliciting a little jealousy from all those white-faced folks back home would be a bonus. Tomorrow we can do a bit more furniture shopping in the morning. I assume we need more than just the few hours we'll put in today. Afterwards I'd love to have lunch at the Holualoa Gardens restaurant. The garden is such a beautiful, peaceful setting. After lunch, I'd like to poke around the galleries and gift shops in the town. I need gifts for my boys. I'll try not to get carried away with shopping so we can have enough time afterwards to go to the coffee plantation just north of town that has the Japanese garden. I love strolling in that beautiful place. We can finish off that visit by having a cup of their wonderful coffee at the pavilion overlooking the infinity pool and that drop-dead gorgeous view of downtown Kona and the coastline. If we're lucky, we might have a clear day so we can see Maui in the distance. I can also stock up on some freshly ground Kona coffee to take home with me."

"What a great idea, Kristin! Those are some of my favorite places, and I haven't been to any of them yet this trip. I would love to pick up some coffee to have at the condo. It's essential to have good Kona coffee when you're in Kona. Coffee bought directly from the growers is better than that sold at the supermarket. I would suggest, however, that we get an early start tomorrow if you are up to it. That way we can have an early lunch, take our time in the galleries and at the coffee plantation, and still have time to get back here for a rest before we meet Walter for dinner. By having lunch early, we should be hungry enough to enjoy dinner. He plans to take us to dinner at Ulu Ocean Grill at Hualalai. It's right on the beach, so the views and general ambience are lovely. The food and service are excellent. I think you'll enjoy it. Since that restaurant is near his home, I suggested that we meet him there. That way he won't have to fight traffic to come here to pick us up and then have to drive all the way back out there. It will also save him a round trip to bring us back here afterward. The reservation is for seven."

"I will have some great memories from this trip," said Kristin. "We've done so much already!"

"Well, we have two more days to build memories. I'll be sorry to see you go. But I'll try to come see you and your family in the late spring or early summer. Maybe we could rent a house on one of the islands off the Carolina coast once the boys are out of school but before the hoards arrive for the summer."

"That would be great! The boys would love some beach time and especially if they can share it with you. How nice to have that to look forward to!"

Chapter 21

A good thing to remember as you go through life is that you should always keep your heart softer than your head.

FRIDAY, FEBRUARY 13, 10:00 A.M.

Walter picked up the phone on the third ring. "Hello. Oh, hi, Susan! What a pleasant surprise to hear from you this morning."

"Good morning, Walter. I called to thank you for the lovely evening last night. Kristin and I both enjoyed the dinner and the ambiance so much. Of course, your company is what made the evening special! Thank you ever so much for spoiling us."

"It was my pleasure. Your daughter is charming, and I'm grateful that I was able to get to know her better. I've forgotten. What time is her flight?"

"Her flight leaves at four o'clock this afternoon. Once she's through security, I'll leave the airport. If you wouldn't mind some company for a short while, I thought I'd invite myself for tea. I can bring some scones to accompany the tea and chase away those midafternoon hunger cravings. I think some company would help me with the transition of her leaving."

"What a good idea! I'd love to see you. If I can distract you from Kristin's absence, I'm delighted to do so."

"Thanks for being so understanding, Walter. You're a treasure! See you about four o'clock."

Hanging up the telephone, Susan turned to Kristin, who had just entered the room. "Finished packing?"

"Yes, thanks. It was a bit of a squeeze since I packed the family gifts in my suitcase. I change planes in Honolulu, so I didn't want too much in my carry-on. In the past, I've found that the Wiki-Wiki express buses are often jammed. I usually walk—or run if it's a tight connection—from terminal to terminal to catch my flight to the mainland. Since it can be a fair distance and outdoors in the afternoon heat, I prefer to keep my carry-aboard luggage light."

"A smart strategy. I usually do that myself. What do you want to do with our remaining hours?"

"Let's just hang out here until we must leave for the airport. A good night's sleep and my early swim have invigorated me. Now I'd like to just enjoy the peace and quiet. I know that when I get home, it's back to the rat race: running the boys around to their various activities, refereeing quarrels, running errands, fighting with corporate America about unauthorized charges, dealing with poor service, and so on and so on. Life has become such a struggle! Electronic phone trees rarely offer an appropriate option for what you called about. People tell you they can't do anything to help once you do get through and then refer you to websites that are supposed to help but often only further frustrate your efforts to resolve the issue!

"As for making financial payments online, which is becoming all the rage, it's a joke! It may be convenient for paying recurring monthly charges, but it can be a trap for the unsuspecting should they ever want to unsubscribe from a service, such as credit card protection or subscriptions to weather alert services. Often there is no way to contact the company and get someone to cancel the service, so you end up paying forever for something you don't want. The consumer is being taken advantage of in so many ways! I just hate it!

"And it's getting harder to have any face time with friends. For starters, people are busy. They rely so much on texting or email that they seldom use the phone—even their mobile—to talk anymore. Getting together over a pot of tea or a cup of coffee is a thing of the past. It seems sometimes that people are even losing the ability to communicate face-to-face. Many people have lost any semblance of manners. Rudeness abounds! Sorry for the tirade, Mom," said Kristin looking embarrassed. "Having time to just sit and have a civilized talk with you here is a real gift. We can chat the morning away. While we do so, I'll memorize this view to remember after I'm at home. That memory will be like a tranquilizer."

"Walter and I have expressed much the same feelings about the state of things. We thought maybe we are just grumpy old fogies. It's reassuring if your generation feels the same way. Maybe they have the energy to try to do something about it."

"I think most of my friends have expressed similar thoughts in the past. Unfortunately I haven't had much chance for a serious tête-à-tête with friends recently. Anyhow, can we have a late lunch? That way I won't need to worry about getting something to eat before my flight. No point in taking a snack either. That just complicates going through the agricultural inspection in

Honolulu. You can just drop me at the terminal in Kona. No need to park and come in with me. Kona airport is such a hectic place in the afternoons."

"Good plan, Kristin. I can't tell you how much I've enjoyed your visit and how much I will miss you once you've left. Would shrimp tacos, a salad, fresh fruit, and Hawaiian rolls be enough to hold you? I have some mango iced tea to drink, unless you'd prefer a cocktail or wine."

"That sounds like more than I need. I'll skip the rolls and nothing alcoholic. Your mango iced tea would be perfect."

The morning passed swiftly. Before she knew it, Susan was dropping Kristin at the Hawaiian Airlines terminal. Both mother and daughter had tears in their eyes as they hugged goodbye.

"I'll call when I get home," said Kristin as she turned to go.

"Have a safe flight, my love," said Susan.

She stood and watched as Kristin got in the line for check-in. Kristin looked back and waved to her mother. Then she turned her attention to the agent at the desk. Susan returned the wave and then got into the car and drove away. Feelings of sadness at Kristin's departure overwhelmed her.

Goodbyes are so bittersweet, she thought. *Two sides of the same coin. Without the wonderful time together, there would be no need for goodbyes. Joy and sadness always seem to go hand in hand.*

As she left the airport, Susan forced herself to stop being maudlin and concentrate on her driving. She remembered that she needed to stop at the pastry shop near Costco to pick up the scones she had told Walter she would bring with her for their tea, so she headed up the hill.

Mission accomplished, Susan drove to Walter's home. No

sooner had she rung his bell when she heard him coming down the hall.

"Hello, Susan," said Walter. "Come in. Your timing is perfect! I was just heating water for tea. I'm glad you remembered to bring the scones," he commented, seeing the bag in her hand. "I'm starving! I played a game of golf with some friends after you called this morning, and it took so long I didn't have time for lunch. I've only had time for a quick shower since returning home."

"You should have called. I could have picked up some sandwiches as well."

"I made us some small sandwiches. Scones and sandwiches? Doesn't that constitute an English high tea? Except my sandwiches don't have the crusts removed to look pretty like those served at a high tea. Marge used to love having the British afternoon tea when we visited England."

"She and I had that in common," said Susan. "It's been years since I was last there, however. I wonder how much things have changed. It seems the whole world has become more homogenized in the past few decades. Many charming old buildings are being razed and replaced by steel and glass towers. Also I've heard that many of the unique customs, foods, and other cultural icons of individual countries have nearly disappeared, except perhaps in remote rural areas. On the other hand, back in Seattle, several recently opened teahouses offer English high tea. They seem to be doing quite well. Several months before I came back to Hawaii, a friend and I went for afternoon tea. We had to make reservations a week in advance!"

"I agree that the world is changing rapidly and, in my opinion, not for the better," said Walter. "Technology is probably one major factor leading to many of the changes. The way people are tied to their cell phones is appalling! I read recently that some people are checking their phones between a hundred and two hundred times a day. How do they get anything done? Apparently gamers stay up all night playing, even though they need to go to work in the morning. As for electronic banking ... never mind. I'm sure you don't want to spend your afternoon listening to me gripe."

"The European Union and the globalization focus of the corporate and political systems also are playing a major role in fostering change," observed Susan. "I often wonder whether anyone will want to travel much anymore if countries lose their unique character and culture. When you read a book like *A Year in Provence* or *Bella Tuscany*, which describe so well the food, architecture, lifestyles, and characters who live in France and Italy, respectively, you can hardly wait to book the next flight there. But if all that is lost, why bother?"

"I do agree, my dear. But back to matters at hand, if you don't mind. I need some food. Excuse me, Susan, while I brew the tea. Perhaps you could put some scones on that small platter next to the one with the sandwiches. Shall we have our tea inside at the dining room table? The sun is already shining on the lanai, so even with the sunscreen lowered, it might be awfully hot."

"That's fine. I see you already have the cups, plates, napkins, and utensils laid out. I'll carry in the sandwiches and scones while you finish up the tea. Is there anything else I can do?"

"If you'll grab a trivet out of that drawer next to you and put it on the table, I'll have a place to set the hot teapot. Then just have a seat. I'll be there in a minute."

Walter followed Susan into the dining room. "Would you like to pour, or shall I?"

"Why don't you pour? I've never had a gentleman pour tea

for me before, unless you count the waiter at the Empress Hotel in Vancouver, Canada."

"It would be my pleasure. Meanwhile, help yourself to sandwiches and a scone. Then tell me how you're handling Kristin's departure. It must have been difficult to let her go. Listening last night to the two of you talking about your many explorations of the island convinced me that you had a great time. You both positively glowed as you talked about your week."

"Yes, we did have a fabulous time. We got to visit so many of the places we love in Hawaii. Each one triggered happy memories, and we reminisced for hours. Why is it that we hardly ever visit these places when we're living here? I find the same thing happens in Seattle. If I have guests, I'll play tourist and take them to the Pike Street Market, the Space Needle, the waterfront restaurants, the aquarium, and so forth. But even though I love going there, somehow I never do it unless I have guests from out of town."

"I've often wondered that myself," said Walter. "Somehow life gets in the way. We fall into a routine of chores and activities. Laziness probably plays a role. Then, too, there are all these time-consuming irritations of daily living that sap one's energy, leaving one too tired to seek out those special pleasures. Just yesterday, I wasted an hour on the phone with my internet provider about a billing error!"

"It's funny that you should mention that, Walter. Kristin was saying this morning that she dreaded going back to her exhausting routines of life and particularly to those sorts of irritants. They are becoming so commonplace. Everywhere there are people out to take advantage of you. It's become necessary to be on guard every minute. I have several magazines I enjoy reading. When I renew, the publisher wants me to use a credit card and be locked into automatic renewal forever-after. I'm not willing to take a chance on dealing with the potential difficulties of cancelling when I get tired of the magazine. Past experience has shown me that they make it as difficult as they can. So I always pay by check at the time I renew.

"And the telephone solicitors! I've learned to say 'I'm not interested' at the start of the call because so many are not what they make themselves out to be. Some just want to get personal identifiers so they can get to your funds. Others are charities that spend only a few percent of what they take in on the charitable cause. The rest goes to administrative costs or to enhance the lifestyle of the founders. I've even heard that there is one scammer that asks a seemingly innocent question to which the answer is yes. If you say yes, they record it and subsequently use your recorded yes to charge you for something you know nothing about."

"It's true," said Walter. "One must be on guard constantly. As for charities, don't get me started. I used to give to a number of legitimate charities that provided services that I cared about. But over the years, things got totally out of hand. They used to send a request for help once or twice a year. Now it's several times a month. Some of them send you stuff, allegedly to say thank you for your donation. This stuff is accompanied by a request for additional giving. I resent them spending money to send me things I don't want or need instead of spending it on the intended cause. In addition, each charity seems to sell your name to several others. Now instead of getting one request for donations every week or two, I get seven to ten in my mail every single day! That's in addition to the phone calls. In the end, the legitimate charities I used to support have lost out. I no longer answer calls if I don't recognize the number, and I toss all the mail solicitations unopened.

"I think, Susan, that one needs to plan for special pleasures and let life settle around them. Perhaps you and I should plan at least one special activity a week doing something we both enjoy. Let's take advantage of lovely Hawaii. For example, I love the crescent beach at the Kona Coast—Kekaha Kai—State Park at Mahai'ula Bay, with its white sand, shady areas for sitting, and turquoise water for snorkeling. If one goes during the week instead of on the weekend, one often has the place to oneself.

"For historical interest, Lapakahi State Historical Park with its remains of an old Hawaiian village is worth a visit. I also like Hulihe'e Palace, once a residence for visiting Hawaiian royalty, and Mokuaikaua Church, the first Christian church built in the islands in 1820. Both are in downtown Kona. Visiting Waimea during cherry blossom season and for the strawberry festival is another thing I enjoy. Even an attending an occasional rodeo there is fun."

"What a great idea, Walter! We should take advantage of being here in this beautiful place. I love both Waimea and the Kona Coast beach park. I also enjoy poking around the shops and galleries in Kapa'au and Hawi or visiting the black sand beach on the south of the island. I've long been wanting to visit the little historic church in downtown Kona that you mentioned. All the years I've been coming here, I still haven't found time to see the inside. And I'd love to revisit the painted chapel outside of Honaunau. It's extraordinary and so unique! And the nearby Place of Refuge, *Pu'uhonua o Honaunau*. The island is so rich in culture and things to do! Once a week for a year wouldn't begin to exhaust the possibilities! Of course I won't be here much longer anyhow. It will soon be time to go back to Seattle."

"Please, can we not think about that yet? We need to follow through on some of the things we've just been talking about doing. And I'd like to have a long talk with you before you make your decision about whether or not to sell and when to leave. My life has been infinitely richer since I met you. Even though I told you the day we met that I'm not ready for commitments, I'm beginning to feel differently. The thought of going back to my life before Susan seems unbearable!"

"Walter, you have become a wonderful friend. I will miss having you in my life. I really enjoy your company. It's become so easy to drop by for a chat when I'm out and about. When something is on my mind, I immediately think about discussing it with you. Your thoughts are always so helpful. But I don't know that I'm ready to think about a future. Your life is here. Mine is in Seattle, except for a few months in Hawaii, if I keep the condo. I admit that not seeing you will be hard. But it all seems so complicated right now," said Susan, looking distressed.

"Don't fret, Susan. I won't pressure you. I understand your reluctance to commit to the future at this point. For now, let's just enjoy our time together. When are you planning to return to Seattle?"

"I was planning to leave at the end of March. But recently I was thinking about pushing the date to mid-April. I've been so busy fixing up the condo that I haven't had a chance to just live and to see how I feel about being here on my own. Of course, now that I've met you, I realize that my parameters for decision-making have changed. Everything has become much more complex. You will clearly be a factor in any decision I make."

"I'm glad to hear that. Would you consider staying through

the entire month of April? That would give us some time for things to evolve slowly so neither of us feels any pressure. Perhaps in mid-April we could revisit this conversation?"

"Yes. Of course. I will gladly put off my departure until the end of April. Time is our best friend right now."

"Thanks, Susan. That gives us several months to just enjoy exploring the island while spending time together. Who knows how things will look by then. Do you want another scone? Or perhaps more tea?"

"Absolutely not! I've eaten entirely too much already. I can skip dinner and just have a piece of fruit before bedtime. I'll carry these plates to the kitchen and help with the washing up before I head home." As Walter started to protest, Susan said, "No, I really am tired and should get back, much as I'd love to stay and chat."

They carried the plates and other evidence of their snack to the kitchen. Susan began to wash, while Walter dried and put things away. Just as they were finishing the last plate, they heard a voice.

"Dad, whatever are you doing?" Turning, they saw a young man coming through the open lanai door.

"Keith!" exclaimed Walter. "What are you doing here? Why didn't you ring the bell?"

"I had a business meeting in Honolulu the past two days. Today's meeting finished early. Since it's the weekend, I thought I'd delay my trip home to California and fly over here to see you. I wanted to surprise you, so I thought it would be fun to pop in the back way rather than ring the bell. I know you usually have the doors wide open this time of year. But it seems that you have surprised me! You have company! Or does she live here?" he asked snidely.

"Keith! What a thing to say! I'd like you to meet my friend, Susan Brooks. Susan, this is my son, Keith, who lives in California with his wife and two children. He's not usually so rude."

"I'm very pleased to meet you, Keith. It was very thoughtful of you to look in on your dad. I'm sure he will enjoy visiting with you every bit as much as I enjoyed the past week with my daughter, who flew out of Kona earlier today. Your dad and I just finished up the dishes from our afternoon tea. I'll head home and leave you two to enjoy your evening. How long can you stay?"

"I fly out around noon on Sunday," Keith replied somewhat sullenly. "I want to spend my time with my dad in the meantime."

"Have a seat, son. I'll see Susan to her car and be back in a second."

"I'm afraid your son looked a bit shocked when he saw us in the kitchen," said Susan as they walked to the car.

"That's his problem. This isn't the way I would have chosen to have you meet any of my children, but it is what it is. Imagine his showing up without any notice! Suppose I had gone on a trip and wasn't even on the island! Keith never was very practical. Always making the grand gesture!

"I'm sure the word that I have a woman friend will spread quickly through the family once he gets home. I'd have preferred to tell them about you myself at a later stage in our relationship. I'm not as comfortable chitchatting with my children as you appear to be with yours. It's probably a man thing."

"Do you think he will approve? He didn't look too happy when he saw us. Maybe he made some assumptions about what he saw that are far from reality. After all, moving from thinking your dad has no woman in his life to finding him with a woman in his kitchen doing dishes as if she belonged there must be difficult, especially since he doesn't know the circumstances.

You really do need to have a conversation about this, difficult as it may be."

"Don't worry. I will talk with him. But even if he disapproves, it doesn't matter to me. I'm finally getting my life back, and even the family I love will not be permitted to interfere. I will try to get him to agree not to tell his siblings until I have an opportunity to talk with them."

"Be cautious, please, Walter. Give him just facts and keep emotions out of the discussion. Our future relationship is still open and uncertain. The last thing you want to do is to jeopardize your relationship with your children because of it."

"Yes, my darling friend. I will be sensible, although I'm a bit annoyed right now. I'm dying to give you a peck on the cheek and a big hug, but for all I know, Keith is watching out the window. Don't want to make things worse. Now scoot. I better get in there since he went to the trouble to come visit."

"Do enjoy his visit. He must love you very much to go to the trouble to come to Kona." Susan got into the car.

Walter waved as Susan backed out of the driveway. Then he turned back toward the house and his son.

Chapter 22

Many of us have learned to avoid speaking the truth in order to keep peace. We need to remember that honesty can be practiced with kindness and love.

MINUTES LATER

Walter reentered the house and walked into the living room where he found Keith sitting in a chair with his legs crossed, arms hugging his body, and one foot tapping impatiently on the floor.

"Keith, my boy," he said, holding out his arms. "Are you too mature to give your dad a hug?"

Keith rose from his chair and reached for his father. "I'm so glad to see you, Dad. I probably should have called to tell you I was coming. I still can't resist the grand gesture, and I thought a surprise would offer you something unique in a string of mundane days. I guess that's how I picture your life. Seeing you chatting away in the kitchen with Susan while *doing dishes*—something I don't associate with you—shattered that picture. I'm sorry I chased her away."

"You didn't chase her away. She was planning to leave anyway. She's had a long, action-packed week while her daughter was here and wanted to get home for a rest. She took her daughter to the airport this afternoon, and I thought that stopping here for afternoon tea would distract her from her sadness at Kristin's departure."

"So have you met this Kristin? You and Susan must be pretty chummy if you've already met her daughter. How long has this been going on?"

"Keith!" exclaimed Walter. "How long has what been going on? If you mean my friendship with Susan, I met her about six weeks ago when I offered her assistance after she sprained her ankle at the Champions Tour Golf Tournament that is held here at Hualalai every year. Funny, it seems longer than that. We've had dinner a few times and went to the theater once. She too is widowed. Her husband died about four years ago. Somehow the common experience of widowhood has made being together comfortable. I guess we didn't look for ulterior motives from each other, since neither of us was looking for a long-term relationship. We seem to fill an empty space in each other's lives.

"As Susan and I talked, we realized that both of us have been wary of spending time with a member of the opposite sex. It somehow felt like a betrayal of our deceased spouses. Also we were suspicious of other people's motives for being with us and feared pressure for commitments we weren't ready for. Yet we missed having the easy companionship we had shared with our spouses. Since our meeting, Susan and I have been evolving a comfortable friendship. We enjoy each other's company without expectations. We share similar taste in music, theater, and food.

More importantly, we have similar outlooks on family, moral values, travel, and a host of other things. Conversation is so natural and comfortable. Susan is adding a whole new dimension to my *mundane* life."

"I'm sorry, Dad," said Keith. "I shouldn't have said that. But the last time I saw you, you were pretty gloomy and not doing much. You'll remember that the three of us kids were urging you to become active and start reengaging with life—playing golf, poker with your buddies, and so on. You do look happier, I'll give you that. But it's as if you've forgotten Mom ever existed. I guess none of us ever thought about another woman in your life. We've certainly never talked about the possibility. And it seems odd that you've not told any of us about Susan."

"Let me respond to those points, each in turn. You are correct that, until recently, I had disengaged from life. Everything is different without a partner, especially when you've lived your life with one partner for more than forty years. Social situations are awkward. People don't know what to say to you. Hostesses try to pair you off with single women. Women on the prowl for a husband chase after you, making you want to retreat into solitude. You kids were correct that I needed to try to reengage, so I resumed occasional golf games with friends. I tried having dinner or playing cards with some of them, but conversation, when not awkward, was downright boring. I preferred staying home listening to music or looking through pictures and recalling my wonderful life with your mother.

"You say I've forgotten your mother. That could never happen. She will always be part of my life. Often when Susan and I are talking, we are sharing stories about our spouses and remembering happier times. In a way, talking about your mother with Susan gives me back that part of my life and fills that vast void of emptiness. So yes, I am feeling better and am experiencing some real happiness for the first time in years. With Susan I can relax and just be myself.

"You also said it is odd that I haven't talked about Susan with any of you three children. Perhaps you have a point. But Susan and I haven't known each other very long, and we have been focused on our present. Who knows what the future may bring. I didn't see much point in talking about her at this point. There is nothing going on beyond fond companionship between two lonely people. For these past few weeks, she has been my own precious secret, and I didn't want to open myself to the kinds of criticism I felt from you today."

"I'm sorry, Dad. I overreacted. When I walked in, the two of you looked like an old married couple working together there in the kitchen and chatting away. At first, I guess I assumed she was living here. From that point—"

Walter interrupted Keith. "I do understand, son, how you might have gotten a wrong impression. Do yourself a favor next time you decide to visit and give me a call first. That way you avoid nasty surprises. For all you know, I might not have been home, but travelling on another part of the island or even off-island. Anyway, Keith, I'm delighted you are here. Can I offer you something to drink? Are you hungry?"

"A mai tai would be most welcome. And I could eat something. It's been a long time since lunch."

"I'll bring you some tea sandwiches and a scone left from our afternoon tea. We can go out for dinner, but not for a few hours yet. I ate too much during our tea because I didn't have time for lunch after my golf game this morning and was starving by the time Susan arrived. I will have a mai tai with you, however," said Walter as he headed for the kitchen.

When Walter returned to the family room, he handed Keith a plate of sandwiches and set the tray with the mai tais on the coffee table, handed one to Keith, and took the other for himself.

Keith said, "So, Dad, tell me about Susan. What do you know about her?"

"Well, as I mentioned, she is widowed. She has two children. Her son lives in California and her daughter in North Carolina. She has three grandchildren, two boys and a girl. She lives in Seattle in the house where she and Scott, her husband, had lived during all the years they were teaching at the University of Washington. She and Scott had a condo here in Kona and used to come during school breaks and during their vacation time. They spent their sabbatical here one year, and Susan said they found it a great place for doing some professional writing. Since Scott's death, Susan has rented the condo for several years as a long-term rental. She couldn't bring herself to come by herself after Scott died. The idea of being here without him was just too painful.

"Susan finally returned to Kona in early January to check out the condition of her condo. Her latest renters recently broke their lease and left rather abruptly. Susan saw this as an opportunity to come and test her emotional reactions to being here. She feared she might not want to spend time here alone, even though she loves Hawaii. She was afraid it might retrigger the pain of Scott's passing from which she was finally recovering. Additionally she didn't know how many of her old friends still lived here or how she would fit in as a single; all their friends in Kona were couples. These are all considerations for her in deciding whether to keep the condo or to sell it. Since she arrived, she has been busy redecorating. Apparently the last renters had smoked and left the place looking somewhat shabby. I think that the work of redecorating keeps her from thinking and feeling too much."

"Have you checked her story?" asked Keith.

"Do you mean did I do a background search on her? I saw no need. The circumstances of our meeting were totally accidental. She had sprained her ankle at the golf tournament. I happened upon her when she was sitting on the ground nursing the pain. I offered her assistance, and things evolved from there.

"When I first saw her condo, it did need refurbishment. Now after a thorough cleaning, repainting, re-carpeting, new wallpaper, blinds, some handyman repairs, and so on, it looks like new. She and Kristin were shopping for some new furniture this past week. It certainly appears that financial constraints are not an issue, although that's not important to me. As I said previously, she is very natural and comfortable to be with. Like me, she is commitment shy. She is planning to return to Seattle in April."

"Are you sure she had a sprained ankle? Maybe she was just using it as a ploy to meet someone."

"Why are you so suspicious? Yes, the ankle was definitely sprained. It was quite swollen and discolored. By the time I returned to her with my golf cart to bring her here, the swelling was rapidly extending beyond her foot and ankle. In fact, she couldn't get her sandal back on that foot. I really feared it might have been broken, but after the swelling responded to an ice pack and the pain to aspirin, Susan assured me that she was sure it was just a sprain."

"What is her source of income?"

"Why are you interested in that? Do you think she's a gold digger? I assure you she is not. She has a pension from her years as a college professor, teaching statistics, plus Social Security based on work prior to joining the university and from consulting work. She owns her house in Seattle, and she travels to see her children and could afford to come here and redo the condo. So obviously she is comfortably off. I haven't asked for an exact accounting of her finances. Why would I? We're just enjoying spending some time together. We're not combining households!"

"Well, if this relationship could become serious ..."

"Sounds to me like you're worried about your inheritance!" exclaimed Walter. "Certainly, if we were to consider marriage, Susan and I would both have to disclose our finances. We'd probably have to consider a prenuptial agreement since we both have children and grandchildren. There would be all kinds of issues to deal with—where to live, what to do with our various properties, and so on. But we've only known each other a short time. Let's not jump too far ahead. Right now, we're providing much-needed companionship in each other's lives. It's part of a healing process. Let me just enjoy that while she's still on the island. When it's time for her to return to Seattle, we'll need to consider what that means to our relationship. Clearly you and your siblings would want to meet her and get to know her and I to meet her son before any commitments could be made. But that's a long way off. Would you like to spend some time with her while you're here, Keith? We could ask her to dinner tomorrow night. Then you can make your own judgement about her."

"That might be a good idea, Dad. I'm afraid I wasn't very friendly when you introduced us."

"I'll call her now and arrange it. Then you and I have the rest of tonight to catch up on your life. I'm anxious to hear about how your job is going and what those grandkids of mine are up to," said Walter as he went to call Susan.

A few minutes later, Walter returned to the living room.

"Ok, Susan will join us tomorrow night for dinner. You and I will pick her up at her condo at six o'clock. We'll have dinner at the Kona Inn, which is reasonably close to where she lives, and it has decent food, especially their seafood. Susan was surprised that you want to spend some time with her. But she was pleased at the invitation. Now, son, tell me about your life. Are you happy in your job? Is everything going well in the family?"

Father and son settled into easy conversation, the subject of Susan forgotten for the moment. The evening passed quickly and companionably

Chapter 23

*When you finally see a light at
the end of the tunnel, make sure
it isn't an oncoming train.*

FRIDAY, FEBRUARY 13, 7:30 P.M.

Bart opened his door in response to loud knocking. Standing outside were Tony and Tony's boss, Jerry. They pushed past him and entered the living room.

"We need to talk," said Jerry. "Not only do you owe me a bundle of money, but now you're giving my guy's name to the fuzz."

"I agree that we need to talk," said Bart. "Please sit down. Can I get you a beer?"

"Yeah, thanks. I'm really dry," said Jerry. "Bring one for Tony too."

Bart went to the kitchen. He took a deep breath to calm his nerves. This was the moment he had been dreading. He needed to keep his cool. *Please, God,* he thought. *Help me to convince him to let me work off my debt over time like I told Tony I wanted to do. I really want to get my life back on track.*

He took two beers out of the refrigerator and returned to the living room. After handing a beer to Jerry, he turned to give one to Tony and asked, "Did you tell Jerry what I suggested when we talked?"

"He did," said Jerry. "No dice. At least that's not enough in itself. Yes, you can pay what you owe me over the next year, but it must be paid completely by then, including the interest, which will continue at the same rate. But to keep you from squealing to the police about my guys, you need some skin in the game. Frank is in Las Vegas on business for the next month. You will take his place as an enforcer until he returns. You get your hands dirty and share risk with us."

Bart paled. "I'm not a criminal. The guys don't need to worry that I'd talk."

"Now I'm a criminal? Listen to me, Bart. I'm a businessman. I make loans and make a profit by charging interest. When people don't pay what they owe, I look for ways to get what is mine. I have been very patient with you. I even bailed you out of the stir last week. After all, if you're not working, you can't pay me. And I protect my people. But I also believe in insurance. Therefore, you will take Frank's place, or else you'll regret it!

"I know you need your day job to pay me, so the enforcement work will be in the evenings. I'll even deduct a hundred dollars of what you owe for each job you do for me. That probably represents about fifty dollars per hour. That's more that you can earn waiting tables or driving a cab. The hours are somewhat flexible, so you can even work a second job as long as you can get free when you're needed. You'll work with Tony."

Jerry stood to leave. "Tony will call you to set up the jobs. See that you are available."

"Yes, sir." Bart watched Jerry and Tony drive away and then reentered his home and dropped into a chair.

"Dear God! What have I done? I've ruined my life. How do I get out of this? I can't leave the island, and there is nowhere to hide. What if I get caught and am sent to jail? How can I beat someone up? I'm not a violent man. A weak man, but not violent. A month, he said. I guess I'll have to take one day at a time. I wonder how often I'll be needed. Please, God, not very often," prayed Bart.

Chapter 24

Never be ashamed to admit that you were wrong. You're only saying that you're wiser today than you were yesterday.

SATURDAY, FEBRUARY 14, 5:50 P.M.

Walter turned to Keith as they pulled into a parking space in front of Susan's condo. "We're a few minutes early. I want you to come in with me. Seeing Susan in her own environment may give you a sense of her that you can't get just from conversation."

"Yes, Dad," said Keith, opening his car door. "I promise I'll behave tonight."

Susan opened the door on the second knock. She looked nervous to Walter. "Good evening, Walter, Keith. Please come in. Keith, it is nice to see you again."

"It is nice to see you as well, Susan," said Keith. "I'd like to apologize for being rude yesterday. I'm afraid I was a bit shocked seeing my dad in the kitchen with a woman other than my mom. But I'm looking forward to getting to know you better. You seem to have made my father a much happier man than he was the last time I saw him."

"I accept your apology," said Susan. "I can understand how surprised you must have been. Walter told me once that he had been pretty morose the last time you were here for a visit. And he said he hadn't told you about our friendship. Please sit down. I'll be ready as soon as I retrieve my purse from wherever I put it. It wasn't where I thought it should be. Would you like a drink or anything while you wait?"

"Thanks, Susan," said Walter. "But we have a six fifteen reservation at the Kona Inn, and parking can be difficult downtown this time of the year because of all the tourists. Perhaps you'll offer us a nightcap instead."

"Gladly. I'll only be a minute, I hope." Susan reentered her bedroom. She sat down in the wicker rocker to think. "Now where could I have put that purse? I remember having it in my hand ... I remember checking to be sure I had my lipstick and some Kleenex. That's it! I had just gone to the bathroom for Kleenex when they knocked on the door. I must have set it down when I went to answer the door."

Susan headed for the bathroom, and sure enough, there on the counter was her purse. Grabbing it, she headed back to the living room. "Found it! We can go!"

When they got to the car, Keith opened the front passenger door and indicated that Susan should get in. "Thanks, Keith, but why don't you sit in front with your dad? You'll have much more leg room. I'll be fine in the back seat," said Susan.

"Are you sure?" he asked.

"Absolutely!" said Susan. "You're a tall man with long legs. You'll be much more comfortable up front."

"Thank you. That's most considerate," said Keith as he

opened the rear door for Susan. "Dad said you were a nice person. It seems that he was right." Keith climbed into the front seat. "Okay, Dad. We're all set. Let's hope traffic is light."

Walter drove up the drive through the condo complex and then took advantage of a break in traffic to ease left into the traffic on Alii Drive. Traffic was moderate going toward town and was moving well. Once in downtown Kona, Walter turned right from Alii Highway. Then halfway up the block, he turned into the parking lot used during the day for the farmer's market. It looked full. However, just as Walter rounded the end of the row, he saw the lights of a car beginning to back out.

"Our luck is holding," Keith said. "A parking spot on the first try! Wow!"

Soon they had strolled the two blocks to the Kona Inn where they were promptly seated at their table facing the green lawn with the sea beyond. "This brings back memories from when we when I was young," said Keith. "We used to come to Kona on vacation, even before Mom and Dad moved here, and came to this restaurant for special family occasions. I loved watching the tourist boats coming into the harbor while the dinner cruise ships headed out into the bay. I'd see huge cruise liners, fishing boats, or other commercial ships on the horizon and think that it would be a great adventure to be aboard one of them. Would you believe that at the ripe old age of forty-two, I've still never taken a cruise? I did promise Jean—that's my wife—that I would take the family on a cruise to Puerto Vallarta in Mexico next winter. She thinks the children are old enough to enjoy it. Apparently with all the amenities offered onboard, they will have lots to do on their own. Jean thinks that perhaps she and I will get some time alone for romance while on board."

"It sounds like your wife would like to see more of you," commented Susan.

"Which way did you mean that?" asked Walter, chuckling.

"What do you mean?" asked Susan, momentarily puzzled.

"Oh! I see what you mean," she said, blushing. "You're a dirty old man, Walter Conway!" she exclaimed, laughing. "Anyway, your wife's plan sounds like fun, Keith. I've always wanted to take a cruise, but my husband, Scott, wouldn't go on one because he had experienced seasickness when he was young. It must have been pretty bad because he wasn't willing to take another chance, even after so many years."

Just then the waiter appeared to take their orders. During dinner, conversation flowed freely as Keith told Susan about his job, his children, and his wife. Susan told Keith about her family and her volunteer work at the library in Seattle. Walter mostly remained on the sidelines, giving his friend and his son a chance to get acquainted. Later, after finishing their substantial portions of fresh seafood accompanied by potatoes, vegetables, and a salad, they refused dessert and decided to stroll the length of downtown to work off their meal before returning to Susan's condo for a nightcap. After several glasses of wine and more than an additional hour of conversation, Walter and Keith took their leave of Susan.

As they drove back toward Walter's house, Keith said, "Dad, I can see why you enjoy Susan. She is very easy to be with. And I believe you are right when you say she is what she appears to be. There are pictures of her family, including her husband in the condo. She seems to be sensible about money. I was impressed when she said that rather than spending it, she and Scott always put the money from renting the condo into a separate account so they would have it for maintenance when needed. I couldn't believe it when she offered to pay for dinner. I think you have found the real deal. I'm sorry I was so negative yesterday."

"You are forgiven, son. I'm so pleased to hear that you like Susan and that your suspicions have been alleviated. I'd have continued to see her without your approval, but it's much more comfortable having your support. I'll try to reach your siblings tomorrow after you depart from Kona, so if you want to mention Susan to them when next you chat about your visit, it's ok. Just don't make more of the relationship than it is. The future is an open book with many chapters still to be written!"

Chapter 25

There are two ways of meeting difficulties: you alter the difficulties or you alter yourself to meet them.

TUESDAY, FEB 17, 6:00 P.M.

Bart sat nervously awaiting Tony's arrival. When he returned home from work that afternoon, there was a message from Tony on the answering machine. "Hi, Bart. It's Tony. We've got a job tonight. I'll pick you up around six. Dress casual. Jeans are good. Erase this message after you've listened to it. See you soon."

Now his head was pounding, and he felt cold, even though he was sweating. He had eaten only a piece of fruit and some cheese for dinner, but it felt like his stomach was going to reject even that. He hated what he feared he was about to be asked to do and had desperately tried to think of a way out. Nothing came to mind. He was also scared. Just as he got up to go look for an antacid tablet, he heard the car pull into the driveway. He opened the door and stepped out. Tony swung open the passenger door of the car. Bart locked his front door and then got into the car.

As he pulled into the roadway, Tony glanced at Bart. "You don't look so good, buddy. Relax. There's nothing to worry about. Tonight we're just going to deliver a first message to a guy who is delinquent in paying. All you have to do is look tough. I'll do all the talking. It's like the first time Frank and I had to deliver a message to you. Except tonight I'm playing Frank's part, and you're me. You were just lucky that you and I had been friends for so long before you ran up so a large debt to Jerry. I was usually able to talk sense into him, so you've never gotten the full treatment. Even having you do this with me represents a huge concession on Jerry's part. I've convinced him you will pay and pointed out that you have never tried to renege. You just had bad luck with Carole refusing to continue helping you out.

"The guy we're seeing lives in Holualoa. He owes Jerry about a grand. When he opens the door, just let me push him into the house and follow me. Close the door behind you. I'll do all the talking. I'm to give him a good scare and a deadline for paying before he faces any serious consequences. Hopefully he will be alone. He's single, so there is no family. If there is someone else in the house, I have a gun. We'll have the guy and whoever else is there sit on the sofa. You can hold the gun on them while I deliver the message. Then hand it back to me, and if everything goes according to plan, we'll leave. Try not to shake while you're holding the gun."

"Okay, Tony. I'll try to stay cool. I'm relieved there is to be no violence."

"I know you are, Bart. You're a good guy, and we've been friends for a long time. I'll do my best to keep you out of anything nasty until Frank gets back. But I can't make any promises. Got to do what the boss orders."

The drive to Holualoa took about forty-five minutes, a somewhat harrowing ride on the winding mountain road in the dark.

"That should be the house, number twenty-one," said Tony, pointing to a modest frame house. "There should be an alley behind the house. I'll pull back there so the car isn't noticed by anyone driving by. Then we'll walk through the yard and knock on the front door."

Tony parked the car, and they quietly walked through the side yard to the front door. Tony knocked.

"Just a minute," said a man's voice. The porch light went on, and the door opened a crack. "Who is it?"

"Got to talk to you, man," said Tony, shoving the man backward and opening the door wider so Bart could enter.

Bart stepped inside and closed the door behind him.

"What the—" exclaimed the man as Tony shoved him. "Who are you? What do you want?"

"Jerry Alonzo sent us. You owe him money. He wants to know when you plan to pay. Who else is here with you?" asked Tony.

"No one!" stammered the man.

"Good thing, Mr. Hunden," said Tony. "We wouldn't want no one to get hurt. Now sit down there on the sofa and let's sort this out." Tony motioned Bart to a chair and took the other one himself.

"You have owed a thousand dollars for the past two weeks on a losing bet you made at the greyhound races two weeks ago. At five percent interest per week, that comes to $1,102.50. What are your plans for paying up?"

"I'm sorry. I meant to pay, but the rent on this house was

due, and the landlord threatened to have me evicted if I were late again. I had nothing left to pay off the loss on the bet. I can give you the interest now and pay half the principal on Friday when I get paid. I can pay the rest two weeks after that when I'm paid again."

"That will be satisfactory, but be sure you do what you said. The interest will, of course, continue to accrue at five percent per week. Our next visit won't be so friendly, I'm afraid," said Tony. "Now get us the $102.50, and we'll leave. Don't try anything funny. We're armed, and there are two of us to one of you. I'll give you a receipt for the payment."

Tony watched closely as Hunden walked over to the desk against the back wall. After rummaging around for a minute, he returned with cash in his hand. "Here's the interest. I'll bring the five hundred dollars by the office and pay Mr. Alonzo after work on Friday."

"Thank you, Mr. Hunden," said Tony. He counted the money and handed it to Bart, who pocketed it. Tony handed Mr. Hunden a receipt. "See you Friday then. Remember, the interest is continuing to accrue until everything is paid off. Have a good week."

Tony walked to the door, followed by Bart, and stepped out into the warm, balmy Hawaiian night. He followed the sidewalk to the end of the block and around the corner to the alley and their car.

As they drove away, Tony said to Bart, "That wasn't so bad, was it? You handled yourself well. Put the cash in the glove compartment."

"It wasn't as bad as I had expected," said Bart.

"We prefer not to get rough unless we have to because they won't work with us to make payment. Most of the guys who owe

Jerry just get in over their heads, like you did. When we show up in person at their home, most are all too willing to give us the cash they have and agree to a payment schedule. That works ok for Jerry. With so many guys losing their bets, he has a steady income coming in, and the interest compensates him for the inconvenience of waiting for full repayment. It's just business."

"How did you come to work for Jerry?" asked Bart. "When I first met you, I thought you told me you were an auto mechanic at the Grand Garage in Waimea."

"I was, and I still am. Jerry likes for all of us to have a legit life. But I've been working for him as a second job for years. My family was Mafia back in New York when I was growing up. My Dad and Jerry were friends. When I announced that I was going to live in Hawaii because I liked to surf, my Dad called Jerry, who had moved here some years before and asked him to keep an eye on me. I had hoped to cut all Mafia ties when I moved here, but as you know, the cost of living is high, and I was always short of cash. Jerry offered me a chance to make some extra cash. End of story."

"So how often do we need to go out like this?" asked Bart.

"Probably two or three nights per week. So if you plan to look for another part-time job, try for something on the weekend. Or you could be an Uber driver. That's very flexible hours. Want to go for a drink before I take you home?"

"Thanks, Tony, but I'm bushed. I was really uptight about tonight, so now that it's over, I'm exhausted. I'm going to bed early."

"I understand. You should be home in another twenty-five minutes. Get a good night's rest, buddy."

Chapter 26

*Life is not measured by the breaths
we take, but by the moments
that take our breath away.*

THURSDAY, FEBRUARY 26, 8:30 A.M.

Susan and Walter had just emerged from the Subway shop with a bag of sandwiches, chips, and water bottles when Susan spotted Sergeant Hanaka coming toward them.

"Good morning, Sergeant," called Susan. "What are you doing here this fine morning?"

The sergeant smiled as he recognized her. "Good morning to you, Susan. Looks like maybe you have plans for this fine day," he commented, indicating the bags.

"Yes, it's part of a program to systematically revisit some of our favorite places on the island. Sergeant, I'd like you to meet my friend, Walter Conway. Walter, this is Sergeant Hanaka, who I've mentioned to you in regard to that business with the carpet in the condo."

The two men shook hands.

"Today we're taking a picnic lunch to the Punalu'u black sand beach on the south of the island," said Walter. "We'll make a day of it. We plan to take the Mamalahoa Highway south from here, down the west side of the island, then return on the east coast through Hilo, and then circle around to Waimea and take the upper road south to Kona, stopping somewhere on our way back for an early dinner."

"I envy you," said Sergeant Hanaka. "When I was young, my friends and I used to spend a lot of time on the south of the island. We'd go to Punalu'u, over to the Kapoho tide pools, or to the hot springs at Isaac Hale Beach Park. It's been a while since I've been to any of those places. By the time I get to the end of my week, I'm worn out. Then family consumes a lot of my time off. I may as well live on the mainland for as much as I take advantage of all that Hawaii has to offer.

"Anyway, you asked what I'm doing here. There was a call this morning from the owner of the Creperie. She reported that when she came to work this morning, she discovered there had been a break-in during the night. I was sent over to check it out. Apparently nothing is missing. I suppose cooking supplies aren't of much interest to a burglar. There were no cash or credit card receipts in the store; the owner takes those home at the end of each day and usually banks the cash on her way to work each morning. She came in earlier than usual today because she has to cater a luncheon at a nearby business."

"So much ado about nothing, it seems," said Susan. "Break-ins seem rare around here. Are there any new developments on our missing person case? I haven't talked with you in a while."

"The results finally came back on Tuesday from the forensic lab. You may remember that we were testing DNA from the sample of the sister's blood against the blood on the rug pad. They are similar enough to be considered a genetic match. It appears the blood was Carole's. I need to get back to the husband and see what he has to say. Also he told me he tried calling her several times after she left, but a check on his phone calls shows that he didn't. He hasn't been in touch to say he has heard from her, and it appears unlikely that he will in the future. I'm assuming she is dead. But without a body or a confession ..." Hanaka shrugged. "Have a great day. I'll be in touch if there are any new developments."

"Thanks, Sergeant," said Susan as they turned to leave.

Susan and Walter put their purchases in the ice box in the trunk of Walter's car and headed out. Traffic was heavy leaving Kona but gradually thinned as they proceeded south through Honalo, Kainaliu, and Kealakekua. It seemed that many tourists were stopping to browse the funky shops and eateries along the way. Once they were at the south end of Captain Cook, there was little traffic. Since it was still early, they decided to detour down into the valley to visit the Painted Church.

The winding drive down narrow Napoopoo Road through tropical foliage and coffee plantations was beautiful. Occasionally they glimpsed Kealakekua Bay through the trees as they descended. After the juncture with Painted Church Road, there were no more cars. When they arrived at the church site, the church was open, but there was no one about. Susan and Walter spent about twenty minutes exploring the paintings in the church, selected a pew toward the back, and sat quietly in the coolness of the interior, marveling at the effect of the paintings done by a long-ago priest. Although the church was tiny, the paintings on the pillars, walls, and ceiling gave the effect of being in a cathedral. Susan and Walter experienced a sense of awe, reverence, and peace.

Finally they returned to the car and resumed their journey. They continued south on Painted Church Road to Ke Ala o Keawe Road, completing the loop to rejoin Route 11, the Mamalahoa Highway. Susan marveled anew at how the vegetation kept changing. The road twisted along the cliff by the sea and climbed in altitude, affecting the climate. Later it straightened as it passed through a high plateau of grass plains and macadamia orchards. Eventually they passed Hawaiian Ocean View Estates, a sparsely populated development in which many people live off the grid. The community had only recently seen new population growth and building activity, as services began to reach the area. Built on fields of old lava, the town spread inland to the east and toward the ocean on the west side of the highway. Scrub bushes and small trees dotted the area.

"I always find this area of the island somewhat intimidating," said Susan. "Can you imagine living with no city-provided water, electricity, sewage, or garbage pickup? I rather cherish my modern conveniences. And the area we're approaching south of the town feels desolate, almost primeval. Even though there has been some plant regrowth in the lava fields over the years, the vegetation is so sparse. It's hard to believe there are still places in the world where only an occasional tuft of grass or scrub bush can be seen."

"I always feel a sense of awe when I'm in this area," commented Walter. "You can feel the power of nature. The people who settled in Ocean View Estates must either have a real pioneer spirit or prefer their own company. I hear some of them are antisocial to the extreme! Of course, in recent years, as property in the more developed areas of the island has gotten expensive, some folks have no choice but to buy down here. It's a heck of a commute for those who work in Kona. At least road conditions have improved in recent years as development spread south. We're nearing the exit for the road to South Point. Did you know that it is not only the southernmost point of the island, but also the southernmost point of the United States?"

"I did know that," said Susan. "And I always noticed a somewhat abrupt change in the landscape after South Point Road. I suppose it happens because the highway turns toward the windward side of the island, so there is more rainfall. We're entering another of the eleven climate zones on the island. That's one of the things I love about this island. So many climates in a relatively small distance! I find it endlessly fascinating."

Soon long grasses began to appear. The highway descended somewhat abruptly into a lush valley with waving fields of grass where cows grazed. Tropical fruit trees and other tropical foliage began to reappear. Susan and Walter decided to stop in the town of Na'alehu at the Na'alehu fruit stand for some Ka'u oranges to add to their picnic basket. While there, they decided to sit on the garden terrace and enjoy a cup of coffee and the shop's famous macadamia nut shortbread.

"Have you ever been to the green sand beach at South Point?" Susan asked Walter.

"Yes. Marge and I used to take the family when we had a four-wheel drive vehicle. It's a difficult drive because there is no paved road the last five miles or so. Without the four-wheel drive, one must walk from a point about four and a half miles from the end of the passable road. It's a beautiful place. Very secluded on a weekday, but it can get quite busy on weekends despite the difficulties in getting there. I haven't been there in years."

"That was one place Scott and I never got to. We didn't have an appropriate vehicle and didn't welcome the long, hot walk. Usually when we came down this way, we stopped to hike the loop trail through the woods in Manuka State Park or stopped at Whittington Park when Scott didn't want to do any more driving. There we'd climb on the rocks or just sit under a tree and just watch the ocean. Occasionally we continued on to the black sand beach. The latter was my preference. I love it there."

"I'm so pleased that we are going to experience it together," said Walter. "Let's hope it isn't crowded. Please watch for signs indicating the turnoff for the beach. As I recall, it's easy to miss the entrance."

"Yes, it is. Because of that, Scott and I usually turned in at Punaluú by the golf course and took the road through the condo area to come in the back way. Have you ever parked by the pavilion that is just past the condos and then stood with your back to the ocean? The view to Mauna Loa is spectacular!"

"Okay. That's what we'll do. I've never seen that view," said Walter. "It's a clear day, so the mountain should be out."

Susan eventually spotted the sign for Punalu'u. They wound their way past the golf course and condominiums to the pavilion parking lot. There they walked to the western edge of the lot where they had a clear view of the mist-shrouded plains with foothills and the looming mountain beyond. Palm trees and acacia trees peeked through the mist in the foreground, looking like ghosts. Unexpectedly the mist thinned closer to the mountain foothills. Mauna Loa could be seen beyond, the snow on its top gleaming in the sun. The effect was surreal.

"Definitely worth the stop!" was Walter's verdict.

Back in the car, they followed the single-lane road through the trees until they emerged at the back of the parking area for the beach. Only about a dozen cars were parked in the lot. Children could be heard shouting from the water's edge.

Susan smiled at Walter. "Not too crowded. We should be able to find a nice shady, private spot under a palm tree at the back of the beach with a good view of the ocean. That would put us next to the freshwater lake so we can watch the exotic ducks, but close enough to the ocean to see the sea turtles sunning on the beach. Does that work for you?"

"Sounds ideal. Make sure you have some footwear. That black sand will be hot for walking on if you want to go for a swim."

"Right you are. However, I'm not sure I'll want to go into water deeper than my knees. The freshwater springs around here can make the ocean water pretty darn cold!"

Susan spotted a clump of three palm trees that cast a good patch of shade. "How about over there?" she inquired, pointing to a spot at the back of the black sand crescent.

"Yes, ma'am," said Walter, leading the way to the spot Susan had indicated.

Soon they had lugged their picnic lunch and beach paraphernalia to their chosen spot. Walter set up the beach chairs and stacked the towels on top of the picnic basket.

"Pick your seat, madam," said Walter.

While Susan made herself comfortable, Walter unearthed two bottles of water from the cooler. He handed one to Susan and then looked around. "Is this paradise or what? That black sand is so striking against the blue ocean! The air temperature is warm but not too hot. There's a gentle breeze to keep it cool, but not so strong as to blow our plates and napkins away when we're ready to eat."

Walter scanned the shoreline by the ocean. "Look to your

left. I see two sea turtles sunning over there by the rocks. Another is just coming out of the water." Then turning, he gazed at the freshwater lake. "Look at those weird ducks!" He pointed to several ducks swimming in the lake. "I've never seen anything like them before."

"I know," said Susan. "They always make me smile. They are so strange looking. Just wait until they come over and start begging for lunch!"

Walter settled in next to Susan. He stretched his legs out in front of him and lay back in his reclining chair. "Didn't realize quite how tired I was from the drive. Forgive me if I doze off on you."

"No problem," said Susan. "Perhaps when we leave I could relieve you and drive for a stretch. We have further to go on the return than the distance we've already covered."

"Thanks," said Walter, closing his eyes. He was asleep in seconds.

Susan smiled as she looked at him. He was so gallant and amiable, so easy to be with and so undemanding. There was no doubt that they were at ease with each other, sort of like an old married couple. She thought back to her life with Scott. Yes, they had also had many times when they experienced this relaxed companionship. But there had also been times when she felt tense or irritated, if not downright angry at some of Scott's annoying behavior. Thus far, she had experienced no such thing from Walter.

Strange, she thought. *Walter is almost too perfect. As if he's always on his best behavior. I wonder when annoying behaviors will surface. He must have some. I can't remember when I first found myself getting annoyed with Scott. Somehow I don't think it was until several years after we were married. I guess it's the constant repetition of things that irritates and leads to intense annoyance. Before that, one is less likely to notice or let it pass as just a momentary irritation. Since it has sounded recently like Walter is starting to think long term, I'd better try to pay attention.*

Susan closed her eyes and focused her mind and body on the sensation of moist sea air and the gentle breeze. She dug her feet into the sand, savoring the warmth on her feet. She began to replay in her mind the weeks since she arrived on the island and her evolving relationship with Walter. Sometime later, Susan's musings were interrupted as Walter stirred.

"Sorry," he commented. "How long did I sleep? Must have been for some time because I'm starving!"

"Only about a half hour. But now that you mention it, I'm hungry too. I'll get the cold food out of the cooler. Then we can use the cooler as a table." Soon she had set out their lunch, together with napkins, cups, cutlery, and plates.

As they were enjoying their sandwiches and fruit, two ducks came wandering over and stood about six feet away watching them.

"I warned you that they would come begging," Susan commented. "I suggest that we don't give them anything until we're nearly finished. Otherwise we'll have all the ducks within a mile radius crowding us."

"I concur. Let's finish our meal. Afterwards, while we clean up, we can toss them some scraps to eat. Once everything is safely stowed, we can go check out the sea turtles. There are four of them now, and then you can go wading. I'm going to stay on dry land. Water has never been my milieu."

Later they walked across the hot sand to the shoreline where the sea turtles had congregated. A fifth one was hauling himself up onto the beach. Staying a respectful distance back from the turtles, they watched the giant animals. Three turtles seemed to be sleeping. Even as people approached, several didn't even open their eyes. They seemed to know that the curious people weren't a threat. Only when boisterous children got too close did they seem to react, and then it was only to shift position.

Susan took several photographs. "Kristin and her children love these creatures. I'm going to send them these pictures."

"Let me take a picture of you too." Walter made a show of getting just the perfect photo of Susan.

"Enough!" said Susan with some exasperation. "I don't particularly like having my picture taken. Let's wander into the wooded area on the east side of the pond and explore."

They investigated the interesting vegetation and then sat on a shady tree stump and watched the activity on the beach from a different perspective. Walter remained under the tree while Susan went wading in the ocean. Eventually they returned to their beach chairs under the palm.

"How about we relax and enjoy the setting for another half hour or so and then get back on the road?" suggested Walter. "I'd like to get through Hilo before rush hour."

"That's fine with me," said Susan, laying back in her chair. "But I will enjoy another half hour here. It's so beautiful!"

Twenty minutes later, Susan nudged Walter. "Do you see that guy with the two children over there by the truck on the dirt road along the shoreline? He has been staring at you for a while."

Walter replied without turning to look, "I've been aware of him for some time. In fact, when I suggested we go look at the turtles, I wanted to get a closer look at him. Checking out the turtles was a ruse that got us closer to his location without being obvious. When I took a photo of you, I was able to catch him in the background. I want to blow up the photograph and confirm that it is who I think it is. When we were walking in the woods, I was able to observe him without being seen. I think he was a member of a gang I broke up when I was working in New York. I was responsible for his boss going to prison. He may think he recognizes me too. Anyway I'm hoping that if we sit here relaxing as if we plan to stay for a while, he may leave. His kids are getting rambunctious. Hopefully he will decide that since I didn't react in any way to seeing him or his staring at me that maybe he is mistaken. I'd rather he didn't see which car is ours."

"You sound as if he could be a danger to you." Susan looked at Walter anxiously.

"One never knows with these guys. They can hold a grudge for a long time. Anyway, don't look so worried. Smile and relax as if everything is fine. Let's talk about the remainder of our day. I was thinking that it's been a long day already. I'm no longer used to long drives on these narrow winding roads. If we leave soon, we'll get to Hilo before rush hour, but too early to have dinner. So I was thinking that instead of taking Route 19 all the way up the east coast to Honoka'a and around to Waimea as we had planned, we should pick up Saddle Road at Hilo and cut through the center of the island. That route has been improved recently and now joins Route 190 well south of Waimea, so it's not a bad drive. It would cut about an hour off our driving time. We can do that stretch of Route 190 another time and make a day of it. Visit the Hawaii Tropical Botanical Garden and Akaka Falls. What do you say?"

"That would be fine with me. I love the botanical garden. They have such interesting plants and birds in the garden. And that path through the canyon along the stream is fascinating.

Finally I love the secluded beach where that stream empties into the ocean. Even though I haven't been there in almost ten years, I can still see it in my mind. That's how much of an impression it made! Shall we have dinner at my place tonight?"

"No. You will be much too tired to cook by the time we get back to Kona. How about we just take Route 180 where it branches off Route 190? We can have dinner at Holualoa Gardens and then trickle down the hill on Lake Street to the Queen's Highway south of town. Then we could go straight to your place. Their food is good, and it's a beautiful evening to sit outside."

"You are a very considerate man, Walter Conroy," said Susan. "Look! That man who was staring at you is leaving with his children—more likely his grandchildren, if he's as old as he looks. I guess he's convinced we're not interested in him. Hopefully he has lost interest in us."

"We can only hope," muttered Walter.

Chapter 27

Good instincts usually tell you what to do long before your head has figured it out.

THURSDAY, FEBRUARY 26, 5:30 P.M.

Bart answered the door to find Sergeant Hanaka standing outside.

"Hello, Sergeant," said Bart. "Come in, please. I'm sorry I had to ask you to come all the way up here, but my boss would have a cow if you showed up at work. I'd probably lose my job. As it was, I was with him when you called, and he wasn't too pleased about my getting a phone call at work!"

"That's unfortunate," said the sergeant. "But as I indicated on the telephone, I need to talk with you about your wife."

"Please have a seat," Bart said, indicating a chair. "Would you like something to drink?"

"No, thank you," replied the sergeant as Bart sat down on the sofa opposite him.

"Have you found Carole?"

"Nothing like that, I'm afraid. What has happened is that the owner of your former rental condo in Kona contacted us. After you broke your lease, she came over from the mainland to check out the condition of the condo. She was thinking of selling it and wanted to determine firsthand its condition and whether she needed to do any upgrades in order to put it on the market. She decided renovation was needed. Among the remodeling she did was replacing the carpets. When her carpet guys pulled up the old carpet, they discovered a large area of brown stains on the carpet pad in the master bedroom hallway. They told her they thought it was blood. Because it represented an extremely large amount of blood, they suggested that she contact the police. At the time of the report, it was brushed off by the office, and no follow-up was done. However, once Carole's sister filed a missing person report, it suddenly seemed relevant. Our lab tested the DNA from a piece of the carpet and compared the results with a test on DNA from a sample of blood donated by Carole's sister. They were close enough to be considered a match. What I need to hear from you is whether there is any explanation you can offer for the bloodstains."

"Yes, I see," said Bart, looking thoughtful. He rose and walked across the room to the window and then turned. "There is an explanation. Some months back, I got home from work to find Carole in bed. She was very pale. 'Are you ill?' I asked. 'No,' she said. 'At least not exactly ill, although I'm feeling quite weak and light-headed. This afternoon, I was having some cramps. I went into the bathroom thinking it was gas and took some simethicone tablets. As I was walking back into the bedroom, I felt a gush of wetness between my legs. I looked down and saw blood. I thought my period had arrived. You know how it is so irregular and initially very heavy when it first arrives. I went back into the bathroom to get a sanitary pad, but after searching for a while, I couldn't find any. I washed as best I could and then grabbed a dry washcloth to catch the blood and headed back toward the bedroom to get a tampon from my nightstand. On my way back to the bedroom, I had a dizzy spell and must have fainted. I woke up sometime later lying in a pool of blood. My clothes were soaked too. I managed to crawl back into the bathroom. I checked, and the bleeding seemed to have slowed considerably. So I got out of my wet clothing, washed, and then came in here and got a tampon. Later I found the pads in the hall closet. After using them, I put on dry clothing and got into bed because I still felt quite dizzy. I must have fallen asleep immediately. I woke up when you came in the front door.'

"I told her I wanted to take her to the hospital. I was scared to death and very worried. Carole refused to go. She thought she must have had a miscarriage. Although it had been three and a half months since her last period, she only recently had begun to suspect pregnancy because of breast tenderness and some nausea. She sometimes skipped periods for several months, so she hadn't yet gone for a pregnancy test. Because of our constant money shortages, she hadn't planned on telling me about a possible pregnancy until she had seen a doctor and knew for sure. She said that the worst of the bleeding seemed to be over and she was feeling better. Although she felt close to normal the next morning, I took the day off work to look after her. The day after that, she said she felt like her old self, so I returned to work.

"Because the carpet was so soaked with blood, I tried to clean it, but without success. Carole remembered that we had seen a piece of carpet in the overhead closet above the TV recess. It matched the existing carpet so I cut out the soiled piece.

After the pad dried, I cut in a replacement piece. There was no extra padding, so that had to stay."

"I see," said Sergeant Hanaka. "That certainly could account for the blood. Do you recall just when this was?"

"Not precisely. Like I said, it was some months ago, maybe six or seven, but that's a guess. It might have been in the summer. I remember that installing that piece of carpet in that narrow hallway was a hot job with no air-conditioning. But of course Hawaii is warm year-round."

Sergeant Hanaka rose. "Thank you for your cooperation. That is indeed a plausible explanation. Did either of you discuss what happened with anyone? It would be helpful to have some corroboration for your story."

"I didn't. I simply told my boss that my wife was ill and I wanted a day off to look after her. I don't know about Carole. She never mentioned telling anyone. She is a very private person. If she had told someone, the most likely person would have been her sister. They are very close."

"I'll check with her. Another thing. When we last talked, you said you had called Carole's cell phone several times after she left but got no response and she never called you back. We checked with the phone company, and there was no record of such call from your mobile phone. Any explanation?"

"I did try to reach her. Perhaps I called from the landline. We had one in the condo because cellular connections were very unreliable there."

"I see. I suppose that makes sense. I'll keep in touch." Sergeant Hanaka turned toward the door.

Bart escorted him out to his car. *Oh, Carole*, he thought after the sergeant left. *How will this end?*

Chapter 28

What can't be cured must be endured.

THURSDAY, MARCH 5, 6:15 P.M.

Tony parked the car in the lot behind the shops in Hawi. He and Bart walked to the south end of the lot and then followed the path along the end building toward the main street.

As they walked, Tony said, "The client lives behind the shops on the other side of the street. We'll join the crowds in the street, walk to the north crossing, and cross there. When we get to the other side, we'll turn south and pretend to be window shopping as we walk down the street toward the visitor center. From there, I'll lead you to his home."

Just as they came around the corner of the building, Tony grabbed Bart and pulled him backward. "Wait a sec," he said, peering intently into the street from the shelter of the building. He pulled a photograph out of his pocket and squinted at it in the dimming light. "See that couple crossing the street from the Bamboo restaurant?"

"Yeah, what of them?"

"I swear that's the man the mob guy from New York saw at the black sand beach last week. He snapped this picture when he was there and distributed it around to guys on the island. We're supposed to be keeping an eye out for him," he commented, handing the photo to Bart.

"I can't tell about the guy in this dim light, but the woman looks a lot like the one in the picture. She's quite good looking for an older woman. Why is he interested in this man?"

"Apparently he was a witness who had a role in sending Morelli, a big capo in New York to jail. Morelli swore to get even. This means a change of plans." Tony watched the couple enter a store in the middle of the block. "The boss said to keep an eye on him if he were spotted. We need to make sure it is the same guy. Do you have your phone handy?"

"Yes, I've got mine here," said Bart, holding it up so Tony could see it.

"Here's what I want you to do. You hang out in the street and try to find a spot where you can be inconspicuous while you get a shot of them as they exit that store. Then you text the photo to me. If I think it is, in fact, the guy the boss is looking for, I'll text you back. Then I'll bring the car around and park it in an empty spot on the street. Watch for me. I'll leave the keys in the car. You get in the car, and when they head for their car, keep an eye on them. When they drive away, follow them to wherever they are going. Eventually the guy will go home. Follow him until you know where he lives. Stay back so he doesn't realize he is being followed. It will be dark before too long. That should make following them without being seen an easier job. Use my car to go home. I'll arrange to pick it up later."

"What about you? How will you get home, Tony?"

"Don't worry about me. I'll go see our client. Then I'll arrange for someone to drive me home. Call me when you get to your house."

"What if I lose them?" Bart asked nervously. "I've never tried to tail anyone before."

"There is a first time for everything. Do what you have to do. Just don't lose him!"

When Tony headed toward the parking lot, Bart nervously made his way onto the street, trying to blend with the other people. He saw the couple framed in the doorway of the shop, ready to leave. Crouching between two parked cars, he took a quick picture as they walked out of the shop toward the street.

As the couple neared the street, Bart heard the man say to the woman, "I know that we both said we were stuffed from our meal at the Bamboo, but here we are next to Tropical Dreams Ice Cream. As you know, there's no better ice cream on the island. I always have one when I'm up here since I come so seldom. It's been at least fifteen or twenty minutes since we ate. Surely you could manage a small serving, Susan."

"Walter Conway, you are incorrigible!" exclaimed Susan, laughing. "I have absolutely no willpower when it comes to their mango pineapple ice cream. I might be able to manage a single scoop. Definitely no more!"

"Why don't you find us a table outside while I go in and get us each a dish? I'll only be a minute."

"Will do, sir. See you in a minute." Susan moved toward the outdoor seating area while Walter entered the store to buy the ice cream. A few minutes later, he joined her on the patio. Where they were sitting was illuminated by a circle of light from the light fixture on the wall just above them.

Bart, grateful for a chance to get a good shot, moved to the far side of the patio seating area to a position where he could photograph the pair while they ate their ice cream and talked. After obtaining several decent shots, he texted them to Tony.

Before long, he received a text. "Good job! Clear shot. It's the guy the boss is looking for. Bringing the car now."

Bart stepped back into the shadows to wait for the car to arrive. While waiting, Bart was able to overhear the couple's conversation.

"Would you be interested in going to Kiholo Bay for our next excursion?" the man asked. "The week after next is predicted to be a few degrees cooler. Since it's necessary to park by the main highway and walk fifteen to twenty minutes on a trail across the lava to the beach, you wouldn't want to go on a really hot day. How about that Thursday? I think it's the nineteenth?"

"Do you know that is one place I've never been? I'd love to go. I've heard it is spectacular!"

"Yes, it is beautiful. It's one of my favorite places on the island. The bay has a lagoon that is a mix of seawater and freshwater that comes from springs. There are lots of turtles and fish. Also, set back about forty feet into the lava fields on one end of the beach is a Queen's Bath that is located in a lava tube. The lava tube connects to a dry cave further in, and there are petroglyphs in the cave."

"It sounds like an adventure. I look forward to it. Thursday the nineteenth would be just fine. Shall I pack us a picnic lunch?"

"Perfect. And I'll bring something to drink and flashlights for exploring the cave. Let's get an early start, say eight?"

"I'll be ready. I'll drive to your place, and we can go from there. Your place is miles closer to Kiholo than is my condo. Shall I …"

Just then Tony pulled into a nearby parking space, got out, and walked away. Bart waited a few moments more in the seclusion of his observation post. When the couple appeared to be preparing to leave, Bart went to the car and got in. Only a few moments later, the couple came strolling down the street past his car. They crossed to a silver Lexus that was parked on the opposite side of the street in the next block and got in.

Bart pulled out of his parking space and drove ahead to an empty lot on the right-hand corner of the block. There he parked so he could determine which direction the couple would take. When they pulled out of their parking space and headed south on Akoni Pule Highway (Route 270), Bart waited until they were about a block south before he pulled out of the lot and began to follow.

There was little traffic, and Bart was able to stay about a hundred yards back and follow with no difficulty. It was also getting dark, so Bart was grateful for the light traffic. As the darkness deepened, however, Bart could no longer see the car clearly. He had to focus on the taillights. He moved closer so he could see the car better. The car turned left onto Kawaihae Road and then right onto Route 19, toward Kona. He felt fortunate that he was able to turn onto busy Route 19 directly behind the Lexus. His heart was in his throat as he tried to keep the car in sight. Cars that passed him in the left lane would pull in front of him whenever he stayed too far back, making it harder to keep track of the Lexus. Bart was afraid that if he stayed too close, he might be spotted.

Finally he decided that in the darkness, the driver of the Lexus was unlikely to realize that he was being followed, so he stayed close enough to discourage other cars from cutting in. His heart was pounding, worrying about what Tony would say if he lost the car. He thanked God that he had the presence of mind to memorize the license plate back in Hawi when he started to follow the car and it was still light. At least, if he lost them, he could give Tony a license number.

As they neared Kona, Bart was able to increase the distance and still keep the car in sight because of the overhead lights along that section of road. The Lexus drove past downtown Kona and eventually turned off on Kamehameha III Road. Traffic had thinned again, and he was able to see the car turn left onto Alii Drive. Once again, he increased the distance between the two cars. After about a half mile, the car signaled a right turn into the condo complex where he used to live. Nervous now and unsure about what to do, he dropped further back and turned slowly into the complex, pausing by the entry to allow the Lexus to turn left and head down the hill.

Following slowly, Bart saw the Lexus pull into a parking space in front of the building at the very end of the drive. That was the building he had lived in! He pulled into a parking space by the swimming pool and watched. The car lights went out, and he saw the couple exit the car and turn toward the building.

Bart quickly left his car and, staying in the shadows, walked toward the building. He saw lights go on in the ground-floor apartment in which he had lived. Quickly he peeked in the condo window to confirm that it was the couple and then crossed the parking lot and ducked behind the dumpster. From there he could see the entrance to the apartment. He didn't have long to wait. Within a few minutes, the man came out and got in his car. Bart waited until the man had started his car and driven partway up the hill. Then he ran to his car.

As the Lexus approached the turn at the top of the hill, Bart pulled out of his space and followed. Bart couldn't see the Lexus turn out of the complex, but when he reached Alii Drive, he could see only one car on the road, and it was headed north.

Bart followed. As he closed on the other car, he breathed a sigh of relief to see that it was the Lexus.

Bart again followed as the Lexus retraced its route back to Route 19 heading north, past downtown Kona and the airport, and then left into the community of Hualalai. Remembering that Hualalai was a gated community with a gate agent, Bart passed by and continued north toward home. He realized that there was no way he could follow the car into the complex. But hopefully, with the information he could give Tony about the guy going to Hualalai, together with a license number for the car, Tony would be satisfied.

On the way home, Bart mused about the fact that the guy had gone to the condo in which he and Carole used to live. In view of what Sergeant Hanaka had said about the owner of the condo coming to check the condition of the place, Bart had to assume that the woman was the owner. What a tangled web this was all turning out to be! He hoped fervently that Tony's associate, Frank, would soon return to the island so he, Bart, would be released from any further obligation to be involved in all of this.

When Bart arrived home, he was exhausted from the strain of the evening. However, before relaxing, he phoned Tony and reported on the evening's activities. Bart relayed the information about the couple going to the condo where he had lived prior to Carole's death and about the man turning into Hualalai. He also gave Tony the make and license number of the car.

Bart heaved a sigh of relief when Tony indicated that he was satisfied with Bart's performance that evening. Once they completed arrangements for Tony to pick up his car early the following morning, Bart settled down in front of the TV with a beer and tried to relax so he would be able to sleep. After all, tomorrow was a workday!

Chapter 29

*The past casts a long shadow.
In the stream of destiny, only the
mad swim against the current, and
only fools bother to swim with it.*

FRIDAY, MARCH 6, 9:15 A.M.

Susan was watering her patio plants when the phone rang. She answered on the third ring.

"Hello."

"Susan, it's Della. Do you have a minute? Can I pop over?"

"Sure, Della. I've not got anything pressing."

"I'll be there in a minute. I need to talk to you urgently!"

Susan looked around the unit. Everything looked tidy. She returned to the patio and finished her watering and was putting her sprinkling can into the lanai closet when she heard the knock on the door.

"Hi, Della," she said, opening the door. "You sounded

concerned. Come in and sit down. What is it? Can I offer you something to drink?"

"Nothing to drink, thank you. I need to share with you something I observed last night. It may be unimportant, but I'll let you decide that. I was sitting on my lanai last evening enjoying the beautiful, quiet evening with nothing but the waves to disturb the peace when I saw Walter's car come down the drive and park in front of your place. The two of you got out and went into your unit. Just after Walter parked, a second car came down the drive and parked in front of the pool. A man got out and walked in the shadow of the building toward your unit. I thought that was odd! When he reached your unit, he looked in the dining room window and then crossed behind a parked car and ducked behind the dumpster. He stayed there until Walter got back in his car and started driving up the drive. The man then ran back to his car and followed Walter. You'll think I'm mad, but I could swear that the man was Bart Selwyn. I glimpsed him briefly when he passed under the overhead light near the pool. It wasn't his car, however. I don't know much about cars, but Bart drives a truck. This was definitely a mid-sized sedan. I couldn't tell you what model or even the color, only that it was a dark color."

"How strange! How would Bart know anything about us? Why would he be interested? I think I should share this with Walter. Thank you for telling me, Della. Another puzzle!"

"I hope you don't think I'm nosey or crazy. I debated a long time before deciding to share it."

"I think it's good you did. I have no idea what could be going on, but as you said, it was strange, just like everything else about the Selwyns seems to be! I'll share what you told me with Walter and see if he can make any sense of it."

Della excused herself and returned home. Susan rang Walter. She recounted what Della had told her.

"That is odd!" said Walter. "Assuming that Della is correct and it was Bart, I don't know why he would be spying on us. If it is someone else ... well, I don't like to think about that!"

"Walter, I think you need to share what you are thinking. This affects us both, you know. Does it have something to do with the man you encountered at the Punalu'u Black Sand Beach?"

"It is possible, but unlikely. That man was a member of a Mafia family run by a man named Morelli. About twenty years ago, I witnessed a crime in New York City that Morelli was involved in. After I testified at his trial about two years later, he was sent to prison for forty years. He vowed to get even for my role in putting him away. I've been told he hasn't forgotten that vow. If that man recognized me and told Morelli, I suppose he could have told the local mob to keep an eye out for me. Maybe someone saw us in Hawi and followed us. But Bart? Unless he has somehow gotten involved with the mob as a way of paying off his debts? It seems like a stretch."

"Walter! Are you in danger? What should we do? I don't want anything to happen to you!"

"Nor do I, my dear Susan. I would imagine that if they don't see me again, they might assume that I was visiting here as a tourist and that I left and went home. They don't know where I live. Even if that man followed me to Hualalai, the gate agent would have prevented him from following me in last night, unless he gave some excuse about going to one of the condos or restaurants, and he would have had to give the name of the restaurant. That presumes he knows something about this resort community. I didn't notice anyone behind me when I came through the gate. He might have given up following me when I pulled in here rather than draw attention to himself. He wouldn't want to make it obvious that he was following me. I shall have to pay more attention in the future when I'm driving. I haven't given any thought in years to being tailed!

"Perhaps we should avoid public places for a while, particularly places where tourists and large groups of people tend to congregate. In fact, we probably should avoid seeing each other for a week or two, just in case they decide to keep an eye on your place, which seems unlikely. If you're not observed coming here and I don't come there, they may give up. No interactions between us for two weeks might reinforce the idea that I was just visiting the island on vacation and have gone back home. Our planned visit to the beach is almost two weeks away. I think that by then they will have given up."

"Anything to keep you out of danger! I can't imagine that you've been living with this for all this time!" exclaimed Susan. Following a lengthy pause, she continued, "I just realized how empty the next two weeks will seem! I will miss seeing you. Are you sure it will be safe to do the trip to Kiholo Bay? I wouldn't want to do anything to put you in jeopardy."

"Maybe that is a good thing, your realizing how much you will miss me! I know I will miss seeing you. Let's be sure to talk frequently. Let me know if there is any sign of someone watching your place. I doubt it will happen, but you never know. I'm sorry to have put you in such a situation. We'll revisit our planned trip closer to that Thursday, but since Kiholo Bay is such an out-of-the-way location, I think it will be fine. We may want to think about meeting somewhere else than here that morning, just to be safe."

"Probably a good idea. I will stay in touch. Please stay safe, Walter!"

"I will, Susan. Try not to worry. I'll stay home for most of the next few weeks to discourage them. A good chance to catch up on some reading!"

After he hung up from his conversation with Susan, Walter called the number for his friend, Jim Breem. When Jim answered, Walter said, "Sorry to bother you, friend, but I think we may have a problem. First, let me reassure you that it doesn't stem from the investigation of the blood on Susan's carpet pad. I've stayed out of that as you advised and let Susan handle everything.

"Susan and I went to the south of the island several weeks ago to spend a day at the black sand beach at Punalu'u. There I spotted someone I am pretty sure was Rocco Carnaggio, a member of Morelli's mob. He was there with what appeared to be his grandchildren. Unfortunately I fear he recognized me as well. I pretended not to notice him and deliberately didn't leave until after he did so he wouldn't know which car was mine. He had come in from the opposite side of the beach area from where we parked, and I doubt he saw me when we first came in from the parking area.

"Several weeks have passed since that day, and I assumed that things were ok, that maybe he thought he was mistaken about who he saw. Then last night when Susan and I returned from an outing to the north of the island, it appears we were followed. A neighbor of Susan's reported that she saw a car come into Susan's complex behind my car and that the driver parked and crept along the building to look into the unit while I was there and then sheltered behind a dumpster. When I left, he ran to his car and followed me out. The neighbor thought that the man looked like Bart Selwyn, but except for owing the mob money, as far as we know, he has no association with them. I have doubts about it being Bart. All this may be a tempest in a teapot, but I thought I should ask you for advice. I'm primarily concerned about Susan. I don't want her at risk."

"Walter, if Carnaggio is on the island and identified you, there is a chance he has put out an alert to the local mob. I'm sure you figured that out. What plans have you made so far for dealing with this?"

"Well, I told Susan we should avoid seeing each other for a few weeks, just in case they are watching her place or mine. Maybe, if I'm not seen around her, they'll assume I was just visiting as a tourist and think I've left the island. Probably wishful thinking. They don't know exactly where I live. I'm sure I wasn't followed into Hualalai last night. But if they got my license plate number, I'm sure they can find out an address through their network. I did think about having Susan pick me up here and drop me at the airport. If they were following and saw her leave the airport without me, it would reinforce the idea that I left the island. Other than that, I'm out of ideas."

"The airport idea might work, but they might go to Susan and try to find out where you went," said Jim. "If we go that route, I can come up with an address in Las Vegas she could give them as your mainland address. That would get her off the hook and allow you to continue living on the island. You would need to take a flight out to the West Coast, so if someone is tailing her, saw you get out at the airport, and stayed to watch you, they could confirm which flight you took. They would probably have someone there on the mainland when you deplane.

"I can arrange to have someone there when your flight comes in. My guy can meet you in the nearest restroom with a change of clothes, a new ID, and bag, so you can leave the airport without detection and check into an airport hotel. Hopefully that will cause a little confusion for their contact at the airport. If they do contact Susan and she gives them the Las Vegas address, they should leave her alone. Meanwhile I'll have booked you a flight back to Kona for the following day under the new ID. You can take a cab back to your house.

"I doubt, however, that they will give up easily. And you can't hole up in your house forever, Walter. So I'd like some contingency plans. I'll have one of our guys get in touch with the local police. Do you think that Sergeant Hanaka is worth working with?"

"I like the guy. From what Susan has told me about her interactions with him, he seems to be a thinking cop. He's low-key, but sharp. I met him briefly. Susan and I were shopping for supplies for an excursion one morning and ran into him at the mall. Susan introduced me as a friend. Since he's been in touch with Bart on several occasions, he may be able to find out about any mob involvement beyond the gambling debts."

"Ok. Hanaka it is. And I'll arrange to get you on a flight out within the next few days. Will let you know as soon as it is arranged. Hopefully this will give you some breathing space while we work on assuring your future safety. Alert Susan to your plans. I'll be in touch as soon as arrangements are made."

Chapter 30

No one is useless in this world who lightens the burden of it to another.

SATURDAY, MARCH 7, 7:30 P.M.

Tony pulled his car into the driveway of Bart's house.

"Do you want to come in for a beer, Tony?" asked Bart.

"Yeah, I could use one," said Tony. "That was a tough one tonight. I thought we were going to have to get really rough. Thank God the guy caved just in time. I think he thought we were bluffing. All it took was that one punch to deflate his courage!"

They entered the house, and Bart disappeared into the kitchen, returning with two cold beers. He handed one to Tony.

"I was relieved when he agreed to start paying," said Bart. "I was afraid you might ask me to hit him."

"Yeah, I could see that. You were looking a bit green. You're not cut out for this line of work. A few more weeks, then Frank will be back, and you're off the hook."

"I look forward to that. But I must say it has been good to have money taken off what I owe Jerry! And you've been great at trying to shield me during these jobs. I appreciate it, Tony."

"What are friends for? Anyhow, Jerry is very happy with what you did Thursday night. The information you got put him in good with the visitor from New York who was looking for that guy. He says he'll knock off another five hundred dollars for that piece of work. Your photos confirmed that he was the guy they were looking for. And having the license plate number and the knowledge that he probably lives in Hualalai is most helpful. The guys are setting up some surveillance to keep tabs on him. They'll watch both Hualalai and the condo of the woman he was with. Funny that she turns out to be the lady who owns the condo you and Carole lived in!"

"You can't imagine how weird it felt to tail him into that complex and then find out she lived in that unit! Knowing the lay of the land, so to speak, made it a lot easier to keep tabs on them there and then tail him out of the complex afterwards. Thinking back on it all, I probably needn't have been so careful. They were so wrapped up in each other that they were unaware of what was around them. Back in Hawi, they were so deep in conversation at the ice cream parlor that I could probably have gone over and sat at the next table without them noticing. As it was, I got pretty close to get that last shot. From where I was standing, I could hear almost everything they were saying."

"Yeah? So what were they talking about?"

"They were planning their next excursion. They're planning to go to Kiholo Bay. Wanted to get some sun, visit the Queen's Bath, and explore the old lava cave. Sounded great. Wish I could go too!"

"They do get around. The New York guy saw them a few

weeks ago in Punalu'u. Last Thursday was Hawi. Now Kiholo Bay! When were they planning to go?"

"I think they said Thursday ... not the one coming up, but the following one. Why?"

"I was thinking that if they see each other so often, it must be getting serious. Chances are, the surveillance team will see them visiting each other before too long."

"What happens when they find him? Why are they so interested?"

"Some big kahuna in New York that he helped put in prison for a long term swore to get even. But this guy disappeared. This is the first time he's been sighted in years. I don't know what they plan for him, but you can be sure it won't be pleasant."

"I'm sorry to be a part of this. He seemed like a decent guy."

"Don't worry yourself, Bart. This guy's fate has been waiting for him. It has nothing to do with you. I'm off. Thanks for the beer. See you soon."

Chapter 31

*Right about the time you're think you're
ready to graduate from the school of
experience, life develops a new course.*

MONDAY, MARCH 9, 6:30 P.M.

Tony and Bart were on their way to a job.
"So what is this about tonight?" asked Bart.
"Some guy was supposed to have paid Jerry a big chunk of change over the weekend but didn't show up. He called Jerry this morning and apologized. Said it took him longer than he thought to get the money. Had planned to deliver it tonight but said he was taken ill this afternoon. Expected to be ill for several days. Jerry said we'd stop by to pick up the money this evening, but the guy objected. Supposedly his wife is looking after him. He says she doesn't know about his gambling. So he asked Jerry if we could come tomorrow night when his wife is at work. Jerry thinks the guy is going to do a bunker, so he is sending us to

stop the guy and collect the money. Could be some rough stuff if the guy is lying and trying to welch."

"I'll pray that he isn't," said Bart.

"Sorry, Bart. Jerry's got a pretty good antenna for this stuff. By the way, I mentioned to Jerry what you told me you heard in Hawi. The information about that couple's planned excursion made him think that the guy knows they are on to him and has tried to pull a fast one. The woman drove him to the airport on Sunday, and he was seen boarding a flight for San Francisco. The guys thought maybe he had been visiting the island for a few weeks and was returning home to the mainland. They talked to the woman, and she gave them an address she said the man had given her. It was in Las Vegas. Someone from the mob was waiting for the flight in San Francisco, but the guy managed to give him the slip. He hasn't shown up at the address in Las Vegas. No one has seen him on the island, but he could have come back while they were busy looking for him on the mainland. When the New York guys heard about the couple planning an excursion for next Thursday, they decided to stake out Kiholo Bay that day. They want us to join them since Frank won't be back yet. We are to go armed. Do you know how to use a handgun?"

"I've never used a gun in my life. Besides, I have to work that day. What are they planning to do? I don't like the sound of this!"

"Sorry, buddy. I'm afraid you have no choice. You'll have to call in sick. We need the manpower. Jerry said he'll forgive an extra thousand dollars for your help that day. I'll give you some training on how to use a gun at the local shooting range one evening this week. As to what they plan to do, I haven't been given that information yet."

"What do you think they plan to do?"

"If I had to guess, I'd say they will either kill him or beat him up so bad that he won't trouble anyone else for a long time!"

"What about the woman?"

"As far as I can tell, she has no part in this except to get involved with the guy. She may have given them false information about him going to Las Vegas, but she may not have known he gave her false information. The address does seem to be a place he owns. Apparently a neighbor the guys talked to near the address confirmed that the guy does live there. So they should leave her alone. Of course, if she's there when they attack him, she would be a witness, and they probably wouldn't want that. But if they attack him in the cave, which is dark, she might not be able to see them. Who knows?"

"You're sure this is going to go down?"

"Assuming he has returned to the island and the couple goes on their excursion as planned, yes. That's what is expected. If he hasn't returned to the island, that changes everything. Let's not worry about it until it's certain. Tonight, we've got other matters to attend to," said Tony, pulling up behind a single, somewhat isolated house and turning off the engine. "Let's go. Just follow my lead. You know the drill."

Half an hour later, they returned to the car.

"Jerry was right again," said Tony. "Had we been a half hour later, we might have missed him. His bag was packed and ready to go. What a wuss! A couple of shots to his pretty face, and he was ready to play ball. You did good, holding on to him tight while I delivered the message. And we got the total amount he owes. Seems he was leaving for good and taking his worldly worth with him. Jerry will be pleased with tonight's work. You may even get another bonus!"

Chapter 32

*Conscience is like a baby. It has
to go to sleep before you can.*

SATURDAY MORNING, MARCH 14, 8:00 A.M.

The doorbell awakened Bart. His head was throbbing. He and Tony had gotten back late from a particularly unpleasant job last night. On several previous evenings during the week, Tony had taken him to a shooting range to practice with a pistol supplied by Jerry. His shooting accuracy was improving, but he hated every moment of handling the gun. Bart worried about what lay ahead. He didn't even have a permit for a gun and would be expected to carry it on Thursday's job, which he dreaded. He had come to hate his life!

Sleep had been slow in coming last night. Tension and worry had kept him awake. Bad dreams had interrupted his sleep several times. Now he had been awakened from his only peaceful sleep of the night. He threw on a robe and then headed for the door and opened it.

Bleary-eyed, he stared at Sergeant Hanaka. "What the! What are you doing here and at this early hour on a Saturday morning?"

"Sorry if I woke you, Mr. Selwyn. I needed to follow up with you on several points and had to be in the neighborhood anyway this morning."

"Can't you come back after you've completed your other business? I didn't get much sleep last night, have a pounding headache, and can't think clearly."

"No, I can't. Go make yourself a cup of coffee. Make me one too. Then we'll talk."

Ten minutes later, Bart and Sergeant Hanaka sat at the kitchen table holding steaming mugs of coffee, the coffeepot between them.

"So what's so important that it couldn't wait?" Bart swallowed two Tylenol with a big gulp of coffee.

"Several things. First of all, I checked what you said about trying to reach your wife after she left you. There is no record of calls from your either your mobile or landline to her phone. In addition, I checked with your workplace. They have no record of you taking a day off last summer. That is when you said you had taken off to look after Carole. Also, no one that I talked with at the condo complex remembered Carole saying anything about a miscarriage. Can you offer any explanation?"

Bart stared at Sergeant Hanaka. He shook his head, trying to clear it. "I can't think with this headache!"

"You don't need to think. Just tell me the truth," said Sergeant Hanaka. "I need to find Carole."

"If there is no record of calls to Carole's cell from my mobile or the condo phone, I must have made those calls from work. I could have been mistaken about the time of year the miscarriage happened. I think I told you at the time that I was only guessing as to when it was. I'm not surprised if Carole didn't tell anyone about the miscarriage. She's a very private person."

"Bart, you know that I can trace your work telephone account and check on calls from that, don't you? I already checked on all your days off from work during the past year. The only days you took off were when you were moving out of the condo. Shall we go over the whole story again? What is it that you're not telling me?"

"What is it you want? I've answered your questions to the best of my recollection. Stop hounding me!" yelled Bart.

"Simmer down, son. Let's talk for a moment about something else. How much money do you owe the mob in gambling debts?"

"What? Why do you want to know that? Why do you assume I owe the mob?"

"Let's face it, Bart. The local mob runs the games. You previously admitted owing money from gambling. The mob would be who you owe for the losses on your bets. They are known to let players bet by putting down only a portion of the bet. They make their money on the interest, which keeps accruing."

"I still owe about seventy-five hundred. I'm to pay it off by the end of the year."

"It's unusual for them to let such a large debt run that long. What connections do you have to the mob other than the money you owe? Why the special concessions?"

"My friend that I stayed with after Carole left does some work for them. He convinced them that I'm reliable. And so he was able to persuade them to let me pay it off over a year."

"What do you have to do for them in return, Bart?"

"Nothing. Just make regular payments, as promised."

"Bart, do you take me for a fool? I want an answer. What were you doing in your old condo complex looking in windows late last Thursday night? Why did you follow a car into the complex and then follow it out again? You were seen and recognized. The man driving the car you followed is being sought by the mob. Can you see where I'm going with this?"

Bart looked at Sergeant Hanaka with a look of horror on his face. "Oh God! I'm dead. They'll kill me for sure! If I tell you everything, can you help me?"

"I can make no promises, Bart. I'll try to do what I can."

"I'll accept that as the best I can do. This could take a while. I'd better make another pot of coffee."

When a plate of muffins and a fresh pot of coffee had been set on the table, Bart asked, "Where should I start?"

"May I record this?" asked Sergeant Hanaka. "That way I can have it typed up as your statement, and you can come down to the station on your own to sign the statement when it has been typed. Are you ok talking to me here without a lawyer present? If you prefer, we can go to the station, and you can call a lawyer. You know that what you say could be used against you in a court of law."

"Yes, I know. But I'm so tired of living this way. I can't bear it anymore! I seem to get in deeper every day!"

"Ok," said Sergeant Hanaka. "Start with what happened with your wife."

"She's dead," said Bart sadly. "I didn't kill her. But it's my fault what happened. It was an accident, I swear!" exclaimed Bart, becoming agitated. "I've had to live with that knowledge ever since. Because of me, the only person who ever loved me is dead!"

"Take it easy, son. Tell me in sequence from the beginning, ok?"

"Yes, sir. You already know I owed a lot of money. The mob was threatening to get rough. As I told you before, Carole refused to help me out because when she did in the past, I didn't stop gambling. My losses were driving us into a financial hole. I was scared. I talked with my friend Antonio Marrato, and we came up with an idea. He and Frank, Tony's associate, would come to my place on a prearranged night when I was sure Carole would be there and pretend to threaten me with bodily harm. The idea was that Carole would give me some money to save my skin. It seemed like such a simple way to solve the problem of getting her to pony up some cash.

"Tony and Frank arrived about seven that evening. It was already getting dark. When I opened the door, they pushed in and demanded that I pay up. Carole heard the commotion and came into the room. Tony pulled out a gun and told her to sit down on the living room couch and stay there. Expecting that she would eventually follow, they dragged me into the bedroom hallway where noise could be kept to a minimum. Tony held the gun on me while Frank pulled out a knife. 'We are going to teach you a lesson,' said Frank loudly. 'You don't welch on Jerry!' He turned toward Tony. 'Shall I cut his face or his hands?' He said, 'Better make it his face. He needs his hands for his work. If he doesn't work, he'll never pay.'

"As Frank turned back toward me, Carole, who had come into the bedroom after hearing their words, ran across the room and grabbed Tony's arm, trying to take the gun. 'No! No! Tell him to stop!' she yelled. Tony gave her a shove, just as Frank turned back toward their direction to see what was going on. Carole stumbled and fell toward Frank who was holding the knife at about waist level, but slanting in an upward direction. Next thing we knew, she was lying on the floor with blood spurting everywhere. Frank and I were both covered in blood.

"'Shit!' exclaimed Tony, looking at Frank. 'What have you done?' He said, 'When you pushed her, she stumbled and fell on my knife, just as I was turning toward you. Bart, can you stop the bleeding?'

"I yelled, 'I'm trying!' I put more pressure on her torso where the blood was spurting out. 'It won't stop! Carole, sweetheart, don't die. I'm trying to stop the bleeding. Help her, God!' Frank grabbed Tony and headed for the door. 'Let's get out of here. You better not say a word to anyone about this if you know what's good for you, Bart.'

"I heard the condo door close, then the car door slam, and finally the car peal up the drive. Carole wasn't moving. The blood had stopped spurting and was now sort of dribbling out. Her skin was blueish-white. There was blood everywhere. I tried to find a pulse, but there was none. She was dead!" Bart was sobbing now, tears running down his face.

"I loved her so much! She must have loved me too. Otherwise she wouldn't have tried to intervene the way she did. Ever since that night, I've had to live with the fact that her death was my fault. And I had to keep it all to myself. Their boss, Jerry, has alluded to what might happen to me if I ever told anyone about that night. Tony and Frank were always around to keep reminding me. Now I'll have to face their revenge! I might as well take the easy way out and end my own life. At least I might be able to rejoin Carole!"

"What did you do after you realized that she was dead?" asked Sergeant Hanaka when he felt Bart had recovered sufficiently to talk.

"At first, I was unable to move. I guess I was in shock. When I finally was able to think, I realized I couldn't report her death because Tony and Jerry were involved. I was on my own and would have to find a way to cover up the whole affair. That meant I had to get rid of her body. Even if I could carry her out to my truck on my own, in that busy condo complex there was no way to do it without being seen or heard. I finally figured out that the only way to dispose of her body was to cut it up into pieces that I could fit into black plastic bags. Can you imagine the horror of cutting up the body of the wife you love?" Bart asked Sergeant Hanaka.

"No, Bart, I can't. Such an act must destroy your very soul!"

"That's exactly the way to put it! I've lived with the pain of that ever since."

"So how did you manage to do it?"

"I sometimes used to do some carpentry work at home in the evening, so residents were used to the sound of power tools. I usually tried not to work after about seven in order to avoid bothering my neighbors. That night, even though it was after seven, I used my power tools to cut up the body and put the parts into heavy-duty plastic bags. I did it in the bathtub to avoid making more of a mess. Fortunately the next day was the scheduled time for the truck to come empty the dumpster.

"Afterwards, to avoid tracking blood around the condo, I put towels from the bathroom over the clean carpet and then took up the soggy section of carpet in the hallway. I put down some plastic sheeting over adjacent areas to keep them clean and over the pad, which was also wet with blood. I remembered that there was a good-sized piece of carpet in the storage area, so I planned to put down the new carpet when all else was finished. Since I had not seen any more pieces of the padding, I left the old one in place. I cut the blood-soaked carpet into small pieces and put it in a plastic bag. Next, I washed down the bathtub and surrounding walls, the bathroom floor, and finally the hallway walls.

"After I changed my clothing, I put my blood-soaked clothes, together with the towels and rags I had used to wash up and the dirty plastic sheets, in plastic bags. I put down another clean sheet of plastic to partially cover the hallway area so I could walk on it. Finally I carried eight or nine large, heavy-duty black plastic bags to the dumpster, one or two at a time. Fortunately the dumpster was only about three-quarters full. I moved a few boxes and put several of the bags under the boxes and then placed the rest on top. Close to pickup time, the dumpster can get quite full. One often must rearrange items to put anything else in. So I doubt anyone who saw me thought anything about it. Afterwards I dumped in some scraps of lumber and cardboard from my truck to partially cover the bags on top. I left replacing the carpet until the next day after work so the pad could dry. Having completed the cleanup, I began planning to move out."

"How long until you moved out?" asked Sergeant Hanaka.

"It was a little over a week. I couldn't bear to stay there and live with those horrible memories! I had to explain Carole's absence and often became quite flustered when asked about her sudden disappearance, thus the inconsistent stories."

"And how did you become involved in working for the mob?" asked Sergeant Hanaka. "What did you do besides tail the couple last Thursday?"

"It started after I was arrested during the raid on the cockfight. It had been clear to Jerry for some time that under the circumstances, I couldn't access Carole's money to pay him what I owed. Now, not only did I owe him gambling debts, he put up the bail to get me out of jail. If I'm not working, he doesn't get paid anything. In the past, I'd always managed to pay him eventually. He made a lot on the interest I paid!

"After you interviewed me and I had to give you Tony's telephone number, Jerry got worried I might tell about Tony and Frank's involvement in Carole's death. He said I needed to get some skin in the game. Frank was going to Las Vegas for a time, and I was told to take his place with Tony on collection visits. I hated every minute of it but had no choice. Fortunately Tony is pretty good at handling the visits so we rarely had to get rough, thank God! And Jerry reduced my debt by a hundred dollars for every night I had to go out with Tony."

"How did you come to be tailing that couple?" asked Sergeant Hanaka.

"Well, Tony and I were on our way to a job last Thursday night in Hawi. Tony spotted this couple and told me that the guy looked very much like a guy some mobster from New York had spotted several weeks before at the black sand beach. The New York mobster thought the guy resembled someone his boss was looking for. But he wasn't sure it was the same person, so he circulated a picture he had taken and asked the locals to keep an eye out for him. Tony thought this might be the one they were looking for.

"He gave me instructions that I was to get close enough to the couple to take several shots with my phone so they could tell if he were the guy they were looking for. I was lucky. They sat under a light outside the ice cream shop in Hawi and were so absorbed in what they were talking about that I was able to get quite close. The pictures were close-up and clear. They were able to verify that he was the guy.

"Tony parked his car on the street and left the keys in the ignition. I was told to get in the car and tail them when they left and report back about where they went. While I was waiting for them to finish their ice cream, I overheard them make plans for a trip to Kiholo Bay for a few weeks from now. They planned to snorkel, visit the Queen's Bath, and explore the petroglyphs in the lava cave.

"When they left, I followed them, as instructed. First, the man dropped the lady off at my old condo. Can you believe! Then I followed him to the turnoff for Hualalai Resort. I couldn't follow him in because of the gatehouse. When I reported in to Tony, I told him where they went, along with the make and license plate number of the car. He later said Jerry was so pleased with the information I gave him after tailing the couple that he took off another five hundred dollars from my debt. Some days later, during a conversation with Tony, I mentioned overhearing the couple's plans to visit Kiholo Bay. He mentioned it to Jerry, who told his associates. Apparently they found it very interesting."

"What information was of interest?" asked Sergeant Hanaka.

"Tony said Jerry was excited about the planned trip to Kiholo Bay. I'm sorry I heard that part. I understand the mob plans to be there when the couple goes. Frank won't be back by then, so Jerry has ordered me to take the day off work so I can go along. He says they need the manpower. I've been told I'm to carry a gun. They've supplied one, and Tony has been teaching me to use it! I don't want any part of what they are planning but don't know how to get out of it!"

"Just what are they planning?'

"I'm not sure. Tony won't tell me anything until closer to the time, just that it's likely to be unpleasant for the guy. I'm not a violent person. I've always hated violence! And now I'm up to my neck. I worry about the lady. What will happen to her?"

"What do you think will happen?" asked Sergeant Hanaka.

"I think they want to kill the guy. If the lady is a witness, they may do her too. I'd do anything to stop this! But I haven't any idea how to do that. They have me in their control!"

"Is there anything else? Any other work for the mob? Anything else about Carole's death?" asked Sergeant Hanaka.

"No, nothing. I've told you all I know. What happens now?" asked Bart.

"I'll have this conversation typed by Monday afternoon. Come by after work to sign it. I'll wait for you at the station. Meanwhile, I'll talk to the chief and the lawyers. I assume you and perhaps Tony and Frank will have to appear before a grand jury about Carole's death. Tony and Frank could be charged with murder resulting from felony/assault. I suppose you could be charged as an accessory for hiding the body and could face charges for hindering a murder investigation by lying to me in the past. But I believe you when you say it was a tragic accident resulting from a staged assault intended to persuade Carole to pay your debts. I will talk to the prosecutor and tell him your story. I will also consult with the judge assigned to the case. Regarding this business with the couple and the plans for next Thursday at Kiholo Bay, I'll have to get back to you. Are you willing to work with us undercover to try to protect them?"

"Yes, just tell me what you want me to do. I'll have to take my chances with the mob. It's better than continuing to live this way."

"Keep us informed about any updates on the plans. I'll keep in touch. We'll try to do this in a way to protect you."

Chapter 33

Failing to plan is planning to fail.

TUESDAY, MARCH 17, 10:00 A.M.

Sergeant Hanaka and FBI Agent Carl Kingston were meeting with the police chief, several deputies, and another FBI agent. Hanaka shared with them the information he had obtained from Bart Selwyn about the mob surveillance of Walter Conway and Susan Brooks. He also informed them about the mob's knowledge of the couple's planned visit to Kiholo Bay on the coming Thursday and their intention to be there.

"I think that Conway and Brooks should cancel that outing," said Sergeant Hanaka. "We don't want them to get killed. Cancelling would also get Bart off the hook. He's terrified about having to be part of it. He's also afraid of what will happen if they find out he ratted. We should at least alert Conway and Brooks and let them make a choice."

"I disagree on both points," said Agent Kingston. "I agree that we don't want them to get killed, but this is a chance to catch Carnaggio in the act. We've been after the bastard for a long time. It's been getting harder to nail him now that he's semi-retired. Let's let him hang himself! Further, I don't think we should alert Brooks and Conway. If we did, they might want to cancel the outing or, alternatively, behave awkwardly and give away that something is up. I propose that the better choice is for us to get there first and get set up so we can protect them. Sergeant Hanaka, you said Bart Selwyn was going to tell you what he learns when he gets his instructions. When do you expect to hear?"

"Bart didn't know. But I would assume he would hear no later than tomorrow afternoon. That would leave us little time to prepare for Thursday morning."

"I think we can prepare now," suggested Agent Kingston. "The only thing that we might have to change is the time we go on-site. I'm sure the mob will want to get there before the couple in order to prepare and be set in their preferred location. We will go even earlier. Sergeant Hanaka, as I recall, you said the couple were planning to go from Walter's place at around eight in the morning. Is that correct?"

"Yes, that's what Bart heard them say."

"Ok. I've been studying the local maps. How about we tentatively plan on going in via the access road at around four thirty. My guys can unlock the gate. We can drive as far as the trail to the lava tube cave and then walk in from there. Someone will need to drive the vehicles out after we've unloaded. We will supply night-vision goggles so we're not waving around flashlights that might be noticed by any insomniacs who are resident in the beachside estates. Those goggles provide far better vision of the lay of the land anyway. I assume that we're not dealing with anything approximating a level path."

"It's anything but level," said Sergeant Hanaka. "The trail is, after all, through the lava fields. Although the path goes right by the cave, the entrance can be hard to see, so those night-vision goggles will come in handy. There is an area toward the back of the cave that is higher and drier than some of the areas on the way in. We can set up our operation there. The tides can inundate parts of the cave closer to the entrance. I'm checking the tide tables," he said, scrolling on his phone. "Susan and Walter will have to plan their visit to the cave during low tide, which narrows the window for events. Communication is going to be a problem in there. Phone and walkie-talkie signals won't be getting through."

"We can take in a mini-generator and a transmitter and run a cord to a micro-signal station that we can bury under some rocks just outside the cave," said Agent Kingston. "That way, those in the cave can communicate with an agent outside who is wearing earbuds and a transmitter. He can alert those in the cave as to what is going on outside."

"We'll need to station some of our folks on the beach, dressed in beach attire, to keep an eye on things," said Sergeant Hanaka. "Low tide is early afternoon that day, so Walter and Susan will likely spend the morning on the beach, sunning, snorkeling, and swimming ... whatever. And then head for the cave after lunch. Once Walter and Susan start preparing to leave the beach, one or two of our guys on the beach can go on ahead to the cave. They can pretend to be checking out the cave while the couple is passing the Queen's Bath. I'm guessing that Walter and Susan will plan to visit the cave first and then return to the Bath to cool down before heading back to their car.

"The mob will also need to check out the cave ahead of time. There's really no place to shelter outside. The lava field there is pretty bare. Several of our advance guys can go into the back of the cave and wait there until the mob has checked things out. There's no reason for them to go all the way to the back. Most visitors only go so far as the petroglyphs, and Bart did say that the couple planned to visit the petroglyphs. After the mob moves back toward the entrance, one or two of our men can linger near the petroglyphs, but in the shadows. Once we get word that the couple have passed the Queen's Bath and are approaching the cave, several guys can leave the cave area and walk back toward the Queen's Bath.

"Once the couple passes them, they can turn around and follow the couple toward the cave, leaving enough distance so as not to be obvious that they are following. That way we'll have the sharpshooters near the back of the cave, some of our guys near where the couple will be examining petroglyphs, and some behind the mob guys by the entrance. I don't think we can do better than that," said Agent Kingston.

"Chief, does your unit have rifles equipped with night vision or do you need for us to supply those? You'll need those if your men are shooting from the back of the cave."

"We have enough, thanks. How about we have one or two police couples in swimming attire among those stationed on the beach?" suggested the police chief. "Too many single guys may look out of place. I can also have a few of our native Hawaiian officers on the beach. Not only do they look like they belong, but they know the area well and will notice anyone behaving strangely, like guys from the mob. It would help to know who we should be keeping an eye on."

"Good idea," said Kingston. "My guess is that one or two people from the mob will also hang out on the beach and then follow Walter and Susan into the cave. That way they will expect to have them trapped. The good news is that since there is no place to shelter outside, they will have to enter the cave and then rely on pistols or knives as weapons. Vision will be limited. If they were to carry bigger weapons, someone would notice. And Bart did tell Sergeant Hanaka that they told him to carry the pistol they gave him and are training him to use."

"Conway and Brooks will be carrying flashlights for use in seeing the petroglyphs," said Sergeant Hanaka. "Unfortunately someone standing behind them, closer to the cave entrance, will be able to see their outline against the light from their flashlights, which is not good. It makes them good targets. On the other hand, unless the mob plans to attack near the cave entrance, where they would chance being observed, they too will have to rely on the light from flashlights to navigate the cave interior. So they too will be outlined by their own lights to be seen both by our sharpshooters in the cave and our men by the cave entrance who follow the couple to the cave. If the mob attacks close enough to the entrance, they will be visible as targets in the light from the entrance."

"Everyone should wear dark clothing when we go in tomorrow night. That will help camouflage us as we move in and then later in the darkness of the cave. Those assigned to beach duty will shed their dark clothing in the cave in the morning before heading to the beach. Sergeant Hanaka, can you arrange for someone to supply the task force with water, food, and the usual beach paraphernalia—towels, sunglasses, duffle bags, and so forth?" asked Agent Kingston.

"Sure thing, Agent Kingston," agreed Hanaka.

"One other thing, Sergeant. Is there anywhere to station an ambulance? Someone is likely to need one before this is over."

"Good thought. We don't have an abundance of ambulances

on the island, but I'll talk with the ambulance service in Waikoloa Village. Perhaps they can keep one available in town or arrange to station one near the King's Shops in Waikoloa Resort, which is nearer the cave. There's no place closer to Kiholo Bay where it wouldn't be seen. We do have a medical officer who will be among those remaining in the back of the cave. He will have a medical emergency kit with him."

Just then, the door opened. "Phone call for Sergeant Hanaka. It's a Mr. Selwyn calling."

The sergeant excused himself to take the call. When he returned, he said, "Bart was calling on his lunch hour. He just heard from Antonio Marrato that he is to be ready to meet Tony and company at five fifteen in the morning in Waimea. That means they will probably arrive in the Kiholo Bay area around five forty-five. So our current plan to go at four thirty could work. If we push back to four, we'd have an extra margin, just to be safe. Bart said he was told to wear beach togs under his street clothing and to take a duffel bag, towels, a water bottle, a snack, and a windbreaker with a pocket that can hold his pistol. Apparently he and Tony are to guard the cave entrance after the couple and the mobsters go in and are to prevent anyone else from entering. That's all he knew."

"Great!" said Kingston. "That should keep him out of harm's way. Our guys can pick up Bart and Tony after the others enter the cave and take them away. And it probably indicates that Carnaggio will be among those in the cave doing the deed. I think we're good to go."

Chapter 34

No one can make promises about the future. The best we can do is calculate the risks, estimate our ability to deal with them, and make our plans.

THURSDAY, MARCH 19, 7:30 A.M.

Susan hastily rinsed her breakfast dishes and set them in the sink. She was running late. Fortunately she had packed her tote bag the night before and put it and several refillable water jugs by the door to grab on her way out. She hadn't seen Walter for almost two weeks. Although they had talked by phone almost daily, she missed him. Walter's voice had been warm and caring during their phone conversations, but communication by phone or texting simply hadn't provided the same level of comfort and intimacy that did his being there. She had been surprised that she missed his physical presence so much.

When Susan had questioned their decision to go on today's excursion to Kiholo Bay, Walter had been reassuring. Susan wasn't convinced that he felt as confident as he sounded about the wisdom of their going. She was feeling edgy and worried, even as she felt excited about seeing him again.

Walter had not left the Hualalai community during the first week after returning from his flight to the mainland, hoping to reinforce the impression that he had left the island and returned to his Las Vegas home. In the past week, neither of them was aware of being watched when out and about. Walter was, however, playing it safe. He wanted to minimize the chance of their being followed on today's excursion. So he had come up with a plan to elude anyone that might be watching them.

He suggested to Susan that since he could load his car with supplies for today's trip in his garage without being seen, he would take care of bringing whatever they needed for the day. He would pack a cooler with water, their lunch, snorkeling equipment, flashlights, beach towels, and other supplies they agreed might be useful for their excursion to Kiholo Bay. He planned to leave his home early and drive to a café in the old industrial area where he sometimes had breakfast when he had shopping to do at Costco or elsewhere in the area. He would have a leisurely breakfast and then head for Costco. Anyone watching would, hopefully, assume he was just following his usual routine and relax.

Susan was to put several empty water jugs in her trunk, as she routinely did when needing to refill her drinking water supply, thus making it appear that she was going out to run errands. She would drive to Costco, refill her gas tank, and then park near the front entrance to Costco. They would enter the store separately and meet in the back corner of the building near the water department at about 8:00 a.m. That section of the store was often empty, particularly early in the day when the store was not yet busy.

Walter had instructed Susan to wear tennis shoes, jeans over her swimsuit, and a lightweight, brightly colored jacket over a white T-shirt. The plan was to meet and then purchase some wine, a few snack items, and a baseball cap for Susan. The latter she would wear when she exited the store alone, sans jacket, and walked to the automotive repair area, hopefully unnoticed. Walter would leave just after her, tucking her jacket into the box of wine and other purchases. He would drive his car to the automotive unit to make an appointment for a checkup.

While he was talking to the attendant, Susan would get into his car, and they would leave together, with Susan keeping down low until they were clear of the Costco parking lot. Since Susan would be sitting on the side of the car closest to the building, Walter hoped they could exit without anyone who might be watching noticing that Susan was in the car. It wasn't foolproof, but Walter thought that since he would be heading north from Costco as if he were headed home, any tail might not get too nosey, especially since Susan's car would remain in the lot. Still he planned to keep his eyes on the rearview mirror to be sure he wasn't followed when they left Costco.

Well, here goes! Susan thought as she picked up her jugs and tote bag and headed out the door. She loaded the jugs in the trunk and put her small tote, which looked like a large purse, on the passenger seat.

After arriving at Costco, she filled up with gas as instructed and then found a parking space near the entrance to the store. She entered and quickly made her way toward the far-right back corner of the building. The light was dim, but she soon saw Walter pretending to look at something on the shelf.

"Walter," she said softly as she approached.

He turned at the sound of her voice, and they instinctively reached for each other, enveloped in a bear hug. "How I've missed seeing you," said Walter against her ear. "I had gotten used to you being part of my life."

"I feel the same," said Susan. "I felt this big hole in my life the past few weeks!"

"If today's excursion goes well, I think we can resume living a normal life," said Walter. "I will welcome that!"

"Are you sure about today?" asked Susan. "I don't want anything to happen to you."

"Nor do I, my dear. Life has been looking up the past few months. I want a happy future for us. Your earlier comment about feeling a big hole in your life these past few weeks suggests to me that you may be coming around to thinking the same way. Am I correct?"

"You are correct, Walter. But many complications remain."

"We can take it slow and easy, but time is closing in on us. It's only a bit over a month before you will be returning to Seattle. Perhaps we can talk about this at our leisure while we soak in the Queen's Bath after we explore the petroglyphs in the cave. Agreed?"

"Agreed," said Susan.

"Ok, my friend. Let's get this show on the road. Time to do our meager shopping and then head for the beach."

Fifteen minutes later, they completed checking out. Susan removed her jacket, which Walter tucked into the cardboard box containing their purchases, and donned the baseball cap. She exited the store amid a group of early shoppers and then headed toward the automotive department. There she spoke briefly with an attendant about the price of some tires. While they were speaking, Walter's car pulled up in front of the entrance, and he came in to make an appointment for servicing. Susan thanked the attendant, said she needed to think about the tires, and got into Walter's car.

Shortly later, Walter got into the driver's seat and started to drive along the building toward the exit. Then he turned left toward the road that bordered the parking lot. A left onto the road, a right at the bottom of the hill, another left, and then a right onto the main highway, and they were headed for Kiholo Bay.

Walter kept an eye on the traffic behind him for the first few miles of the drive and saw no sign of any car following them. He was pretty sure that if they had a tail, he would have seen the car coming out of the industrial area not too far behind them.

"I think we have the day to ourselves, Susan," he announced. "It's a beautiful day, and we're together. What more could we ask?"

About fifteen minutes later, Walter turned left across the highway and pulled into a gravel area alongside the southbound lanes where two other cars were already parked.

"Doesn't look too busy yet," he observed. "Time to load up and begin our hike. It's not too hot, but by the time we reach the beach, we'll probably be ready for a dip." As he unloaded, he handed Susan a backpack. "That contains our beach towels, snorkels, and so on. Shouldn't be too heavy for you. Let me know if you get tired, and I can take it."

He next removed a rigid, oblong object with straps and several outside pockets. Seeing Susan's puzzled glance, he explained. "This is a cooler backpack that I designed. Since it's difficult to carry a regular cooler on long hikes, I devised a lightweight one you can carry on your back. I've used it a few times now, and it seems to work pretty well. May have to patent it one of these days!"

"Walter, you amaze me. I'm constantly seeing new dimensions to your talents!"

"Good! If I can keep surprising you, maybe you'll want to hang around. Designing this thing was something to do. It kept me from dwelling on my sorrows after Marge died." He closed the trunk, checked to see that the car was locked, and then turned to Susan.

"The trek begins. A good thing you have that baseball cap. It will be a hot twenty minutes or so, but what's at the other end makes it worthwhile. I'm so glad I will be the one to show it to you for the first time. The trail is pretty narrow and hard to see in places. If you don't mind, I'll lead, and you can follow behind me. The lava to the sides of the trail is pretty rough, so it's hard to walk side by side."

About twenty minutes later, they simultaneously breathed a sigh of relief as they stepped into the shade of the palm trees that lined the back of the crescent beach. It felt at least twenty degrees cooler than it had on the hot lava trail. Both of them were soaked in perspiration. Ahead a deep stretch of pure white sand stretched the width of the crescent and glistened in the sun. The white sand beach framed the most breathtaking aqua-colored bay that Susan had ever seen. What appeared to be a small island with a few palm trees was set about a hundred yards from shore, slightly to the right of center. A second island, treeless, was situated on the left side of the bay. The water was generally calm, with only occasional gentle waves lapping the shoreline. A gentle breeze stirred the palms. About a dozen people could be seen, several wading in the water or swimming, a couple with two children walking along the shore, and a couple sitting on a beach towel talking.

"Seems like a lot of folks for two cars," muttered Walter. "Must have parked further down along the highway."

"Oh, Walter, it's paradise!" exclaimed Susan. "I feel like I died and went to heaven. This is well worth the hike. No wonder you love it."

"Did you know that this was once a freshwater/brackish fishpond? It was built in 1810 during the reign of Kamehameha the Great to replace one destroyed by the Hualalai lava flow in 1801. I once read that it had stone walls up to six feet tall and as wide as twenty feet. The pool was two miles in circumference and held a myriad of fish species. Most of it was destroyed by the 1859 Mauna Loa lava flow, which flowed thirty miles to here, filled in most of the pond, and destroyed the southern wall, creating the present lagoon. The freshwater that originally fed the pond came from springs that still feed the lagoon. When we go snorkeling, you will find what seems to be a pane of glass suspended horizontally in the water about a foot below the surface. That is the freshwater floating on top of seawater, which is heavier."

"I had no idea! I'm so glad you know the history. It seems that those early Hawaiians were very inventive and managed their environment well to produce an abundant food supply!"

"Indeed they did." commented Walter. "Ok, I suggest we find somewhere to settle. Pick your spot. There's lots of space so we can get some privacy. I would prefer shade to sun, if you don't mind."

"That would be my preference also. How about over there under that clump of scrub trees in front of those palms on the far side?" Susan pointed. "Those trees are big enough that we can sit in their shade. It's close to the water yet provides an expansive view of beach and that beautiful multicolored aqua water. Also that cluster of rocks in the water in front of that area may attract turtles looking to bask in the sun."

"Great choice. Since most of the folks on the beach seem to prefer this end, it will be more private as well," said Walter.

Arriving at their chosen spot, Susan spread their beach towels under the trees. After they removed their street clothing, Walter handed Susan a bottle of cold water from the cooler before sitting down. "I think I need a rest from the exertion of getting here and a chance to cool down before I'll be ready to get in the water. What about you?"

"I'm happy to sit and drink in the view while I cool down and rehydrate," said Susan. "Could you imagine living in this spot? I don't think I would ever want to leave home. We both have lovely views from our respective homes, but this is really special."

Walter waved toward the back of the beach. "The shame of it is that most of the owners of those estates back there don't even live here. They just come to visit for a few weeks a year. Yet they keep the gate on the only access road locked most of the time so we peons have to hike in. What a waste! I suppose the positive aspect is that most people are too lazy to hike in the heat so the beach is rarely too crowded."

About thirty minutes later, they decided to go snorkeling. The variety of fish species was astonishing to Susan. Even though she was tiring by the time Walter suggested they take a break, she was reluctant to leave the water. Once she lay on her beach towel, however, she was instantly asleep.

Once they both had awakened from their naps, Walter suggested they had earned an early lunch. Susan realized that she was ready to devour anything in sight, even though it was only eleven. So Walter unpacked their lunch—fat deli sandwiches, kosher dill pickles, kettle chips, juicy pears, and chocolate cupcakes. A bottle of cold Kona Longboard Ale was the finishing touch. While they ate, they enjoyed the sight of turtles climbing on the rocks to sun, sometimes pushing another off the rock in an attempt to find a comfortable spot.

Shortly after they finished eating, Walter suggested that this might be a good time to clean up the leftovers from lunch and then walk to the cave to see the petroglyphs. He observed that the beach seemed to be getting more crowded, and he thought it might be a good idea to see the cave while others were having their lunch. Also it was now low tide, making it easier to view the cave. They would stop for their soak in the Queen's Bath on their way back here to collect their belongings.

Susan and Walter repacked the cooler and then left it with their extra towels, snorkel equipment, and street clothing under the trees. They carried only a beach towel, a flashlight, and, since Walter warned that it could be cool in the cave, a shirt. Both wore their tennis shoes since they would be crossing some lava.

They walked along the back of the beach to benefit from the shade of the palm trees. Once they reached the opposite side of the beach, Walter located the narrow trail through the lava that led to the cave and led the way. Susan followed behind. Walter told Susan that once they passed the Queen's Bath, he would have to move slowly and keep an eye on the surroundings because the entrance to the cave could be difficult to find. The trail continued on for some distance beyond the cave, so they wouldn't want to miss the entrance and continue hiking on in the heat.

As they passed the Queen's Bath, they saw several young men soaking in the water. Later, just as Walter was beginning to think that he had missed the cave entrance, he spotted two Hawaiian men coming from the left and realized that they must have just left the cave. Relieved to have found the entrance, he nodded to the men as they passed and then turned to wave Susan forward.

As he did so, he noticed several other beachgoers some distance behind Susan on the trail. "Drat," he commented. "I was hoping we'd have the cave to ourselves. It's not usually so crowded on a weekday!"

Susan and Walter paused to don their shirts. Susan tied her beach towel around her waist. Walter tossed his over his shoulder. Then they stooped to enter the low entrance to the cave. The early section had areas where the ceiling had collapsed, letting in light from outside. Some areas were quite wet from puddles left by tidal inundations. As they proceeded, the ground rose somewhat and became dryer. It was also getting darker.

They heard voices ahead and soon saw flashlights coming their way. They moved to the side wall and waited for the couple they could now see coming toward them to pass them by. After turning on their own flashlights, they continued on their way.

"The petroglyphs should be coming up soon. They are mostly on the left-hand wall," Walter commented, turning his flashlight to shine the light on the wall ahead of them. "There, I see them," he said, pointing to the area where his light was now shining. "Walk ahead of me, Susan. I'll hold the light so you can see them."

"Thank you, Walter. There are really a lot of them, aren't there?" commented Susan. "I see human figures. Those there look like fish. What do you think these were meant to be?" She pointed to some indecipherable forms.

Just then, they heard steps coming their way.

"Darn!" exclaimed Walter. "I was hoping we'd have some time to examine these in peace. I've heard stories about what they represent and wanted to explain them to you."

A shot rang out from behind them, from the direction of the cave entrance, and they heard the sound of a bullet hitting the wall.

"Walter! What's happening?" yelled Susan.

More shots followed immediately, some from behind them nearer the cave entrance and others from deeper in the cave. Bullets continued to ricochet off the cave wall.

"Get down!" shouted Walter, pulling Susan to the ground with him, extinguishing his flashlight and then hers, which she had dropped when he pulled her down. He tried to cover her body with his own. Then he felt warm moisture against his skin. "Susan, are you all right?" he asked anxiously.

"I think one of the bullets hit my left side," said Susan. "It hurts, and I can feel blood soaking the side and sleeve of my shirt."

Another shot whizzed by where they had been standing moments before. Then they heard a yelp, followed by a moan, a thud, and people shouting from the direction of the cave entrance.

The sound of running footsteps came from the back of the cave. As several men passed Susan and Walter, a voice ordered, "Trooper, stay here and see if you can help them. We'll see what's happening further out." The sound of footsteps receded.

"I'm Trooper Carter from the Kona PD," said the voice of the man ordered to stay with them. "Are the two of you all right?"

"What the hell is going on?" demanded Walter. "I think my friend has been shot! She seems to be bleeding."

"I think it is safe to turn on your flashlight so we can assess the situation. The shooting seems to have stopped. Sergeant Hanaka thought that it sounded like we hit one of them. I think the others may be trying to flee."

"Sergeant Hanaka? Who is it behind us? I gather the police were in the back of the cave?"

"Yes, the police and the FBI. We had men by the mouth of the cave as well, so they won't get far. Hand me your flashlight so we can check your friend. Once things are under control, I'm sure Sergeant Hanaka and Agent Kingston will fill you in on the whole story."

The trooper shone the flashlight on Susan. Her eyes were closed, and she was very pale. There was a pool of blood forming on the cave floor by where she lay. He pulled up her shirt and pointed to where the blood was seeping out. "Take your beach towel, Mr. Conway, and use it to exert pressure over where the blood is coming out. I'll grab the medical kit and call for an ambulance," said Trooper Carter, turning toward the back of the cave.

"Susan, can you hear me?" asked Walter, touching her cheek but continuing to exert pressure on her wound. "Please talk to me. I need to know that you are all right."

Her eyes fluttered open. "Walter, are you okay? Were you hurt? Please be all right!"

"I'm fine, dear one. It's you who is injured. How are you feeling?"

"I'm so cold. And so tired! My side hurts. I just want to sleep!"

"Susan, listen to me. You've been shot and are bleeding. That's why I'm pressing on your side. It's also probably what's making you feel cold and tired. But until the ambulance arrives, it's important that you don't give in to the tiredness. Try to stay awake, please. I'll put my shirt and beach towel over you to give you some extra warmth. I can still use the corner of the towel to staunch the bleeding. Try talking to me to help you stay awake."

Just then, Trooper Carter returned. He placed a compression bandage over Susan's wound. "We had some blankets with us to keep warm. Here are two that you can wrap around your friend, Mr. Conway. The ambulance is on its way ... should be here within fifteen minutes. Agent Kingston is getting the gate unlocked so it can drive in. Meanwhile, I have several of our colleagues coming in from outside the cave with a makeshift stretcher that we can use to carry your friend out to where the ambulance must park. We want to get her out before the tide starts coming back in. We'll try to minimize the roughness of her trip out of here since I'm sure any bumps will exacerbate her pain. Unfortunately we have no pain medicine except Tylenol until the ambulance arrives."

"Thanks, Trooper. Let's get on with it," said Walter, taking Susan's hand as the men arrived and lifted her onto the stretcher.

Chapter 35

*Contentment lies not in fulfilling all
that you could ever wish for, but in
realizing how much you already have!*

FRIDAY, MARCH 20, 10:00 A.M.

Susan sat in her hospital bed, surrounded by Walter, Sergeant Hanaka, and Agent Kingston. She was feeling much better. Her wound had been cleaned and bandaged when she arrived at the Kona Hospital ER the previous afternoon. She had been unconscious when she arrived but revived quickly after she was given IV fluids. Once she was conscious, pain medication had been administered. The doctor had decided to keep her overnight for observation; her blood pressure had remained quite low. Further, the FBI had requested that she be permitted to stay for her protection until they had wrapped up their operation. Walter had stayed overnight in her hospital room. Sergeant Hanaka and Agent Kingston had arrived about fifteen minutes ago to fill them in on the events of the previous day.

"So," said Agent Kingston, "the reason you weren't being followed this past week wasn't because the mob bought Walter's ruse of leaving the island, but because Bart Selwyn overheard the two of you planning your Kiholo Bay excursion when you were in Hawi. He happened to mention what he heard to his friend, Tony Marrato, who told the local mob boss, Jerry Alonzo. Jerry, in turn, had been watching for you at the request of Rocco Carnaggio, a colleague of the mob boss, Vincent Morelli, whom Walter's testimony sent to prison. If Bart hadn't told Sergeant Hanaka about the planned hit on Walter, yesterday might have turned out very differently."

"So we have Bart to thank for our lives," said Susan. "To think that all that sneaking around yesterday morning was unnecessary!"

"Neither of you should ever need to worry about doing anything like that again. Carnaggio led the group into the cave and was killed in the cave. We intercepted Jerry and all the members of his organization who were there. When word got back to Morelli at the prison that Walter had escaped vengeance, he lost it. He started yelling and then hitting anyone in his proximity, prisoners and guards alike. When he didn't respond to orders to stop, one of the prison guards shot him. He died an hour later. He was the instigator of the order to find and kill Walter, so with him gone, Walter can relax and enjoy the rest of his life."

"What about Bart? What will happen to him?" asked Susan.

Sergeant Hanaka spoke, "I am convinced that the story he told me about the death of his wife is true. I interviewed Tony and he corroborated Bart's story in every detail. I believe it was a tragic accident. The assault on Bart by Tony and Frank was staged by agreement of the three of them. It was not an actual assault with intent to inflict bodily harm. I hope to convince the DA of that. If I can't, he could still see some jail time.

"There is still the issue of Bart not reporting his wife's death and disposing of the body. It's understandable why he did that: he was scared to death of trouble with the mob and saw no other recourse. He's suffered severely from the whole experience. He truly loved his wife. He seems sincere in his desire to receive treatment for his gambling problem. His experiences these past few months have affected him profoundly. If and when he's cleared of any charges relating to his wife's death, I'll arrange to get him into a residential treatment program. I plan to testify on his behalf during the legal proceedings. If he has to serve some jail time, I hope we can get him treatment for his gambling addiction while he is in prison.

"It won't be easy, but we will try to have a death certificate issued for Carol Selwyn. If we succeed, Bart can inherit her money, clear the remainder of his debts, and have enough left over to start anew somewhere else. He's thinking of going to school. He would like to study to be a physician's assistant. He feels like, if he can contribute to saving some lives, he can atone in part for his role in his wife's death.

"Because he told me about yesterday's plans to attack Walter in the cave, we were able to pick up him and Tony while they were standing guard at the cave entrance before the shooting started. There will be no charges against the two of them relative to yesterday's events."

"Because he ratted on the mob, they could seek revenge, especially if Frank and Tony are sent to jail for their part in Carole's death or if Jerry and his associates are sent to prison for yesterday's attack. Therefore, my boss has agreed, in the event Bart does not go to jail, to put him in the witness protection program and move him somewhere else for his anti-gambling treatment and then school," said Agent Kingston. "We'll try to expedite the court review of Carole's death to move things along. If he does get prison time, it will be harder to protect him, another point we will make to the DA."

"What about his friends, Tony and Frank? Do you think they will be sent to jail?" asked Walter.

"If Susan's death is officially declared accidental, they might escape with no more than a lecture from the judge for their stupidity in agreeing to stage the incident, or I suppose they could be charged with manslaughter," said Sergeant Hanaka. "Either way they'll have to spend the rest of their lives living with the fact that they were responsible for her death."

"It sounds to me as if everything is nearly wrapped up," said Walter. "I can't thank the two of you enough for your efforts to protect me and Susan! All's well that ends well! Was it Shakespeare who said that? Anyway, with Morelli gone, I can breathe again. It's like getting my life back. Even though Marge and I had a good life after I was put in the witness protection program, I never stopped looking over my shoulder. Yesterday when I couldn't spot a tail after leaving Costco, I got careless, thinking I had outsmarted them. My radar failed me when I noticed the excessive number of people at Kiholo Bay. I passed it off without much thought because I was focused on showing Susan all the special features of that place. I'm glad I will be able to live without constantly being on guard. Thank you both so much!"

"Thank you from me too for keeping Walter safe," said Susan. "The possibility of losing him made me realize how important he is to me. And thank you for getting me prompt treatment for my gunshot wound. I am honored to know both of you."

"I think the two of you need some time alone. So we'll say goodbye," said Agent Kingston.

"We wish you well," said Sergeant Hanaka. "Susan, if you are inclined to play detective again in the future, I'd be honored to have you help me with my investigations," he said with a twinkle in his eye.

"I think my days as a detective are over, Sergeant Hanaka. But I'll keep your offer in mind. Goodbye, and thank you for everything you've done to help."

"Alone at last!" said Walter once Hanaka and Kingston had left the room. He turned to Susan and then took her hand as he sat in the chair by her bed. "Have you any idea how devastated I was yesterday when I thought I might lose you? Susan, I love you! I don't want to live without you!"

"I love you too, Walter! I had lots of time to think these past few weeks. I realized that life without you in it would be even emptier than my life just after Scott died. Where do we go from here? I'm due to fly back to Seattle in about four weeks. We'll be thousands of miles apart!"

"Not if I can help it! Susan, may I come for a visit and stay with you in Seattle for a few weeks once you've settled back into your home and life there? That will give us leisurely time to make plans, and you can determine if being around me twenty-four hours a day will drive you crazy. Or is that too big a step? I did promise you yesterday that we would evolve our future relationship in slow steps."

"Of course you may, Walter. I think it's being away from you that will drive me crazy. There's so much we need to do. We haven't even met each other's families!"

"Yes, that is a crucial step. How about I stay with you for a few weeks and then we take a trip and make the rounds of our children and their families? At the end of that obligatory trip, let's go away together to somewhere special for some uninterrupted time together. We can think about where that should be.

"After that, we can deal with next steps. I want to marry you. If you decide that's not what you want, I'm happy to continue our relationship on whatever basis you want. I can live with you without being married. If that's too much right now, let's figure out how to spend as much time together as possible—in Seattle, here in Hawaii at my home or your condo, or dividing time between Seattle and here—or wherever else works for you!"

Susan started to interrupt.

"I know getting married is fraught with difficulties," said Walter. "We'll have to deal with the legal issues of protecting our children's inheritance, ownership of our properties, and so forth, but we shouldn't let solvable issues like that get in the way of our happiness. We'll live one day at a time, savoring each moment! I believe we can find our way. Are you willing to embark on the journey?"

"Oh yes, Walter. You are the best thing that has happened to me since Scott's death. I want to be with you, to try to make you happy, to build a future! I love you."

"And I love you," said Walter, gathering Susan into his arms and kissing her at length.

When he finally released her, she gently caressed his face. Then as they gazed longingly into each other's eyes, she smiled and said, "Let the journey begin!"

ABOUT THE AUTHOR

Barbara Valanis is a retired professor, epidemiologist, and health services researcher. She has previously published epidemiology textbooks, as well as numerous articles in professional journals. She and her husband currently reside in Melbourne, Florida. In the recent past, they spent winters at their condominium in Kailua-Kona, Hawaii, the setting for this book.

Printed in the USA
CPSIA information can be obtained
at www.ICGtesting.com
LVHW050102110124
768640LV00008B/210

9 781480 875890